"FUNNY..

OUTRAGEOUS ...

The Condon cult knows that he is an earnest man using every writing weapon from brass knuckles to Sioux pogamoggans against his fictional adversaries . . . he is deadly serious about the pollution of our atmosphere by sham and hypocrisy . . . It might take the reader as long as four seconds to figure out how many big male stars there are who come from Wales. If further hints are needed, the superstar is married to Caterina Largo, a screen queen."

Herbert Mitgang,
The New York Times Book Review

"The plot is hallucinogenic, the characters are monstrous, and the style is Beverly Hills baroque. Yet Condon's grotesque farce is often merely truth . . . deserves a place on the shelf that includes Nathanael West and S. J. Perelman." *Time Magazine*

"Marvelously funny . . . a riotous barrage."
—*San Francisco Examiner*

"Condon is one of the most gifted of contemporary writers . . . Behind the inspired nonsense of *The Ecstasy Business* a social critic is at work." —*Kansas City Star*

Richard Condon

THE
ECSTASY
BUSINESS

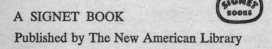

A SIGNET BOOK

Published by The New American Library

Library of Congress Catalog Card Number: 67-14467

This is an authorized reprint of a hardcover edition published by The Dial Press, Inc.

SIGNET TRADEMARK REG. U.S. PAT. OFF. AND FOREIGN COUNTRIES
REGISTERED TRADEMARK—MARCA REGISTRADA
HECHO EN CHICAGO, U.S.A.

SIGNET BOOKS are published by
The New American Library, Inc.,
1301 Avenue of the Americas, New York, New York 10019

First Printing, October, 1968

PRINTED IN THE UNITED STATES OF AMERICA

In fond memory of
Hal Horne

Let us go down to the peep show,
For a taste of life and sex to see,
Let us go down to that place of dreams,
For a peek at the business of ecstasy.

The Keeners' Manual

1

EVEN for a film star, not to mention the greatest film star of his generation—which he was—Tynan Bryson had an extremely weak grasp of reality. He was as at home playing a chrysanthemum-raptured shogun of the old East as he was as a shotgun-ruptured sheriff of the old West. Or as a Cardinal, either of the Church or of the St. Louis ball club, and he had played both. He was Everyman in an Elizabethan ruff, as a waterfront tough, or a ducal gruff, and in spades. In forty-six starring films he'd had only one failure, and that was because a Hungarian director, groping for the meaning of multilevel America, had persuaded him to portray Thomas Jefferson as Richard Nixon might have played him.

Bryson sometimes tried to seize reality, but he had to grasp upward beyond his reach through the quicksand of his existence. He was an unzipped fly caught in forever amber. Everything in his life was out of proportion. He owned one hundred and eleven tennis rackets, sent to him by adoring fans after his triumph in *Sneaker* (retitled *Plimsoll* in the British Commonwealth), in which he had played alone to win the Davis Cup from the Australian doubles team. Such victories made him uneasy with the jagged formlessness of real life. He wanted to be what he played, not for his art, for he was not a Method actor, but because according to the laws of being a hero in an American motion picture, he must always win.

Bryson sat at a large corner table under a portrait of Lutatius Catulus, the consul who had commanded more galleys than any other Roman, in a New York restaurant called The Galley, which had lapis-lazuli fixtures in its washrooms, enormously muscular half-naked waiters dressed as galley slaves, and two hundred and ten customers at each meal. He signaled for the table captain. "What is this Cream of Toheroa Soup, please?" he asked.

"That is our New Zealand mussel soup, sir. Extremely rare and very tasty."

"Sort of like winkle soup?"

"Something like that, sir."

"Six dollars is a lot for winkle soup."

"**Not really, sir. The maximum legal catch for these little** fellows is twenty, sir. And they may only be dug up with the hands or with a piece of wood no larger than four by eight inches. Then it takes the big jets nineteen hours to fly them in."

"Is it a large bowl?"

The lawyers flanking Bryson at the table were snarling conversationally. They were honed, sleek men with aggressions like battering rams under testudos of blandness. Their voices had toothed ratchets and circular persistence. Bryson didn't hear them. He decided to try the soup, then returned to the menu, which he read aloud: "Pheasant of the Golden House on a Silver Shield in Gilded Plumage, Roasted with Exquisite Sauce, Serves Two, Twenty-One Dollars." His voice had a high, irregular tonal pitch. Sometimes it reached almost a falsetto, then dropped a full octave with the next sentence. Being a British voice, it lacked glide and was distinctive because of its choppy change of pitch.

Two months before, one day after he had completed his performance as the dying but triumphant Italian labor leader in *Strike!,* Bryson had collapsed with hepatitis in Castellaneta, Italy, the birthplace of Rudolph Valentino. At odd moments, especially when eating, the bitterness of this experience fell on him like a peregrine. He interrupted the lawyers.

"I agreed to visit Valentino's statue," he blurted, "because Goldberg said it would be a nice gesture on my part. Did you ever spend five weeks in a clinic in Castellaneta, Italy, with little brown nuns staring through the oval windows of their habits? I nearly died in that place, and for the first ten days the damn press kept yammering that I was feigning the whole thing for publicity."

The Blackfoot Indians had had a system of mockery which could make life intolerable and drive anyone out alone on a quest for death or war honors with which to redeem himself. It had been the most subtle and sophisticated method of mocking ever known until the star system of the film industry. Bryson felt mocked. Sometimes he was able to comfort himself by measuring his profession against the way his father's brother had made his living years before in South Af-

10

rica, where he had castrated sheep with his teeth. His uncle had been able to explain the job away blandly. "I mean, it wasn't my idea, lad. That's how the boys on the top wanted it done because it was the year before Bordizo pincers were put on the market. A knife or a razor simply made them bleed too much."

But as time went on, even though he was a king in a great palace, or more likely because he was, Bryson felt more and more mocked—so much so that he hadn't been able to look at his face in a mirror for more than eight years.

He was six feet three inches tall, and had teeth like a pale fist under a mustache more famous than Stalin's. He wore his hair in a high pompadour which was fixed with a glossy spray. His smoke-gray belted jacket was piped with black silk and marked with his initials *under* his lapels, where only a dry cleaner would see it. The suit had been cut by an Italian tailor in Paris out of English cloth, paid for with American dollars and then copied by a Japanese in Hong Kong in four other patterns. He was a shade more handsome than Alcibiades before the Greek had started to drink. The eyes of all of the women in the room—twenty percent for sexually based reasons, eighty percent because it was known that he earned several million dollars a year—and those of one Cypriot busboy, took on a crazed glaze as they stared at him.

Bryson's metabolism was juggling depression and elation. He was depressed because of the lingering melancholy that is an aftereffect of hepatitis, and because of the heartlessness of his ex-wife. He was elated by the lust emanating from the mewing women around him and because the first piece of writing he had ever done, a starkly rhymed description of his boyhood as a winkle-picker on the Welsh coast, commissioned by the world's largest greeting-card company, had been reviewed ecstatically the day before in all media.

The table captain, in high suede boots, walnut stain and a galley master's whip looped across his chest like a bandoleer, plugged a portable telephone into the wall behind Bryson. As he leaned over, he smelled of iodoform. "Hamburg, Germany, is calling you, Mr. Bryson," he said. His voice was discreet, but the woman at the next table heard him and she passed the word until the room buzzed.

Bryson blinked. Hamburg. Albert McCobb was in Hamburg. He had read it that morning in *Variety*. His eyes went as expressionless as Christmas-tree ornaments. His business sense, which could have been symbolized pictorially as an endless beach of razor blades beside a sea of ammonia filled with unspeakable monsters, took over at once. The name of

11

Bryson's own company was Hold Productions Inc. Ltd. S.A. He had vowed long ago that once he got money in his hands he was going to hold it and keep holding it. He hated even to have to let it rest in banks temporarily. Holding the telephone, he slipped into the character of Dan Grandy, confident board chairman in *Board,* which had grossed nine million two, and said, "Yes, Albert?"

A Glaswegian voice, scarred and pitted by a thousand scalding bowls of porridge, roweled into Bryson's wincing ear. "Are you all right, Ty?"

"I'm steadier, luv. But Goldberg was very wrong in forcing me to come to New York."

"What did he want?"

"Ships just opened. He had twelve Norwegians row a Viking longboat from Oslo in those heavy wigs, but when they got to Staten Island the captain had all of them shave and change into neat blue serge suits. Then they came into New York by subway instead of sweeping past me and the mayor and the press at the Battery, where we were standing in a driving rain."

"Pity."

"Yes."

Their voices were light-hearted with a persiflage that concealed anxiety for a way of life in which they needed to remain ever wary. It was a world where balding men spent most of their lives kissing telephones, and dissembling by calling each other "baby" and "sweetheart," while they called beautiful women "Listen" or "Look." Since he was British and wanted to be more straightforwardly friendly, Bryson called everyone, including elevator starters, "luv."

"It is seven-thirty in the evening here," Albert said.

"Oh, please, Albert." Ty's drawl was so relaxed that the vowels were as long as novelty frankfurters. Glottal stops staggered through McCobb's speech, but somewhere, buried in the spiny sounds, there were fruity European undertones, as though he were secretly taking a crash course in Polish at Berlitz.

"Are you cured? Are you all right, Ty?"

"I'm tired, luv. My skin looks like a banana, but thank all above, O'Gorman is in town and he's devised a make-up so that I can at least walk out in public."

"Walk?"

"I walked here from the hotel and only eight people recognized me. Then a passing lady cab driver waiting for a light at Fifty-fifth was kind enough to tell me that my fly was open."

Not a word of this was true, McCobb knew. If anyone had told Bryson his fly was open in public, he would have run back to his hotel to call his analyst and dig for meanings. Ty was so adhesive to his subconscious that when film production had forced him to travel so much during the second and third years of his analysis, he underwent simultaneously an Adlerian analysis in Paris, Otto Rank therapy in London and a combination of Hayim Steinthal and Lévy-Bruhl in Rome —all the while mailing tape recordings of random free association to his permanent analyst, Dr. Abraham Weiler, in Beverly Hills. Weiler was a pre-Freudian with a few cosmetic tints of Harald Høffding and Frederic Wertham.

"No matter, Ty," McCobb said from Hamburg. "You've gained a fan and there's nothing odd about forgetting to button your fly."

"Caterina certainly wouldn't agree, luv. Or Stekel, who might have made allowances for a characterical phase but would have distinguished between the anagogic and catagogic phases."

"*Casey* Stekel?"

"Do you know what 'catagogic' means, Albert?"

"I've not your ability to memorize lines, lad."

"It means 'gutterward.' Sex is masked in every action, and we—"

"Tell me about your liver."

"What can I say? I was very depressed when I got off that ship and found Caterina's book on sale everywhere."

"Does she mention you?"

"*Mention?* Great God, Albert! I'm on every page!"

"Libelous?"

"I am lunching with lawyers right now."

"Lunching with *lawyers?*"

"I couldn't help it. Their chambers are being painted."

"Has anyone seen you?"

"On the West Side?"

"Nonetheless, you must leave separately." There were splashings over the phone. Albert was calling from his bathtub, the base of the telephone high over his head as it rested on his domed stomach.

"What are you eating, Ty?"

"We haven't ordered."

"What were you thinking of eating?"

"How can I think of food?"

"You've got to eat, lad. Let me talk to the *chef de rang.*"

"Albert, for heaven's sake!"

"Don't waste time please, lad. This is an overseas call."

13

Bryson gestured, and the table captain came to him with the speed of a cheetah and took the phone. He listened carefully, and then hung up reverently. "That was Albert Mc-Cobb, master of suspense," he said. Though the captain had been in the center ring for twenty years, feeding the top animal acts of his time, McCobb could still provoke awe in him.

"I thought it sounded like him," Bryson snarled.

"He ordered lunch for you from Hamburg, Germany."

"I'll have the hamburg," the younger lawyer said.

"Albert doesn't give a damn that I just beat hepatitis," Bryson said bitterly to the older lawyer, who had a face like a deflated football.

"When a man calls, prepaid, from Hamburg, Germany," the lawyer said gravely, "just to order lunch for a friend, that man is something to be cherished. In my humble opinion," he added arrogantly.

Ty knew then that his own lawyers were in McCobb's pay. They had chosen the restaurant only a half-hour before, and yet Albert had been able to locate him instantly. Slipping back into the characterization of Dan Grandy in *Board*, he went crafty and cool. "What do you think he really wanted, Judge?" he asked.

The judge shrugged as if the restaurant had just gone over a bump. "I know Mr. McCobb only by reputation," he answered evasively.

No actress in Tynan Bryson's time had achieved real star rank—that is, true box-office bankability—unless she had played opposite him in at least one picture. Despite his former wife's celebrated allegation, "Scratch an actor and you'll find an actress," made during the proceedings for their second divorce, to which *Paris-Match* had sent a team of nine writers and photographers, Bryson had slept with all but one of his leading ladies, the discard having turned out to be a female impersonator, the best-kept secret in worldwide show biz. It was this pitiable inability to say no to any beautiful, not-so-beautiful, even ugly woman, which kept shattering Ty's marriages to Caterina Largo, who for over a dozen years had been the hottest female star since Bellatrix in Orion.

Bryson simply did not know how to cope with Caterina's vindictive and reckless jealousy. After each divorce he had tried to remain a gentleman, no matter what the provocations at the trial had been. After the first divorce he had told the *U. S. News & World Report* with his usual restraint, "Mrs. Bryson is a mirror raper." After the second divorce he was quoted by anthropologist James Cerruti, of the *National Geo-*

14

graphic, as saying, "Mrs. Bryson is a pterodactyl encased in a huge wax flower which has no smell." (Largo hated his affairs with other women, but she detested being called Mrs. Bryson even more.)

After each divorce Largo had released photostatic copies of a forged birth certificate which falsely established his age as eleven years older than he really was. Each time, to save his public image, Ty had to have his mother interviewed on *The Ed Sullivan Show* to deny the slander. The second time Largo did it he sued her and won damages of six hundred and fifty thousand dollars, which really hurt her because she had enormous sentimentality about money. Consequently, when they married for the third time the yellow press had said she was marrying him for her money.

Dr. Abraham Weiler testified for Ty in closed sessions during the third divorce in an attempt to place in proper proportion Largo's charge of satyriasis against her husband, a charge which received increasing emphasis in the court record of each divorce action. According to the psychiatrist, Ty required more emotional stimulation than any other patient he had ever encountered. "The patient is a man who requires constant reassurances of affection in order to keep from falling into the wasting disease called marasmus," said Weiler under oath. "He must be assured in physical terms that he will not starve from his acute, unending recognition hunger. His perpetual sexual forays must not be considered as those of a man who merely enjoys the pleasures of sexual contact with hundreds, perhaps thousands, of women; these actions are forced on a man who needs *social* intercourse to abate his extraordinary fear that he will not be appreciated."

Ty knew that he loved Caterina Largo very, very much. But what he felt for himself was something even more exalting. He was a pope in the actors' religion: the humble adoration and celebration of self. Only Bryson was real to Bryson. The public was an unreliable fantasy, and though he adored his former wife, he sometimes had to rush to the nearest fan magazine to remember what she looked like when they were apart. But he was so real to himself that he maintained a library of over five hundred thousand feet of tape of his voice talking on and on through his every hour of psychoanalysis. He played back selections from this collection to himself every weekend to gain "insight," and when he traveled he was never without eight or ten hours of recordings of himself explaining himself to himself.

It was fairly deadly stuff. "I am remarkable in that way," he said, for example, on Tape 4871, "in that I do not go

15

into a shoe shop to raise false hopes cruelly among the shop assistants, who are perhaps dependent upon commissions from such sales for their livelihood. Nor do I believe, *au fond,* in ready-made shoes, because their styling is frequently static. I hire someone to scout the entire shoe market for me, and then he prepares an album of photographs and sketches. The selections I make from this are then sent to the wholesalers, and twenty or thirty pairs of the actual shoes are then delivered on approval. In that way I prevent anxieties on the part of shoe clerks, and though it does cost me considerably more time in the end, I feel I have saved another human being from worry. After all, what we do not see we cannot fear. In my humble opinion."

Many of the detailed accounts on Bryson's tapes were lies, but this was because of his cinema-conditioned thinking. He had to embellish truth to provide himself with the proper entrances and exits and to enhance his life. He was so busy and so isolated from the world by his fame that beyond his work very little except random copulations and his divorces from Largo ever happened to him. He was consistent, however; he told the same basic biographical lies to each analyst. The truth was that he had been born John Bryson near Pontryhydfen, Wales, where he won the All-Britain Winkle-Picking Competition in his late teens. This not only placed him in the top class of British professional winkle-pickers, but earned him a berth as Right Forward Picker on the All-England team, which won three successive test matches with Australia and which, in his last season as a picker, brought the World Cup back to Europe. With his accumulated bonuses he emigrated to New York in 1950 at the age of twenty-six, and was discovered for films on his second day in the United States by a neorealistic Italian director who was shooting a low-budget sleeper called *Little Dog* on the streets of the upper East Side. The world took Ty to its bosom for the sequence, which he had no idea was being shot, of him looking into the pet-shop window and losing his heart to the canine of the title. His first starring picture, for Albert McCobb, followed, and from the very beginning he became the biggest box-office attraction of his time.

Bryson watched and he learned. He struggled and reached to understand audience psychology. He became the professionals' professional. He absorbed the working of every department of film making as though each were to become his specialty. But perhaps his greatest acquired skill was in negotiating contracts. As his own business adviser, he modeled his performance on Sir Herbert Beerbohm Tree's characterization of Shylock. But through all this, he remained filled with an unquenchable curiosity and compassion about himself, if about nothing else. But he was also perpetually frightened, abjectly anxious. Everything terrified him, not merely such phobias of ordinary people as sudden noises, being shot at, taxes, dentists, politicians and saw-toothed fish. He needed to change his disguise to escape the terrors of living, and this made him nearly distraught with shyness and distrust, for he had to depend upon acting to provide shield and mask.

That evening, safe in his hotel apartment, Ty wrote to his mother, who would be momentarily in Athens when the letter reached her. He complained about the inventory of charges (such as the preposterous allegation that he had written business letters to her in baby talk) which Largo had made against him in her new book.

I am not devastated, Mama, you may be sure, for her lies hang like candy arrows in my flesh. But I am hurt, and that I resent because it is what she intended. Please study this list of harmful exaggerations, dear Mama; then cable me collect saying you will consent to appear as the Mystery Guest on *What's My Line?* I will send a camera crew to your next stop, at Tel Aviv. All you will need to do is to smile pityingly and deny Caterina's lies categorically. I will have a print made for screening aboard ship for your friends.

Ty wrote to his mother daily because he felt she was dependent on his letters. She sent him a monthly post card in return. He felt guilty because he saw her so infrequently. She lived aboard cruise ships and was always on the move across the world. Sometimes he would get Mother's Day and Navy Day confused, but he always remembered her on one or the other with a $2.75 greeting card, which Goldberg's people were able to get for him wholesale in Valencia, Spain.

When he had finished the letter he played with his stamp album for a while, grinning with pleasure because neither Largo nor the California courts knew he possessed it. He tried to keep at least one stamp album in the house vault of the hotels he used around the world, because stamps were relaxing and a sound way to study geography. Afterward he thought of toppling the chambermaid, but by the time the masseur left it was eleven o'clock and he was tuckered out. Some nights he didn't think he could keep his eyes open until the masseur arrived because he was so tired since the hepatitis. The masseur could not come before eleven, since he worked at a twenty-four-hour vegetable market on Lexington Avenue, but it was worth the wait because the man was deaf-and-dumb.

By eleven twenty-seven Ty was in bed. He had ignored thirty-six telephone messages from women lonely enough to want to stop by and be cheered up for the night. Wearing white silk pajamas with broad mauve stripes, he slept on his back, his mustache erectile. His coiffure was protected by light gold-wire filament as soft as wool, another by-product of the breakthrough in alloys as America answered the challenge of outer space. His eyes were secured from falling out of his head by a sturdy eyeshade in Chinese red, with "Hello, there!" printed across it in silver sequins. It had been a present from Largo out of her share of the community property. His underchin was cuddled to his jawbone by a sling of apple-green stretch silk. Against the bright yellow pillow case, he resembled the flag of an emergent African nation.

It took four long rings of the telephone to waken him. He ripped off the eyeshade in panic, leaped out of bed and ran to the window. Thirty-four stories below the streets were empty; it was deepest night. He thought of rushing downstairs and decapitating the telephone operator, then toyed with the idea of setting fire to the hotel's curtains. How dare they ring his telephone! He would demand that they call the managing director of the hotel every half-hour in reprisal. All at once the explanation came to him. It must be McCobb. Only Albert could get through the defenses of such a hotel. McCobb held the switchboard operators of every major hotel in the world in bribe. Ty picked up the phone, and gritting his teeth, spoke into it with icy control. "Yes, Albert?"

"Ty? Did I disturb you?"

"At ten after four in the morning? Don't be silly, luv."

"The *chef de rang* told me, when I called back, that you had eaten every bit of your nice lunch."

There was a longish pause.

"Ty? Are you there?"

"Yes, Albert."

"Feeling better, are you?"

"What the hell are you doing in Germany and why do you keep making these ludicrous calls?"

"The continental première of *Ghastly* is taking place here in Hamburg," Albert said.

Albert made the world's most successful suspense films. One of them had turned to gray the hair of an entire third-grade class in Clermont-Ferrand, according to a scientific
18

experiment conducted by the French authorities. All of his films were classical cinematic achievements, discussed in universities and woven with long hair into many awed essays and books, particularly by the French.

"We made *Ghastly* two years ago," Ty said.

"Nineteen months, actually. And the reason I've been calling is to tell you that I've decided to make a film in Hamburg."

"I would have much preferred to have read that in Suzy Knickerbocker."

"But I am designing the film for you."

"Out of the question, luv."

"And I have worked everything out with The Bungler, your agent, pending your approval."

The exasperated expression on Ty's face suddenly changed. His eyes narrowed and his mouth tightened. Money was at the heart of all art, and the thought of it quickened his pulse and cleared his mind. "I have an entirely new deal, you know, Albert," he said in a steely voice.

"So The Bungler told me. You are to become the first star ever to be paid a hundred percent of the gross, part of which is to be leased back to Goldberg, who is then to pay me, the owner and creator of the film, in Ghanaian aluminum delivered shipside in Dutch Guiana with Canadian bills of lading. The Bungler assures me that it has all been worked out with Washington, including the funneling of your hundred percent of the gross through Liechtenstein, Iranian and Zambian corporations, then into a commercial account in Luxembourg before transfer to your numbered accounts in London and Geneva. He assures me that my own tax position will be enormously improved and that I am to get a bonus, the size of which is to depend upon the amount of paper losses you are able to pile up in the venture. Of course it won't wash."

"There is one other condition, luv. Something I had forgotten to tell The Bungler."

"Really?"

"I have this magnificent idea to carry on my name, if not my work, after my death—"

"In the event of such an absurd contingency."

"In this new wrinkle I will be paid the first year's premiums on a life insurance policy on which I will borrow the maximum one can get for a face value of, say, five million dollars. The beneficiary will be the Tynan Bryson Foundation, a public relations firm which, after my death, will be devoted solely to keeping my memory alive."

"I see. But why do you want to borrow on the policy?"

"So that I can invest it in the market. Capital creates greater capital, and all my profits will be used to keep paying the premiums on the policy. Immortality is easily possible in this market."

"The Bungler also explained, in his vicious way, that you must have approval of casting, technicians, financing terms, stills, exhibition contracts, advertising, the co-producer if any, popcorn brands, the cinematographer, the script—and that Goldberg's own reader, Elizabeth Shannon Phillips, must be assigned to you for the duration of the filming."

"But I always get that—except Goldberg's reader."

There was a splashing sound as McCobb pushed a boat away from his pinkness in the Hamburg bathtub.

"Who will play the woman?" Ty asked.

"Name her."

"What kind of part is it?"

"Yours?"

"The woman's."

"There is none. This is a jockstrap picture. You play triplets, each reared separately in a contrasting environment. You all meet for the first time as inmates in a state prison. One of you is, of course, a secret agent; one a clergyman who is there incognito to gather research for a sociological study; one is an actual criminal. I may be able to get Mc-George Bundy to play your father."

"Why not De Gaulle?" Ty asked sarcastically.

"He wants a hundred percent of the gross."

"What sort of contrasting environments?"

"Republican, Democrat and Communist."

"Luv, you know I won't play a Communist."

"Ty, hear me out. You will be the first actor in screen history to play simultaneously the hero, the villain and the hero's best friend while earning a hundred percent of the gross."

"But there's no woman!"

"I'll write one in."

"In a prison picture?"

"I'll adjust the story if you insist upon a leading woman."

"Luv, I'd be crazy to carry the blame for a picture myself! In fact, if I were going to play it—which I am not—I'd have to have two leading women."

"All right. We'll do that."

"Albert, how can you call me in the middle of the night and talk business? I'm a sick man, I practically just got off the *Queen Mary,* and on top of that Caterina's book is driving me crazy."

"Why not write a book of your own?"

"Come off it, luv. I can't write, and you know it."

"That defeatist attitude was not conveyed by the reviews of your greeting card, lad. They compared you to Toynbee. Besides, I'd help you with the book; after all, I have a certain reputation for construction. You could call it *Biography of Three Marriages* and break Caterina's back in every chapter."

"They should read what a room looks like after she has walked through it. It resembles a garbage-strewn sty."

"You see? You've got to write it, lad."

"Albert, I can't go on talking like this. Among other things, someone is trying to kill me."

"Did you say kill you? Did you say *kill?*" For the first time in Ty's memory Albert's aplomb was shattered. "What has happened? Tell me. Have you reported this to Goldberg?"

"The first time was just before——"

"The *first* time!"

"It was just before we finished *Strike!*, when Goldberg let me have the *palazzo* outside Rome. The police say I was drugged before I went to bed, so that the criminal could enter and work beside my bed all night, setting up a huge piece of white marble embossed with raised gold letters . . ."

As Ty told the story in a flat, bored voice, he relived the horror of that sunny Roman morning. He had awakened, as always, at seven o'clock. As he swung out of bed his feet stopped in midair, then lowered slowly to the great plaque as long and wide as his bed, a tremendous metal-and-marble placard that transformed the floor beneath him into a great memorial. Half believing that he was still asleep, he read the six-inch-high letters:

> BRYSON! I AM GOING TO KILL YOU!
> IT WILL BE A FILTHY DEATH!
> FIRST I WILL TAKE YOUR FACE AWAY,
> THEN I AM GOING TO KILL YOU!
> THE VISIBLE WORLD IS NO LONGER
> A REALITY, AND THE UNSEEN WORLD
> IS NO LONGER A DREAM!

Bryson decided this was just the sort of puerile joke that his agent, who was unexpectedly his houseguest, might spend five hundred dollars to bring off. Donning swimming trunks, he set off toward the pool across the gardens. Ambling through the hedgerows of the exquisitely green garden with parterres, he turned down gentle steps into a long, formal slope to the swimming pool.

His agent, Junius Dollar, was making his approach to the end of the diving board. His wife, Gertrude, who never left his side, was seated in a wicker chair at the far end of the pool. Junius Dollar happened to be an agent who could execute fantastically improvised somersaults, half gainers and full twists. Before Ty's eyes he rose on the last step of his approach, came down heavily on the diving board and was catapulted approximately ninety-six feet into the air in a lovely parabola which would have ended abruptly in the distant rock garden had not his wife, an extremely plucky little woman, run across the greensward like a great outfielder, shading her eyes from the sun, and caught him as he came down.

"Great God!" McCobb said. "What happened to her?"

"She snapped two ankles and suffered a double hernia."

"But . . . that is a frightful story!"

"The point is, luv, if The Bungler and Gertrude had not happened to arrive the night before—quite unexpectedly—it would have been me on that diving board."

"But how—"

"The police investigation uncovered a diabolical mechanism which had been attached to the board. It was a launching device used to fly small planes off Fujihawa-type submarines in World War Two. If The Bungler had not weighed so much—about two forty-six—if he had weighed one hundred and eighty pounds as I do, he would have been propelled approximately one hundred and sixty-three feet up and dropped squarely on the stone roof of the *palazzo*, two hundred and ninety feet away."

"My God!"

"It was a terrible morning, and I got hepatitis almost immediately afterward."

"What has Goldberg done about this?"

"Goldberg moves in mysterious ways, as you know."

"I shall call him at once. Didn't you say that there had been other attempts, that this one was only the *first?*"

"Albert, I simply can't go through it all again on the telephone. It is four forty-five in the morning and I am exhausted."

"Very well, I shall ask Goldberg. But let there be no argument about this: you mustn't be alone. You must come to Hamburg, where I can provide a security force. I'll help you with your book and you'll help me with my film and we'll keep you safe. The only important thing is to keep you safe."

"But what about my new terms?"

"We'll just have to work that out somehow."

Bryson had been feeling his loneliness as intensely as if he were locked inside a refrigerator on the city dump. It was becoming a complicated business just to get dressed; if he stayed in New York he might not be able to get out of his pajamas for months. He needed to be taken in charge; he needed to be with good friends. Exhaling slowly, he said, "Provided you solemnly believe that we can work out the deal, I'll go."

Albert sighed. There was no price tag on what Ty would permit other people to spend to save his life. "All right, then," he said slowly. Ty was the only positive assurance of profit left in the business; if he had ten more pictures left in him it could mean a hundred to a hundred and fifty million dollars' gross. Goldberg made it on that gross. If Bryson was struck down before he made six more films, the loss would be perhaps a hundred and fifty million dollars. Under these circumstances he supposed he could get Goldberg to agree to Ty's new deal. "This is how you will be organized," Albert said. "Make notes, please. The contracts will be at your hotel at seven fifty-two tomorrow morning. Do not sign them. Read them on the plane and we'll chat about them when we meet. The limousine will be at the hotel to take you to the airport at nine-three."

"Please be sure to arrange a stopover in London, luv."

"Why?"

"I'm afraid that the hepatitis has burned up my hormonal implant."

"Is that Sir Herman Levin in Harley Street?"

"Why, yes."

"I will fly him to Hamburg."

"He is fantastically expensive just standing still in Harley Street."

"I will pay for it," McCobb said, and Bryson stopped protesting. "Now hear this, Ty. The hotel valet will enter your room at eight-three to pack your bags. The waiter will arrive at eight-nineteen with scrambled plovers' eggs and a dish of the *chipolatas* you enjoy so much."

"Aren't plovers' eggs fattening?"

"No matter. Four ounces at most. We'll sweat that out in

23

the sauna I am building for you here. Not to worry. You **bring out** the best in people, Ty. You know that."

"I suppose I do, luv. Dr. Weiler says I do. Technically speaking—"

"Tell me in Hamburg."

"I'll bring the tapes of that session. It's fascinating."

"Thank you, laddie. Sleep warm, old friend."

Bryson hung up, lay back in bed, shook two sleeping pills out of a dark-brown vial, pulled his chin strap into place and lowered his eyeshade. It was one minute past five. No one was going to talk him out of being the first actor in history to be paid a hundred percent of the gross, he thought grimly as he popped the pills into his mouth absent-mindedly.

2

THE AMERICAN CULTURE which gave the world the motion picture had grown so complex that American males were unaware of the changes in fashion of their sexual ideal. First there was the Grant Wood pioneer woman of Anglo-Saxon stock, uncomfortably angled and spare, knobby under her Mother Hubbard. She was the prodigious worker who pulled the Conestogas to the Pacific when the horses had been shot by Indians, and by the time she got a chance to sit down, she had begun to fill out. Then came the great waves of Italians, Swedes, Germans and Slavs—great-handed farm women with the sort of breasts which would one day exemplify Mother's Day and provide the frantically busy American male with an instant sex symbolism, so that as he rushed across the landscape he could pause, yell "Holy cow, what knockers!" and leap on, fully aroused. Time is money, after all.

Then came the moving-picture camera, and Caterina Largo's fortune and fame, indeed immortality, were assured. But Largo had more than the greatest set of supernormal stimuli ever shown on a fifty-by-eighty-foot Vistavision screen in glorious Technicolor. She had wonder calves for the Oriental market, and a behind stuffed with the golden fleece of erotic dreams for the Mediterranean peoples. She had shoulders so flawless that they reminded Swedish men of winter nights in boarding schools, and English women of golden hockey captains. Her hips—well, no Frenchman under ninety-one had ever been able to recall the complete plots of her pictures because they were blinded by tears in their contemplation of the sanctuary adumbrated within the rocking cradle of her hips.

Largo had something for everybody, and certainly everybody had something for Largo.

Albert McCobb believed that proper casting was the most difficult part of film making. It was not simply a matter of persuading precisely the right actor to play a part, but to secure his services at a price commensurate with breaking even. Nonetheless, casting was the part of film making which he enjoyed most.

Real stars were as rare as the caviar from yellow-bellied sterlet, and they had the assets of small suburban banks. To secure the professional services of Caterina Largo for the film he was preparing in Hamburg, McCobb waited until the last day of shooting of the epic she was currently making at Indian Head, Saskatchewan, in which she played the role of the first woman Mountie of the Royal Northwest Police. It was called *Always Get Your Man,* but would be released as *Timber* because Goldberg believed in short titles.

To reach Largo in the most dramatic manner possible was an involved process. McCobb had Goldberg's Italian manager cable her from Florence in his name. The cable asked her to telephone McCobb at 9 P.M. (2 P.M. in Saskatchewan), at the Ristorante Sabatini on Via Panzini. It was an irresistible appeal.

Years before, when her work in European films first brought her to California to play the peasant girl Rifke in *Hopeless* for McCobb, it was discovered that Largo was a direct descendant of the Medici. She became evil-tempered if it was suggested that this was just press-agent fill. Largo knew more about the Medici than the head guide at the Pitti Palace. In time it was universally accepted that she was a Medici —particularly by the surviving men in that great family. Bryson mocked her claims before television newsreel cameras following their third divorce, citing the wording on the tombstone of Anna Maria Ludovica as "The last of the royal race of the Medici," but he could prove nothing and no Italian newspaper would believe him. A gossip columnist who had covered World War II from his typewriter in New York wrote that she had starred in pictures in Germany and had

25

been a friend of Dr. Goebbels', but the lawsuit which she and McCobb instituted established that she was only fourteen years old in 1944, and they had split a settlement of two hundred and seventy-seven thousand dollars. McCobb gave his share to the German war orphans; Largo gave all of hers to a German refugee in exchange for a chamois bag filled with uncut diamonds.

Largo and Tynan Bryson met when they appeared together in *Hopeless*. While exerting his inevitable droit du seigneur on the evening of the fourth day of shooting, they each discovered that they had been tricked. What had appeared to be simple lust turned, before their horrified eyes, into enchaining love. They were married for the first time during the shooting of their second film for McCobb, a tremendously successful thriller called *Awful*.

If Largo was not delighted to make the call to McCobb at the Ristorante Sabatini in Florence, she was curious enough to place it exactly on time. She liked to acquire unexpected information and unanticipated emotions, and she was accustomed to casual conversations with McCobb changing the course of her life.

When the call came in to Sabatini's, Unger, Goldberg's Italian manager, had it switched to Hamburg without informing Largo. McCobb took the call in his bathtub, where he was restaging the Battle of Lepanto in miniature. Largo was under a hair drier in the suite Lord Tweedsmuir had once occupied in the Imperial Hotel at Indian Head. As she spoke to him she imagined the taste of the *strozzapreti* of her homeland, and the instant she heard his voice she cried out, "What are you eating, Albert?"

Largo's voice had several strata to it. There was the gutter layer, which could have been part southern European, part American show biz. The next level was beautiful; though her voice held harsh tones and she often spoke argot with obscenities, her phrasing was delicately shaded and controlled. It was the good-woman part of her voice, and though she had acquired it, it had become her own music. Largo's teacher of English had been a tiny linguist from Dublin named Peggy Flinn, who had so softened the stridency of Largo's speech that she now spoke English with a slight Irish accent.

"I am having some *chiocciole nel tegame,* actually," McCobb replied.

"Oh, Albert! Let me speak to Signor Sabatini, please."

From his bathtub, McCobb handed the telephone to an Italian character actor who was standing by, desperately needing to go to the john and tortured by the splashings of tub water. He greeted Largo jovially, if nervously, in a broad Tuscan dialect, described the weather in Florence and the depth of the Arno. She wept softly under the hair drier until hurriedly he gave the phone back to McCobb and rushed out.

"How is the food in Indian Head, my dear?" Albert asked kindly. Largo sobbed louder.

At crucial moments McCobb always dealt with actors either when they were in restaurants or by telephoning from restaurants because it was his theory that actors' most deep-seated memories were of their early, hungry days, and because of the cruel diets they had to endure endlessly to remain underweight for the cameras. Largo would never suffer from athrepsia; in fact, she relied on a metal corset fashioned sentimentally from one of Garibaldi's cannon. Italian food was her vision of eternal life.

"Never mind, my dear," Albert said. "I am having this identical meal flown to you in New York. Will you be at the hotel or at your flat?"

"New York? I'm going to Palm Springs."

"No, no. New York. I have settled every contractual point with Francis A. O'Connell."

"What contract?"

"We are about to start our ninth picture together."

Largo laughed gaily. "Impossible."

"Not at all."

"I'm exhausted. I've made two pictures back to back. I'm going to sleep for a month."

"Oh, by the way, Ty is writing a book."

"What book?"

"He calls it *Biography of Three Wives*." Albert waited a few beats. "He read me a few tidbits from the first chapter this morning." Silence. "He calls the first chapter 'The Great Sow.'" Silence. "He plans a chapter on your personal hygiene; according to him, you rub apples of raw garlic under your arms every night before retiring."

"Albert!"

"You must strike before he does. That is, if you care. He has no contract yet, so why not appropriate his title and have your own publisher announce it as your next book? That could stop him."

Largo began to laugh, sounding like a bagpipe underwater. "He will double up with pain!" she yelled into the telephone with delight. "How do I do it?"

"You must go to New York at once and talk to your publisher; insist on a front-cover ad in *Publishers' Weekly*. Then

27

fly to Hamburg and I will lay on a monster international press conference to announce the book in a glamorous continental setting."

"He will turn orange! He will weed his rug in fistfuls!"

"And I will send Basil to New York to smooth the way and take care of everything."

Albert had known it would not really be difficult to persuade Caterina to make the picture. She had the time, and her price, seven hundred and fifty thousand dollars, always made her feel rested and strong.

When Largo hung up she was humming. Her best dreams continued to come true; she was Tynan Bryson's endless punishment, a goal that took character, strong will and an unswerving belief in justice.

Once when Bryson was at the studio she hired a dry-cleaning truck to call at his house on Cabrillo Drive and take away all his clothes. Fifty-six suits, twenty-three suede vests, one hundred and nine shirts, two hundred and forty-one ties, and more underwear than was issued annually to the Swiss Guards at the Vatican, had been shipped to Boys Town in Italy. When he returned that night, all he had to wear was the Robin Hood costume in which he was dressed, and for three days he had to endure the humiliation of ready-made underwear and off-the-peg shirts until his haberdashers and tailors, working overtime, rescued him.

On another occasion Largo hired pickets to follow him wherever he went for three months. Their signs demanded to know whether or not he was a sympathizer with Red China, and he had been forced to get a court order to call them off.

The previous autumn she had convinced two insurance companies that Bryson was a bleeder, and production on the picture he was making for his own company had to be stopped at a cost of forty-three thousand five hundred dollars a day while he flew to London from southern Yugoslavia and cut himself savagely with a razor in the presence of insurance-company doctors.

That winter she sent mechanics to his garage in the dead of night to take his four automobiles apart entirely, intermixing all parts in a pile on the floor. Two days later she bribed his butler to give him sleeping pills at breakfast instead of vitamin tablets. It was during the shooting of a high-speed, mile-a-minute farce, and he nearly broke down in terror that his talent was gone. This time his production company lost fifty-one thousand two hundred dollars a day for five days because nothing shot during that period could be used.

Largo fought to hurt, if not to win. While she fought she

felt very good because in her own way she was with him every hour of the day and night. She was acquisitive for grudges and possessions, and wherever she could she took them with her. She traveled back and forth across the world, an angel of mercy for independent film producers, always with one hundred and thirty pieces of luggage, never more than ninety of them filled with the telephone books which Bryson had picked up at a bargain in Lawrence, Kansas, during their first marriage. Though she had the usual star's paraphernalia—a Lear jet, a helicopter, seven cars scattered around Europe and four in the States, her own ski lift and a hydrofoil—she always listed her occupation as "homemaker" on any application, partly in wistful longing and partly because she and Bryson owned houses in Beverly Hills, Palm Springs, New York, London, Florence and the Algarve. Theirs was the only triplex penthouse in New York with a small but well-banked roller-skating track. But they needed everything they owned to satisfy the corps of income tax engineers who toiled and intoned over such expenses as shoeshines and safety matches, and who forbade them to tip lavatory attendants without getting a return receipt.

The London house in Heath Street had eleven bathrooms fashioned from the choir lofts of seven Ukrainian parish houses. The bedsteads in the high-ceilinged rooms had bases of pink marble with gilt frames, which Sotheby's had authenticated as having come from the cavalry dormitory at Versailles. The dining room in the Algarve house had full-scale replicas of Michelangelo's *David* in each corner only because the City of Florence had so far refused to sell the original to Goldberg, who had promised to lease it to Largo. Caterina's table service was of carved jade executed with gems from designs by Da Vinci. She had almost as many fur coats as all the white bears in the Arctic, and shoes enough to start a revolution, were the inventories to become known, even in an affluent country.

Beyond these mundane things she had her face, her body and her incalculably womanly spirit—together more precious, more luxurious, more sybaritical, more illusory, more sensual, more unforgettably formed and more exquisitely endowed than all of her other possessions. She was so glamorous that even her hangovers had an exotic mystery.

But it was all wasted. When Largo and Bryson weren't married, her only real pastime was wheeling and dealing. She lived only to torture Bryson or to lie in his arms. She would rack her mind to try to discover by what genetic or environmental curse she had been burdened with the bleak happiness

29

or the merry anxiety of the one-man woman. While she waited another turn with Bryson, always relying on the calendar to wear him down until he would be hers and only hers, only the pursuit of money gave her any respite. She speculated in painted canvas and formed marble. What a man had created for the price of a bowl of lasagna she bought for eighty to two hundred thousand dollars and resold to the first buyer for a fat profit. She accumulated objects over which men had agonized and starved: nudes by Ingres and Eisenhower, jeweled crosses, the pottery of Bernard Palissy, agonies by Géricault, cords of woodcuts, furniture by Boulle, a stone hunting lodge in Abruzzi which hadn't been touched since the days of the Hohenstaufen emperors in 1240. Her stock market bets were handled by a Parsee wizard in Geneva. Between them, they shuttled tons of the same shares back and forth with every quarter-point rise and dip, and Largo always came out dusty with gold.

In between, she dabbled in Calcutta real estate, underground parking lots in Brussels, and a twenty-one percent interest in the largest gambling house in London. Away from Bryson she was always sad, but accumulating so much money and so many possessions relieved her peckishness.

3

BRYSON came awake to a hammering sound from somewhere nearby. He realized gummily that he had taken the sleeping pills much too late. He seemed to be glued to the bed, and could move only with great difficulty and then in slow motion. He began to worry that somehow he had been transported back into *Carnal,* in which he had been drugged because he possessed a vital paper which could prevent or start the greatest war in history. Enemy agents disguised as Chinese laundrymen had come to his hotel room to steal the paper. He looked around. It couldn't be, and yet it was the same room, a replica of the set in *Carnal.* The hammering on the door had been just like this in *Carnal* too. He must have been projected back into the movie somehow—in which case he had a terrible fight on his hands.

Sunlight came into the room, and the eyeshade wasn't really working; how typical of Caterina to have given him a faulty eyeshade. He slid it up over his forehead with an effort, and while the racket at the door continued, tried to think of how he had fought off the effects of the drug in *Carnal*. What secret paper could they be after? He had no such paper.

Somehow he got out of bed and began the immense journey to the door with what must have been powerful electromagnets, imbedded in his slippers. His mind was like a deserted bird's nest. Perhaps the hotel had caught fire, as in *Fire!*, which had grossed six million six and which . . . The set in *Fire!* had been a replica of this room too. The pounding on the door grew louder; yet he could make his way toward it only at the speed of a manacled centenarian. The intricate designs in the Persian carpet beneath his feet passed under him at the speed great cities move under a jet plane flying at forty thousand feet. He worked on the chain lock with slow persistence until it fell away and the door opened. There was no one there.

Something struck his ankle sharply. He looked downward and stared into the face of a dugong attached to a tiny female human body under a rose corduroy hat which seemed to feature a large fishbone as panache. The face snarled at him through teeth which resembled a careless stack of racing oars in a pooorly maintained boathouse. "Where the hell were you, honey?" the face said. "I been knocking and knocking."

"Whassamattah?"

"I like your style. Sign here." She handed up a sheaf of typewritten pages and a thick-barreled pen. Bryson crouched, leaned the batch against the door at waist level and began to sign wherever she held her finger. But after three signatures he realized that there was something wrong. "Whaddam I signing?" he asked thickly.

"Come on. Three more copies."

"Who are you?"

"Sally Capistrano, but they call me Swallows." She leered up at him. "I'm a junior partner with Bernstein and Ennis. I was Harvard Law, and I say that with a lotta pride." She tapped the pages with an iron finger. "Sign. Three more."

"But . . . whaddizzit?"

"Come on! I don't have time! I gotta be inna federal courthouse, Foley Square, by nine."

"Leave then. Go." Bryson backed away and tried to close

31

the door but she was on top of him in an instant, stamping on his bare instep with a burgundy suede space shoe. "Sign, you actor!" she shrilled. "You mimes are all alike. Give you a deal whereby you get the lion's share, you could make a million, maybe two, and you scream. What am I, some kinda fan? Some kid?" She pushed her short hairy arm into his stomach and jammed him against the wall. "Sign! You think because I'm Harvard Law I'm some kinda soft touch?"

Ty signed. He wasn't intimidated, but people were gathering outside in the hall and stared at him in his pajamas, with the sequined eyeshade on his forehead and his chin strap down and the gold netting over his hair. What bothered him even more was that they might think he had brought such a woman into his rooms for lewd purposes.

"A copy for you, movie star," Miss Capistrano said. She slapped one of the thick documents into his hand and reached up to pat his throat. "Call me at the office any time after five, you hear? We'll have a belt and maybe a little kiss-kiss." She slammed the door and was gone forever.

Bryson stumbled into the living room, fell into a chair, lifted the sheaf of papers to eye level and focused. It was a contract citing Albert McCobb as party of the first part. But Albert had insisted that he sign nothing. There must be a misunderstanding. Albert was in a bathtub in Hamburg and a valet was coming in any minute to pack his bags. Ty moved slowly to the bedroom, more in a drift than a walk, and laboriously set aside his traveling clothes, leaving the rest to be packed. He sat down in the tub as though he were descending the north face of the Eiger, then reached up and turned on a cold shower. He made it hot, then cold again. After five minutes this seemed to help, and his head was clearer as he began to shave with a Swiss machine which resembled Telstar.

Though he felt a desperate need to telephone Dr. Weiler, he managed to dress himself single-handedly. But when he opened the bathroom door with a democratic greeting for the valet, the room was empty. And where was breakfast? Albert was always very precise about these things.

When he dialed the valet, an olive-choked Greek voice answered. "Yas?"

"This is Tynan Bryson in 3524, 25 and 26. Where are you?"

"In the basement."

"Why aren't you here?"

"You want a suit packed up, or laundry?"

"You were supposed to be here at eight-three to pack me."

"Pack you in what?"

"To pack my luggage!"

"Nobody told me. Who did you talk to, mister?"

"It was all arranged last night from Hamburg, Germany."

"What?"

It had sounded strange even to Bryson as he said it, but it was impossible to convey to a civilian how McCobb worked. "Let me speak to the head of your department," he said abruptly.

"I am head. And the boy is sick today."

"All right, then. You will please come at once to 3524 and pack my bags. I have a plane to catch."

"Mister, not before half past ten. I'm all alone and I have to make eight suit pickups and thirty-one laundries." The line went dead.

Bryson dialed the hall porter to ask if plane tickets had been left for him. They had not. He pressed the room-service bell and the floor waiter appeared at once.

"Where is my breakfast?"

"Sir?"

"Plovers' eggs and *chipolatas*."

"Did you order last night?"

"The order was placed last night." Ty felt dizzy; the humiliation was simply too much. But he was not going to explain that his breakfast had been ordered from Germany.

"What is a *chipolata*, sir?"

Bryson ordered a cup of chocolate. When the waiter left he sat down on the floor in the deepest depression he had felt since leaving Castellaneta. He couldn't possibly call Dr. Weiler; it was only a quarter to five in California. He tried to remember how to go about packing sixteen suitcases; it had been too long and he had lost the knack.

The telephone rang, and he reached up to the table. "Hello?"

"Ty? Albert, here. Everything on schedule?"

To his alarm, Bryson's eyes filled with tears. He had tried to do too much since leaving the hospital. He should be resting and marshaling his strength.

"The valet never came, luv," he said, "the waiter doesn't know what a *chipolata* is, and all the bags are unpacked. There is no plane ticket here. A nightmare of a woman forced me to sign something which had your name on it. It's been very difficult, because I took two sleeping pills after you called, not realizing how late it was, and—"

"But this is outrageous! I'll find the people who botched this and—"

33

"No, Albert. Please. Just get me out of here and never mind about the rest of it."

"I'll tell you, I am going to fly to New York today and rip the shirt off the managing director of your fine Fifth Avenue hotel."

"Fifth Avenue?"

"You are at the St. Regis?"

"No. No, no! I'm at the Tower." Bryson shook his head like a wet collie.

"My God! Please forgive me, Ty. I have botched absolutely everything. Just give me ten minutes on the telephone. Basil is in New York on a little errand, and he'll see that everything lands feetfirst, you may be sure of it. Please forgive me, Ty. I am so sorry."

"But—"

"Yes?"

"But you keep calling me here—at the Tower, I mean—not at the St. Regis."

"Well, after all, Ty, I just tell the operator to get you, I don't specify *where*."

In twelve minutes Basil Schute was on the line, very crisp, very military British. "Awful balls-up at the St. Regis, Ty," he said. "Valet packed a honeymoon couple and shipped all their luggage to Hamburg and the man threw the plovers' eggs at the waiter. But not to worry. All you have to do is walk straight out of your apartment and forget everything. Goldberg's men are zeroing in now to handle the packing, and the luggage will be aboard the plane with you. No time to lay on another limo; just this once, if you will take a taxi to the airport. It has been paid for and is waiting below for you right now."

Ty read the contract as he walked to the elevator, as he crossed the lobby, as he stepped into the taxi and as the ride to the airport began. He adored reading contracts. McCobb had actually signed it, which meant that Goldberg had agreed to pay him a hundred percent of the gross. What a precedent this contract would set! But why had Albert and Goldberg agreed without a fight? He smiled like a timber wolf. What would it do to Caterina when she learned that he was the first film actor in the world to be paid a hundred percent of the gross? He was more important than any actor in the history of the world. He smiled like a hyena.

"Where are you on Vietnam, Mac?" the taxi driver asked.

"What?"

"I said, are you a hawk or a dove?"

Ty leaned forward, slid the glass panel shut and returned

to reading the contract. The driver slammed the glass open immediately. "What the hell was that for?" he asked.

"My dear man, what the foreign secretary of your union instructed you to deliver to your passengers today is of little interest to me. I am busy with these papers. Please remain silent and we will forget the whole thing."

"Yeah?"

"Slide the window shut, please."

"Yeah?"

"Oh, for heaven's sake! Stop at the next corner. I shall change cabs."

"Whaddya talk like that for? You some kinda faggot or something?"

"I am British. We all talk like faggots. Stop the cab."

"I am paid, buddy. You go where I'm paid to go."

"How much were you paid?"

"Fifteen bucks. You wanna double it?"

Bryson rolled down the window beside him, inhaled deeply and then sang out in a strong baritone, "Police! Police!" The cab stopped abruptly, directly beside a convenient cab rank.

"What are you, some kind of fink?" the cabbie screamed. Bryson entered another cab two steps away, then summoned the first driver with a crook of his finger. The man leaped out and came toward him belligerently. "You will give me fourteen dollars and twenty-five cents. The remainder is your five-cent tip," Bryson said.

Suddenly the second driver shouted, "Hey! You're Tynan Bryson, the movie star!"

"Yeah?" the first cabbie said. "He is?"

Bryson wriggled his outstretched fingers, and the driver took out his wallet and laid the money on it. "I would appreciate it very much," he said, "if you'd give me yaw rautograph."

"Certainly. What is your name?"

"Marty Macklefarb."

Ty unscrewed a black fountain pen. "Have you something I might write it on?" Macklefarb looked through his pockets, but the only paper he had was his hack license. He handed it to Ty, who rested it on his attaché case and wrote: "Up yours, Marty Macklefarb—Sincerely, Tynan Bryson."

The driver stared at it and blushed. "Gee, thanks, Mr. Bryson," he said shyly.

"That's all right."

"But what *do* you think we ought to do about Vietnam?" Macklefarb asked anxiously.

"Why not write to your President?" Bryson said graciously.

4

TYNAN BRYSON's greatest conceit, and such a superlative can hardly be measured in terms of human reference, was his belief that he possessed an almost supernatural ability to assess the total character of anyone he ever met in a few seconds. This gift, he felt, was imbued by a Greater Power to only a few really great actors of each generation. He had been encouraged in this opinion by his agent, The Bungler, who had planted the identical idea in the mind of every one of his clients. Consequently there were fifty-seven film actors who believed that they knew more about human nature than Freud, Socrates and La Rochefoucauld combined. Since each had chosen The Bungler to represent them, and since The Bungler had convinced them that where people were concerned, they *knew* they never erred, they were impelled to think of him as the perfect agent.

But in point of fact, Bryson's judgment was so faulty that he trusted anyone who appreciated his work. "*Pravda* is a basically sound newspaper," he would say. "They have liked both of my pictures shown so far in Russia." Hence he did not quite trust McCobb because Albert would not tolerate his attempts to mangle every script by rewriting (Bryson told anyone who would listen how he had actually written the script, as it was seen on the screen, of virtually every picture he had ever appeared in). Also, McCobb always seemed to be managing him.

On the other hand, in Bryson's uncanny judgment Basil Schute, McCobb's right-hand man and production manager, was open and true-blue. As Ty entered the terminal at Kennedy Airport, he could see Basil flirting with a beautiful stewardess across the large room. He was tempted, but restrained himself and made a beeline for the life insurance machines to perform his usual rite of propitiation.

He made the Salvation Army the beneficiary on the first fifty-thousand-dollar policy, then endowed in an equal

36

amount the NAACP, Methodist Missions and the Organization for Rehabilitation and Training. He decided not to include an actors' charity lest it put a stain of selfishness upon his gesture. If the plane still insisted upon crashing, he would have bought splendid post-mortem public relations for a very small sum.

Basil was still shivering the drawers of the stewardess, but he came to attention as Ty approached. "Good morning, Ty. You're looking quite fit. Fräulein Schmeckle, may I present Mr. Tynan Bryson?" Ty bowed, and the girl winked with her off-eye.

"Here is your plane ticket, Ty. And Mr. McCobb wishes you to have this hundred-dollar bill—will you sign this receipt for me, please?—for spending money at the Frankfurt airport, where there will be a seventy-minute layover."

"Oh, really, Baz! Albert knows I always fly direct!"

"Only when the plane schedules co-operate. But not to worry. Plovers' eggs and *chipolatas* will be waiting for you in the lounge there."

Ty had stopped listening. He was surrounded by the public, which always produced a chemical change in his unfailing courtesy. Basil knew that Ty was shocked, because since he entered the building, no one had recognized him. Anonymity was so totally alien to Bryson's way of life that tremors of anxiety started at his toes, and his mouth dried up. Then and there he decided that the production was going to have to fly Dr. Weiler to Hamburg for the duration of the film, or he simply wouldn't be able to finish it. Only five feet away, a swarm of pimply people were hopping from foot to foot in a manifestation of group lust for the sight of a celebrity—but they seemed to be looking right through him.

"Who is this bunch waiting for, Baz?" he asked as casually as he could.

"Oh, probably some school team returning victorious." Basil did his best to appear relaxed, but Ty could see that he was embarrassed and uneasy.

"I don't agree," he said, glaring beadily at Basil until he sidled over to the nearest rotten little punk, gripped his arm and snarled in his ear. The boy cringed, and Basil's head jerked furtively in Ty's direction, Ty saw, though the gesture had been subtle. The acned face stared directly at Bryson without recognition; he could have been John Bunny or Dustin Farnum. This is what purgatory must be like, Bryson thought. It was a remake of that scene from *Tension*, in which he was an upperclassman at West Point and his roommate had discovered that he was not a WASP and the whole corps of cadets built a wall of silence around him. How had he coped in that script?

But before he could think it through, Basil was back. "Just a lot of kids," he said with an overlarge gesture.

"I am aware of that. What are they hanging around for?"

Basil shrugged as if he were trying to lift his torso off his hips.

"Dammit, Baz! I mean, what difference does it make to me who they're waiting for?"

"Well, Ty . . . you see . . . well, damn it all, the boy says that Largo is due in from Canada in about a half-hour."

"It's not fair!" Ty shouted. He looked wildly around, then broke into a run toward the departure gate with Basil and Fräulein Schmeckle in pleading pursuit. Ty was overtaken at the passport counter, his face like granite.

"Surely, Ty," Basil said, "you don't think this is my fault?"

"It's all right, luv. Let us forget it. Good-bye. See you in Hamburg. Good-bye, Miss Schmeckle."

"But I am your stewardess for the flight," she said, pushing her bosom at him.

"She is going to see that you are very comfortable," Basil added emphatically. Then his passport was stamped and Fräulein Schmeckle walked him to the plane well before the flight was called, telling him soothingly that his films were among the most important things in her life. As they sat alone in the huge plane, Ty noticed for the first time how remarkably pretty she was. And so healthy and interested. Because she was clearly a fan, he asked her if she would be able to attend the European première of *Ghastly* in Hamburg two nights later. She said that she would be very, very honored, so he kissed her. Could they count on being alone for a while? he wondered. The would be alone for at least seven minutes, she said. Would it be possible to lock the forward door and put the seats all the way back? he asked. Oh, yes, she replied, that would be quite easy to do, but why did he want to do it? He would show her why, he said.

After Ty had boarded the plane Basil returned to the waiting room to find the rotten young punk. "Good work, Gar," he said. "Now call Mr. Keller and tell him I want a discreet mob in front of the St. Regis at eleven-thirty."

"How many?"

"Twenty-five. Tell him I want a top-notch respectful demonstration. Well-bred, enormously admiring young people. No rough stuff. They may surround her, but everyone must say please—and no clothes-tearing, understand?"

"I dig." The boy turned and pumped his right arm high over his head. "Now hear this," he shouted to his people. "Back to town. Regroup at the St. Regis at eleven-twenty."

Basil went into the bar to wait for Largo. He wore a blue blazer with brass buttons, a symbol of Alvaro's Restaurant in the King's Road. He had a large head, resembling the Norfolk tradition in cartoons of John Bull, over a wandlike body. He wore a close-cropped ginger mustache, and his movements were as quick as if he had studied dancing at the monastery of St. Vitus. When the occasion arose, he had the most piercing voice and terrifying manner of any assistant director in the industry. He had been Albert McCobb's assistant, production manager and go-between for a dozen years.

Largo arrived from Toronto at ten-seventeen, sixteen minutes after Bryson's plane took off. As she walked out of the customs area, people dropped packages; men bit their lips to keep from moaning piteously, and furtively tried to adjust their clothing. She was so beautiful that no one could possibly ever get used to it, least of all Basil Schute.

Largo walked directly to the bar and sat on a stool beside Basil, pleased that he had kept the faith by not making any fuss so that she could walk across the airport unnoticed, just like anyone else.

"Mexican beer?" she asked tentatively. "How are you, Baz?" The bartender had the bottle opened before she finished speaking. She took a sip, then leaned over and kissed Basil on the temple. "You think of everything," she said. "How long will we be in New York?"

"Ten-one tomorrow morning."

"McCobb said he was sending me a meal from Sabatini's."

"It's at the hotel. Do you want to see a show tonight?"

"Any good fights?"

"Yes, actually. In Brooklyn. Armory boys, but they mix."

"I'll say they mix. Let's have dinner at a Joosh delicatessen."

"Katz's? The Stage? Downtown or uptown?"

"Schmulka Bernstein. I can smell it now. Where's Bryson?"

Basil stared into his orange juice. "I suppose it was speaking of the lights that reminded you," he said. "He's in Italy, I think."

"No, he's here. Goldberg brought him here to open *Ships*."

"Then he's in New York."

"That's what I asked you. Where?"

"Why?"

"Why what?"

"Why do you think I'd know where he is? Or give a single

damn? You're in love with him and I'm in love with you and I detest the man. Do you mean you want to *see* him again?"

"Knock it off. I want to make sure he reads my book. I have a rigged copy which opens at five passages that will send him to bed retching."

"In that case we must find him."

It took Largo ten minutes to get from the curb on Fifty-fifth Street into the lobby because there were twenty-five polite but eager fans waiting for her in front of the hotel. "I swear to God I don't know how they find out when somebody is going to hit town, but it certainly makes you feel good. I mean, yesterday I thought that I'd be in California this morning. How do they find out? It's crazy!"

In her large corner suite, slipcovered in ivory and over-looking Central Park, she called her publisher before she sat down. "How's it doing, Pepe?"

"Great. I mean *sensational*. The Spanish-American War Veterans Book Club took it this morning, and the jobber in Chicago says he'll take twenty-six hundred extra copies if you'll write out the first chapter in longhand for display material. Isn't that fantastic?"

"No good, hon. He'll put it in a safe and then sell it as a holograph in a couple of years, and I won't get a quarter out of it."

"No, no. You don't do anything. We'll have a girl in the office copy it in longhand."

"Okay, but no resale, you hear? And Pepe—"

"Yes?"

"I started on another book. I have a great title. *Biography of Three Husbands*. Like *Inside Bryson*."

"Mamma mia!"

"I didn't know you spoke Italian. But I want the cover of the next *PW* for the announcement. Can you get it?"

"It just·so happens that we have reserved the cover—for this poet—a Pulitzer Prize-winner—"

"Good. Then tomorrow in Hamburg—"

"Germany?"

"Where else—Basutoland? McCobb will set up a big press conference where I'll announce the book and throw in a few grislies. We'll get great space. A deal?"

"Fantastic. What about the contract?"

"So call Francis A. O'Connell."

"You'll indemnify us against libel? Bryson is a suer, as you know."

"Bryson is a sewer, as I know. S-e-w-e-r. He won't take this book to court, Pepe, because when he reads it he'll go right home and shoot himself."

That night, after the fights in Brooklyn, after Basil had dropped her off at the hotel, Largo called her garage to send a car around and drove uptown through the park. It was a lovely, clear, cool night, the kind which New York occasionally delivers unexpectedly, and everything about it made her feel wistful.

She let herself into the apartment, hoping against hope that he would be there. The enormous flat was musty. All of the furniture and pictures on the walls were covered with sheets. She trailed across the great spaces of the enormous rooms to the kitchen, pulling her huge sable behind her. The kitchen was spotless because the cleaning woman was instructed to keep it ready for use. The spaghettini from Torre Annunziata was where it should be. She hung up the fur coat in the walk-in refrigerator between two legs of lamb, and then drifted into the kitchen to prepare something that Bryson liked.

As Largo cooked, she reflected that this was probably what she had been meant to do if she'd had a different face and another figure. Money bought places like this, and that was fine, but *spaghettini all' amatriciana* was better. What a rotten thing to be hooked on one man when sex was such a glorious pastime. What a rotten thing to be able to cook so well and to have to eat alone. The film business was such a lot of crap.

She savored the spaghettini under her iron corset, and at one twenty-five she locked the apartment door behind her and drove back to the hotel. She always felt like crying when she left one of her houses. They were such forlorn places.

Carrie-Ann Blongett's agent called her at Schwab's to say that Albert McCobb had just telephoned from Germany to offer her the second lead in the next Bryson picture. Miss Blongett's reaction had more chambers than a housefly's eyes. "Tah musta done it," she said in her specially induced Dixie accent. "He's the only man big enough to tell McCobb—and Ah mean, including Goldberg."

"Watch it, baby. You could be on a bugged phone."

"*Maybe* McCobb knew Ah'm alive, but no bets. Believe me, Harry, Ah don' care what they pay, but fix up a precedent this one time—you know? And first class on the plane. Right?"

5

WHEN it was granted a charter as a free city state and port by the Emperor Barbarossa in 1189, Hamburg covered two hundred and eighty-eight square miles, making it the largest of the small states of Europe; larger than Andorra, Bremen, Liechtenstein, San Marino, Monaco and Vatican City. During the bombing in World War II, its asphalt streets had boiled, cooking thousands. It was rebuilt into the most beautiful city and largest industrial center in West Germany. Its fine new buildings, its opera house, its beautifully landscaped parks and famous zoo, and the lovely lake around which it hovered, made it unique in Europe.

The Pacific Seasons Hotel was on the quay overlooking the Inner Alster, one of the two segments of the lake whose water flowed through the city and into the Elbe. It was the finest hotel in northern Europe, and the reason McCobb had chosen Hamburg as the location for his film was the incredibly large size of its bathtubs and the high quality of its *Snuten und Poten*. He was such a food snob that he not only favored Roquefort cheese, for example, but refused Bleu de Bresse and Danish Blue cheese because they were non-ewe.

But the bathtubs were the main attraction. McCobb had brought a sizable part of his famous collection of miniature ships of war to the hotel in seven fitted trunks because he anticipated a long shooting schedule. He had fleets of tiny Greek galleys, to recreate the Battle of Samos; triremes like those which had fought at Actium; ships of the line which had gone out with Drake to stop the Spanish Armada; Arab corsairs and Spanish treasure galleons. These little navies were armed and could fire miniature cannon. Two years previously, while reenacting the Battle of Jutland in one of the magnificent bathtubs of the Savoy Hotel in London, where non-swimmers and the chicken-hearted bathed in the soap dish, McCobb had wounded himself with a broadside from a German light cruiser. In commemoration, he awarded himself the Distinguished Service Order, executed by Buccelatti of Rome, and carried it in the large pocket of his dressing gown with his night cheque book and a signed copy of *Jane's Fighting Ships*.

McCobb's sole interest was in maneuvering his fleets so that the wrong side won, thus reversing history. He had devoted a lifetime to writing screenplays wherein the most moronic actors had emerged triumphant, and he realized that for the sake of international culture, this would always be so. But he needed relief from this mockery, and so he fought time and history and reversed them in his fantasies.

Being extremely well padded, McCobb was able to sit in the tub for hours wearing a rubber suit to keep warm. He had originally been attracted to his hobby because of his admiration for navies. There was something intoxicating about a service which had the cool to designate its principal officers as "admirals." "Naval persons would have us believe," he once lectured Basil, "that the title is derived from the Arabic *emir-al-bahr*, or 'lord of the sea,' which occurs in the *Chanson de Roland*. But when one acquires real understanding, the very walk of superior naval persons and their insistence upon arrogance as a way of life impel one to believe that the title is derived from the same root as the word 'admired.' Take the wondrous ambivalence of the title *commodore*— from *comode*, meaning 'convenient,' because *commodore* is a rank which is not recognized, but which is convenient. Compare the luster of 'admiral' with the vagueness of 'general'; the prideful address of 'able-bodied seaman' with the secretive shamefulness of 'private.' Contrast 'fleet' with the dead designation of 'corps,' and the defeatist dichotomy of 'division.' Furthermore, naval persons eat much better than those other clods."

Early on the morning of Bryson's arrival in Hamburg, McCobb lowered himself into his bathtub and began to dictate into a machine. "Furthermore, merely because Lady Maureen Nichols is of the peerage does not alter the fact that taxes will be due on this pension fund, and should be put aside. Send a letter to this effect to her Montague Square address. The correct spelling is quote M-o-n-t-a-g-u-e close quotation. Since there are both Montagu and Montague streets as well as Montagu Place, Mews, Row and Mansions, in addition to Montague Place, Court and Close, many of these in different postal districts in London, be sure that you get this right."

Snapping off the machine, McCobb turned to his ships. But he couldn't begin the maneuvers; something was niggling at his mind. He snapped the machine on again. "Please use the prettiest postage stamps you can get for this one, Miss Silverschein," he dictated. "The letter does seem a bit cross, and I want to be fair."

He turned back to the tub, undecided whether to recreate the commando raid mounted by Sir Robert Holmes for Charles II off the shores of Vlieland and Terschelling. It was an interesting problem because Holmes had used a minute force to attack more than one hundred and fifty richly laden Dutch ships, but the ways in which Sir Robert could have been defeated were so varied that McCobb did not feel he could choose the most humiliating before going to the airport to meet Ty. He toyed with the idea of re-enacting the ramming action by the Austrian Admiral Tegetthof against the addled Italian commander off the island of Lissa on July 18 to 20, 1866. He lay back in the warm water, paddled his pink feet and thought about this, but in the end, because of the lack of time, he decided to stage the handling of the mutiny aboard H.M.S. *Marlborough* by its admiral, the Earl of St. Vincent.

The crew of the *Marlborough* had objected to St. Vincent's order to hang one of the ship's company, and the *Marlborough*'s worried captain had so informed St. Vincent, played on this occasion by Admiral Albert McCobb. He glared down at the quarterdeck of the flagship lying off his right knee and roared, "Do you mean to tell me, Captain Ellison, that you cannot command His Majesty's ship *Marlborough?*" The sounds of his bold voice caromed off the tiled walls of the bathroom. "For if that is the case, I will immediately send aboard an officer who can."

Quickly McCobb ran up the tiny signal flags on St. Vincent's flagship which ordered the rest of the fleet to turn all its guns on the *Marlborough;* then he positioned the fleet in a circle around the pariah. "The *Marlborough* is to be fired upon until all indiscipline ceases!" St. Vincent shouted. "And it is to be sunk, if necessary."

He waited tensely, imagining the drama aboard the *Marlborough*, conscious of the eyes of the men of his fleet following his steely gaze across the choppy waters of the bathtub. Slowly, in his imagination he saw the body of the seaman being run up the yardarm. "Discipline is preserved, sir!" he snapped at Captain Ellison, then slid back under the warm water, his rubber pants skidding along the bottom of the tub.

Albert McCobb looked like everyone's idea of Bacchus, except Caravaggio's. He was short and round, and as pink as a
44

white carnation left for days in Châteauneuf du Pape. While living in the Arctic and the near Antarctic he gradually became opinionated because of lack of conversational opposition. This was his forte. People tended to nod at him rather than answer, and few can contradict with a nod. In the world's film community his position was roughly that of a deity in a similarly primitive society. The French, of course, fell into religious comas after seeing his films; they would totter out to write essays and ponderous analyses of his work and character. Two Paris book shops and one in La Colle sur Loup, Alpes Maritimes, specialized only in books about and by him, including the McCobb line of horror comic books in twenty-three languages and the McCobb magazine *Heinous*. A young French film director of some European reputation, Joseph M. Reynard, had traveled eleven thousand two hundred and two round-trip air miles from Paris to the Beverly Hills Hotel to interview McCobb in a shockingly small bathtub. They worked together for three and a half weeks, whenever McCobb could spare the time. The result was published in five hundred and fourteen pages under the title *La Danse McCobb*. It won the Médaille Cinéaste and the Prix Eulalie Goncourt, named for the grandniece of the literary brothers, a woman who had seen *Duel in the Sun* forty-two times. The book soon became required reading in the secondary schools of France.

A few excerpts from this authorized biography will suffice to demonstrate its subject's insight and the mastery of his art:

The two fundamentals of film making which the serious director must master are the actor and the audience. If the director cannot bring himself to enter the fantasy that every actor is, or was at one time, an individual, then he will not succeed. It is true that if a layman listened to a group of actors feeding, he would not be able to tell one from another. Yet the director must hypnotize himself into believing that many actors do have skills and characteristics, just as he must understand that his audience possesses only herd instincts and will obey blindly the orders of their leading mares in a herd of closely knit family parties. Just as it is fatal for the director to assume that the actor is not anonymous, it is a deadly mistake for him to assume that the audience is composed of a group of individuals.

Early in my own career, I once watched six actors at the Warner Brothers Studios in Burbank, California, for a total of 135 hours, spread over ten days and nine nights. I often slept out in the open only thirty yards from them, and I became fascinated by two aspects of their behavior. First I studied their heads and came to recognize certain unmistakable expressions. Second, I took written notes on their "vocabulary" and set down foundations for a "dictionary." They spoke almost entirely in terms of sex or money, though frequently getting them alarmingly confused—with some reason. They proved to be capable of nattering at each other for hours about "sport shirts," and of bickering about their "grosses." All of them lied about how much they could drink. Some of them could whistle and hum attractively. Though in public they were prepared to fight other males for the right to sign a feeding bill, they hated to share anything . . .

With the audience, of course, it is all sharing. Visual information is the most important thing for an audience. What it sees at a given moment is more significant to it than any experience from memory, however new. Even when the visual contradicts what all the audience's other faculties tell it it is true, it will be dominated by its visual impression. In this respect the audience closely resembles a herd of chimpanzees . . .

Aside from the mirror, the visual sense of an actor is used for protection only. Whenever actors are together in any social congregation, particularly in their restaurants in the actor preserves of Southern California, they never face each other; instead they sit back to back, with their heads looking outward in different directions. This is known to naturalists as "star formation." It enables each individual member of the species to widen his field of vision and hearing, and provides greater security against actors' predators—the public and agents . . .

No one, no matter how dedicated, can be expected to live among actors for any sustained period, but it is vital that the director go to their hotel rooms to "converse" with them at least once a day, just as a falconer, talking continuously, will take his bird for long walks on his arm. No actor is able to listen, in our understanding of that sense, but they can learn to differentiate between praise and censure by the tone of one's voice, and even, after a time, can learn to imitate the director's voice and gestures in some of the easier scenes.

On page 486 of *La Danse McCobb*, Reynard asked the master of suspense if there were any common characteristics which might reveal an undiscovered star actor. After much thought McCobb replied that there were:

The head must be round. The eyes should be set on either side of the nose, just above the center of the face. The mouth should be directly below the nose. If possible, there should be a forehead. These are the secrets of why some actors are loved and others are not.

McCobb's eyes were small and blue. He had a sandy beard, shaped like a spade in the style of the Earl of Essex in 1620, and his lips were as pendulous as double church-bell hammers. He was so subtle that he listened only to contrapuntal instruments in symphony orchestras and deplored monosodium glutamate. He was fifty-two years old, nine years older than Tynan Bryson. He ate with a heavy fork and set an air-express table: *pappadums* from Poonjiaji in Bombay; *camarones secos* from Leonusas in Madrid; clover honey from the Buckfast Abbey in Devonshire; *croquignoles* and almond *massepains* from Becret in Rheims, and so on and on. In the days of the covered wagon he might have been gaunt and spare but the plentitude of food flown from every corner of the world had made him pumpkin-plump. The plumpness had made him more sedentary and the repose had made him more thoughtful.

McCobb was such a successful director that Goldberg was willing to pay the extra expense for his habit of traveling with two complete sets of everything from luggage to aspirin and including all clothes. The first set would be picked up by Goldberg's men on the first leg of the journey, and the contents of all the bags would be unpacked and pressed in a chosen hotel. The second set of luggage would get the same treatment in the second city of the itinerary, and as McCobb left the first stop his bags would be flown ahead to a third city. In this way he never had to fret about finding a porter. No other man in the industry had earned this privilege.

So much nonsense had been written about McCobb's bizarre background that it was impossible to separate the facts from the press-agentry. Originally known as "The Bard of Antarctica" because of his two-volume autobiography, *Cold!*, he had come into international prominence after World War II in the Falkland Islands Dependencies, where he was gleaning cross-bred wool from Romney and Corriedale sheep on Cape Disappointment, South Georgia Island, a few degrees from the Antarctic Circle.

When Lafarge Fein brought his film-production unit of

thirty-seven people to South Georgia Island to film *Cold!*, McCobb was said never to have seen a motion picture. Then Fein acquired hysterical amnesia, brought on by excessive alcohol treatments taken to ward off the cold, and fled on a freighter bound for Mombasa with a Filipino dental-floss tester whom he subsequently married, leaving the costly production unit stranded by weather until the following spring. None of the film people had the courage to take over from such a legendary artist as Lafarge Fein. Luckily, McCobb didn't know any better, and because he had written the book on which the film was based, Goldberg cabled authorization from him to direct the picture.

Cold! won twenty-six Academy Awards the following year, grossed $13,547,892 and made McCobb the hottest film director in the world. The picture told his life story movingly. He was the only child of a Scottish father and an Eskimo mother. His father, a sergeant major in the British Army, had met her at the ill-fated Sled & Sledge Expedition at London's Crystal Palace in the summer of 1914. Though they were never to learn each other's language, they fell deeply in love, and it was only because the sergeant major was posted to France abruptly at the outbreak of World War I that they did not marry.

In 1915 McCobb's mother, made ill by cooked fish and the tropical English winters, took the little boy who was the product of her love for the sergeant major north by northwest to live in his grandfather's igloo in the Arctic. Here he grew up quite happily, and the reason for his adult residence near the Antarctic Circle was only due to a sentimental error. To the growing boy in the Arctic almost everyone else in the world was a southerner. Through a chance reading of Joel Chandler Harris' *Uncle Remus*, which had been left behind by Matthew Henson in Peary's party, young McCobb became fascinated by the Deep South. To someone at 90 degrees latitude north with a scanty knowledge of geography, it seemed logical that this region must be somewhere in Antarctica, and thus it was natural that he confused Harris' Georgia with South Georgia Island of the Falklands.

When he was nineteen, McCobb's entire family passed on after a tragic brush with a pet polar bear who had matured within the igloo. The young lad journeyed southward to Greenland by kayak, thence by tramp steamer to Boston, from which he shipped out to southern Argentina and finally Cape Disappointment. He began to write *Cold!* in 1937, when he was twenty-two, but could not finish it until 1945 due to the impossibility of keeping his hand outside his mit-

48

ten for more than five minutes at a time. In late 1945 a Boer sea captain took one of the two copies of the work north, to Philadelphia, and passed it along to his mistress, whose husband was the president of a publishing company. *Cold!* was eventually published in thirty-one languages, including Twi, and serialized in *The New Statesman*.

In 1947 McCobb, newly hailed as the world's most talented and exciting film director, left the Falklands and his beloved sheep. Since then his reputation had only grown, and he had dominated the industry for twenty years.

As Albert finished dressing, Basil Schute telephoned from New York.

"Ah, Baz. Good. Is Caterina in hand?"

"All correct, sir."

"And the airline stewardess?"

"Entirely *d'accord,* sir. She refused to be paid, but I think we'll have to find a small part for her. She's film simple. However, she has confirmed by cable that Ty has invited her to the première tomorrow night."

"When do you take Caterina to the airport?"

"In ten minutes, sir."

"Splendid. An Executive jet will pick you up in Frankfurt. Let Goldberg's people get a cargo plane to transport her baggage."

"Yes, sir."

"Take her directly to the Tembo Room in this hotel, and—"

"Is that Tem-*bo,* sir?"

"It means 'elephant' in Swahili, and don't ask me why a German hotelier came to choose it. Richard Gallagher will have the press on hand so that she can talk about her new book. It will shatter Ty."

"I must say, sir, that I admire enormously your campaign of psychological warfare against Ty. Your insight that he does his best work only when harried, confused and totally insecure would win you plaudits from Freud himself."

"Odd sort of aberration, isn't it? He must have hurdles. If we can drive him again to the verge of insanity with humiliation and frustration, he may win another Oscar."

"I know you can pull it off, sir!" Basil said warmly.

As Ty emerged from the airline terminal in Hamburg, he saw Albert waving from within a cavernous Mercedes 600 which had been converted into a two-seater. Bryson was wearing a canary-yellow waistcoat and a whale's-tooth black-and-white sports jacket under a chocolate Tyrolean hat with a

49

one-inch brim. He was looking indigant because he was sure that no one had come to meet him, but the instant he saw McCobb he sagged into a post-hepatitic slouch and waved back feebly.

"*Allo*, Albert," he said languidly. "I say, this *tonneau* would make a nice flat for some young couple with two or three children."

"You are looking marvelously fit, Ty. I cannot believe my eyes."

"You don't think I look bright-yellow?"

"Nothing we can't correct in the printing." Albert took the baggage checks from Ty's limp hand, gave him to a Goldberg man standing by, and the car moved off. "We expect a marvelous première tomorrow night. In fact, I have every reason to believe that Walter Lippmann may be there."

"Really?"

"Then we can begin shooting the following morning. The sets are wonderful."

"Have you cast the two women?"

"I'm still rewriting."

"When will I have a script?"

"You'll have to take it in pages and scenes for the first two weeks or so."

"Dammit, I hate that."

"We'll work it out."

"But when one's conception of a characterization starts out muddy, it stays muddy."

"It will be crystal-clear."

"Has the doctor arrived from London?"

"What doctor?"

"What doctor? My hormone shots! I'm two months late with this implant as it is, and—"

"Oh, *that* doctor. He's waiting at the hotel."

As they entered Ty's rooms Albert said, "I've had them do over your apartment here entirely, with inlaid tiger oak, patapsko pomla, avodire, bubinga, zebrano and black-bean wood."

"How nice."

A tall, dark man full of plump and aplomb was waiting in the living room of the suite. McCobb introduced him as *Mr.* Ornstein-Zec, explaining that British surgeons charged by guineas and insisted on being addressed as laymen.

"How do you do," the mister said.

Ty hesitated. "But I expected Sir Herman Levin——"

"He is at a medical convention in America," Mr. Ornstein-Zec said smoothly, far too smoothly. "I have your dossier and I know your hormone mixture. Please remove your trousers and lie down."

"But—" However, Albert patted him gently on the arm and nodded when Ty looked at him. Ornstein-Zec busied himself with his satchel, and then turned to his patient with a most peculiar expression on his face and a transparent, inch-long vial in his hand which could contain anything, Ty suddenly realized, including deadly poison. The same scene had occurred in *Dope* and he would have been murdered—my God, the set was identical with this room—had not Caterina shot the lock off the door.

"Albert," he said shakily, "do you realize that this room is identical to the set you used in *Dope?*"

"Well, yes. I have used only two interior sets in every one of my pictures—this one, which I have just done over so that you could get used to it again, and the New York suite."

"I didn't know that."

"Tremendous savings, of course. In fact, Goldberg has been talking about using the same two interior sets for all the company's films."

"You will lie down, please," Ornstein-Zec's silky voice with its unmistakable Spanish accent interjected. Hands guided Ty insistently to the sofa, and he stepped out of his trousers and stretched out on his stomach. "In this tiny vial," the disembodied Mediterranean voice continued, "we have a few estrogen crystals to ward off arteriosclerosis, for skin tone, to keep rheumatoid arthritis out of the joints, and to keep us from rushing off to the loo after just one beer. Yes? Plus a few crystals of testosterone so that we may continue to be kind, kinder and kindest to beautiful ladies. No?"

"You look like an actor I worked with in Spain about eight years ago," Ty said. "In *Bull*. Remember, Albert?" Ornstein-Zec's eyes flicked over at McCobb.

"I remember the chap!" McCobb exclaimed. "He was a genuine duke."

"It was perhaps my brother," the mister said. "Your left buttock, please, Mr. Bryson."

While Ty wondered where the poison would strike first, Ornstein-Zec deftly inserted a trocar, chattering softly as he worked.

"Dig, dig, push, push," he said. "The implant goes in the upper and outer part of the gluteal region, between the posterior fascia of the gluteal muscle and the periosteum of the pelvic bone by means of a trocar and a cannula. No stitches. No pain because of the local anesthetic."

In seven minutes the mister was finished. As he departed,

Albert asked if he might use Ty's phone to call O'Gorman in the States.

"Is O'Gorman on this picture?

"Yes."

"How did he get away from Caterina?"

McCobb blinked. "Who do you mean?"

"He is her make-up man. She has him under personal contract."

"Oh, that. Caterina has just finished two in a row, and since she's gone to sleep in the Springs for a couple of months, O'Gorman is free." He picked up the telephone, murmured into it, listened and then said, "There is a New York call coming in for you, Ty."

Ty got into his trousers and took the phone. "Hello?"

A strange, remotely familiar old voice with an undefinable accent said, *"Bryson! I am going to kill you! It will be a filthy death! First I will take your face away, then I am going to kill you! The visible world is no longer a reality, and the unseen world is no longer a dream."*

"Who are you?" Bryson shouted.

"Ty! What happened?" Albert cried with alarm as he saw the fear in Bryson's face.

Ty dropped the telephone onto the rug. "Another threat. The same words." He sat down carefully. "You and Goldberg are going to have to work something out with Dr. Weiler. I'm going to need a lot of solid psychoanalytical reassurance if I'm going to finish this picture. You'll have to move Weiler here for the duration."

But Albert was tracing the call. The operator said that it was a routine person-to-person from New York, and that she would try to locate the number in New York.

When McCobb hung up he said, "Dr. Weiler is an important doctor with many other private patients dependent on him and a great deal of hospital work besides. But we should be able to arrange daily sessions with him by telephone."

"To Los Angeles?" Ty brightened instantly. "Oh, I say! No one has ever done that. Why, we might even make 'Medicine' in *Time*."

"You said there have been other threats and attempts to murder you. Do you remember how soon after the threats the actual attempts were made?"

Ty began to quiver. "Never longer than twenty-four hours," he quavered. "And the second attempt was made five minutes after the threat."

The six-seater jet plane brought Largo and Basil into the

Hamburg airport at eleven-nine in the morning. There they transferred to a helicopter, and reached the hotel at eleven twenty-seven. "I will turn you over to Dick Gallagher in the Tembo Room," Basil said as they entered the lobby. "*Tembo* means 'elephant' in Swahili."

They ascended to the mezzanine and walked toward a door inscribed with gold letters. "It's the Tempo Room," Largo said. "*Tempo* means 'time' in Italian." A tall man who had been hovering at the entrance came toward them in a stately manner. "Dick!" Largo exclaimed and embraced McCobb's press agent as he led her into that sort of public room which should be seen only at night, filled with white wood, pink drapes, gold furniture and red carpets. Largo sat down on a Louis XIII chair on the orchestra dais, facing a seedy band of about fifty newspapermen, and press and TV photographers. Largo took her shoes off to make the press more comfortable. The huge chair was apple-green. Largo was dressed in summer ermine and wore her heavy red hair in the style of a peruke. Her large, wet mouth held their eyes. There was a moment of total silence while the men in the room wondered where along life's path they had taken the wrong turning.

The press coverage was motley but universal, consisting of the Hamburg papers and magazines; the West German TV services; NBC and BBC crews; the Australian *Vogue* representative on her way home from covering the collections at Riga; AP, UPI, Reuters, Agence France Presse; a man from Goldberg's company house organ; a crew of nine reporters and photographers from *Paris-Match;* and a severely dressed young man from the *Osservatore della Domenica.* Everyone had a handout which had been done in McCobb's own typewriter face: the O's were tiny human skulls, the T's were gallows, and the I's *poignards.*

The most impatient journalist was Ludwig Berg of the *Hamburger Zeitung,* who had a deadline problem because he wrote very slowly. He blurted out over the heads of the working photographers, "Is it true, Fräulein Largo, that you are going to write yet another book about Herr Bryson?"

"Just a minute, buddy," a photographer screamed. "When we're through, you start—not before."

"Take it easy, boys," Gallagher said and nodded to the interpreter.

"Take it easy, boys," the interpreter shouted in German.

"Why is there an interpreter? Largo speaks German," someone yelled.

"The interpreter is for me," Gallagher answered amiably. "I have to know what she says."

"She says," Largo told them with a smile, "that I only write these books to help Mr. Bryson with publicity." This got a good laugh. "Bryson and I were married three times, so it is fitting that there be three books." She repeated the statement in German.

"Honey! Not yet!" the NBC cameraman yelled down from a platform near the windows. "Don't answer them yet. Look up here, honey. Yeah, good. Higher with the dress. Ah, good. That's nice."

"Just one more, Caterina," a tall photographer with a bandit's mustache and a Texas accent implored while he took six rapid pictures.

"Come on, come on, fah Chrissake!" the AP man shouted. "Get these guys outta here. They never finish."

"What does Herr Bryson think of your books?" a reporter asked.

"I hope you fellows will tell him all about my books," she answered. "Then we'll find out what he thinks."

"Cheat up this way, honey," the NBC man yelled. "Keep talking. We got you fine—just cheat a little more toward us."

"Miss Largo," someone asked, "would you consent to appear in another film with Tynan Bryson?"

Largo glowered. "Never! No one could ever understand what an unpleasant experience that is. I mean—physically. It is not generally known that he rubs garlic apples under his arms and refuses to bathe during a picture."

"Garlic?" the *Newsweek* stringer, a free-lance food writer on the side, repeated involuntarily.

Largo shrugged helplessly. "He is an emotional cripple, and this is only one of his little aberrations."

"Since this is only the second book," a matronly woman asked, "shouldn't it be called *Biography of Two Husbands?*"

Largo smiled, waited and swept every face in the room below her with her eyes. Her superb timing alerted everyone to the juiciness of what was to come, and the audience leaned forward. "Are you sure Mr. Bryson has been my only husband?" she asked clearly as the TV cameras whirred, the pencils flew and even the photographers at the bar in the back of the room paused between gulps of free beer.

6

AFTER leaving Largo with Gallagher, Basil went directly to McCobb's rooms. The master of suspense was standing in the classical position of Fleet Admiral on the Bridge as Basil entered. Facing the Alster, he glared broodingly out the window, his back to the door.

"All correct, sir," Basil reported.

McCobb spun around. "All is *not* correct, sir," he said. "How dare you exceed your authority? How dare you conduct yourself so with my star without specific orders from me?"

"Miss Largo and I were models of comportment, sir—"

"I am speaking about Tynan Bryson!" McCobb roared. "I should have you run out of this business, you heavy-handed—"

"*Quiet!*" Basil's fearsome assistant director's voice rattled the glass objects in the room. McCobb looked startled. Basil asked, "*What* has been incorrect, sir?"

"I refer to the crudely managed telephone call from New York in which you thought it might be helpful to threaten Ty's life."

"*Sir!*"

Albert's indignation dissipated in the face of Basil's blazing rectitude. "I thought—well, dammit, Baz—I mean, he was threatened! The worst of it is that this is only one of a sequence; someone has actually tried to murder him three times already. Since you knew I was harassing Ty to get the best possible performance out of him for this picture, I naturally—"

"I followed each of your orders to the letter. As always. Nothing more, nothing less."

"I am sorry, Baz."

The statement dismayed Basil. It was the first time in almost fifteen years that he had heard McCobb utter an apology. "May I have that in writing, sir?" he sneered at Albert.

"It could be auctioned off in the industry for a pretty penny. Rather like De Gaulle apologizing. Grotesque."

"Spare me, Baz. We may be in bad trouble. If you did not make that murder threat, who did?"

"It certainly wasn't Caterina," Basil said stiffly.

"I am not suggesting that it was."

"Undoubtedly it was someone who had just seen *Jefferson*. And if it is a real threat rather than his own attention-getting ruse, then I feel the need to celebrate." He went to the bar and poured himself three fingers of Scotch. "And dammit, sir," he said aggrievedly, "it is the Tem-*po* Room, which is Italian for 'time,' not the Tem-*bo* Room, which is Swahili for 'elephant.'"

"I am happy you have cleared that up," McCobb said gratefully. "Swahili seemed so wrong for this hotel. Now, about the première tomorrow night. Please sit down and do forgive me for all I've said. Ty must be seated on the left side of the auditorium, and Largo on the right. Very important."

Basil sipped his whiskey and nodded.

"The air stewardess understands her role?" McCobb asked. "Can she divert Ty so that he won't see Largo in the theater?"

"She can. By the way, do you want Largo to see Carrie-Ann Blongett?"

"I've altered course there. Carrie-Ann will not be invited. Ty's and Largo's cars must arrive at the theater no more than five minutes apart. The film must begin the instant she is seated. Gallagher will move both of them on the double past the photographers. The worthwhile shots will happen later anyway."

"I'll help there."

"Who will escort Largo?"

"We have the North German water-ski champion. More Teutonic than Preminger. Chap named Philippe von Klarnet."

"Excellent. Ty detests Germans. Does Klarnet speak English?"

"Not a word."

"Better and better. Is the stewardess beautiful?"

"My own stock, sir."

"*That* beautiful?"

"Yes, sir."

McCobb sighed. "You have real authority with women, Baz."

"Not always, sir. Sadly."

"A really pretty girl with Ty will bring out the tigress in Caterina at the confrontation scene with the press. Are all

56

police arrangements finalized? Have you arranged for the crowds the police will have to handle?"

"Yes to both questions, sir. Eleven busloads of young people are being trucked in from Lübeck, where the West German government is secretly training their own Beatles in some balance-of-payments scheme."

"Let's buck that information along to Whitehall, shall we? What do you suggest for Ty's entrance?"

"I thought that from the time he steps out of the limousine until he disappears into the theater, we could have the mob of young people singing Luther's 'A Mighty Fortress Is Our God.' I could translate what they are singing as Gallagher and I hurry him into the theater."

"Smashing."

"Do you want the police to lose control of the crowd when Largo and Ty leave the theater, sir?"

"No. Only the one girl—just that single turn we have planned for the lobby."

"She is rehearsed and ready, sir."

"That's the crucial moment—the moment which will propel Ty into one of the greatest performances of his career and which will stimulate the world press into an orgy of titillation. It will be the first time Ty and Caterina come face to face since the last dreadful divorce proceedings. Needless to say, Gallagher has arranged fitting coverage." McCobb seemed to be purring.

Ty slept late on the day of the opening of *Ghastly*. It was enervating to his system still to be living in a hotel and he was feeble from the terrible anxieties which greeted him on awakening each morning. As he swallowed one of the striped pills Dr. Weiler had prescribed for early-morning dread, he wondered if someone who had paid to see *Jefferson* was trying to kill him. Because he knew he must not think about his own murder until the stripey had taken effect, he ran through the inventory of obstacles which he might be able to place in his own path that day. But something warm and wonderful, something very pleasant was trying to reach his consciousness. Finally he remembered and began to chuckle like a leaking submarine: he was about to enter a regular, sustained, transoceanic, transcontinental psychoanalysis.

Ty swung himself out of bed with alacrity. The stripey was working. He opened all the blinds and let the glorious late-spring morning burst into the room. He padded to the bathroom and brushed his teeth, then trotted back to the telephone and fixed the attachment of the portable tape re-

corder to the telephone apparatus. He did five minutes of cal-
isthenics, then sat on the edge of the bed, and breathing
deeply, gave his happy instructions into the phone. "Tynan
Bryson here," he said in a resolute voice, the voice of the sort
of a man to whom England would entrust its queen, if the
script called for it and the part could be cast.

A telephone operator at the large switchboard in the basement of the hotel waved her hands with helpless excitement
and said, "Frau Fringl! Frau Fringl! He is on the line!
Quickly!"

A middle-aged blond woman plugged in instantly. "Yes,
Herr Bryson?" she said. The three other operators listened
rapturously.

"Please get me Dr. Abraham Weiler in Encino, California
—Yew Ess of Ay—at State 8–5320. I'll hold."

"My niece is crazy about you, Mr. Bryson."

"What time is it in California, luv?"

"Midnight, sir. We will call you, Mr. Bryson, don't hold.
God bless you, sir."

In twelve minutes Ty's phone rang. Dr. Weiler was chewing something when he said hello.

"Dr. Abraham Weiler?" the operator said. "Hamburg, Germany, is calling you."

"Who? *Germany?* What?" The doctor swallowed noisily.

"Mr. Tynan Bryson is on the line."

"Is it paid?"

"We are paid in Hamburg. Go ahead, Mr. Bryson."

Ty switched on the tape recorder. "Hello? Dr. Weiler?"

"Call me Abe. I'm no Adlerian, but a rejection of rapport
can give me inferiority feelings just the same. Listen, so what
are you doing in Germany? I had you down for a session tomorrow. Shall I cancel?"

"Abe, I'm in terrible shape. I have to start a picture tomorrow, so I talked to McCobb and he talked to Goldberg and
they okayed daily treatment by you on the telephone. Is that
okay with you, Abe?"

"Well—"

"It's historic! You'll be in every psychiatric journal!" He
would be shattered if Weiler did not agree.

"In every psychiatric journal I've been arreddy. Besides,
I'm not so sure my patients would like me to conduct sessions
with a patient in Germany. And look! Across the room even
my wife is shaking her head. That's no rejection of you, you
unnerstand. Since 1934 we haven't even bought anything
German."

"Abe! I'm a human being! I need help! I'm in a terrible

58

depression. Tomorrow I have to start a new picture, my wife is libeling me, and someone has threatened my life three times—my God, four times! They've tried to kill me three times."

"So okay, an oath is an oath."

" 'My God' is not an oath."

"The Hippocratic oath, boobie. Our credo. I want to know the exact wording of those threats. Maybe some of those words have bad associations for you."

"Believe me, Abe, all these particular words have bad associations for me. I have the exact text right here, and—"

"Say! I read Caterina's book! *Very* good. I like that frank, honest stuff."

"It wasn't honest! It was fiction!"

"Well, listen. So I also like that kind of fiction."

"Not if a woman writes it! Wyoming was the first state in the union—maybe the first place in the world—to grant women the vote. And what happened? They marched backwards. They voted to abolish the federal income tax—"

"You *like* paying income tax?"

"They've voted that the U.S. must get out of the U.N. and that the U.N. must get out of the U.S., they've voted to abolish the authority of the Supreme Court, they've demanded a repudiation of the disarmament agency, they've—ah, what's the use?"

"Women are nice, remember that, Ty."

"Caterina is so irresponsible that she could be a political boss in Wyoming."

"Hitler wasn't a lady, remember that. Stalin was a fella, not a girl. The percentage of ladies' pictures on post-office walls is very low. It's natural that you are a little touchy because of the divorces, but what's a little thing like three divorces from the same woman? Every marriage has three major schisms, and in your case the publicity helped you at the box office."

"Abe, please be fair."

"Are you lying down?"

"No."

"So lie down. Freud had his reasons. I'll wait."

Ty stretched out on the bed.

"Which way are you facing?"

"East, I think. The Baltic is on my left."

"All right, I'll face southwest. The Pacific is on my right." Ty could hear a chair scraping. "All right. We will begin. While you talk you must remember your frame of reference. You are Everyman, doomed to wander across the world

59

seeing yourself, right? Caterina is your woman; therefore she is Everywoman, who is pushing you out into the world to find yourself. When you find yourself, you will find her there. Clear? You must face the enemy. He is within. She knows that, but you aren't so sure. What is this enemy? You cannot distinguish the unreal from the real. Each time you take the easy way you go deeper into the unreal. Find reality, boobie, you hear? So . . . Now we will start with the wording of the threats. Please read each word separately and then freely associate with each word."

7

THAT MORNING Albert joined Largo for breakfast. He arrived with his own waiters because he enjoyed eating what was known in the hotel trade as an English breakfast, a euphemistic designation because thanks to their taxes few Englishmen could afford such a meal and those few could not possibly have digested it.

Albert greeted Largo warmly and then ordered the five rolling tables to be lined up. He moved along the rows of silver dishes arranged on two levels, lifting silver lids and confirming his order.

"Ah, Durham bacon cake. Caudle, flummery, ale jelly. Rissered haddie! Huntingdon fidget, Bucks bacon badger, stargazey pie and slapjack. Delicious!"

"Don't wait for me to order," Largo said. "You go right ahead."

McCobb gestured absent-mindedly to a waiter. "Take Miss Largo's breakfast order, please." Suddenly he looked stricken. "They haven't sent the Bedfordshire clanger, the Hindle wakes or the bockings!"

"Here they are, sir," the headwaiter said smoothly, "with the Somerset rook pie, the bog star, the jellied eels and the Tonbridge Mushroom Ketchup."

"But you've forgotten the jugged rabbit and the Burlington whimsey."

"And the grilled whale *entière*," Largo added severely.

"Dammit!" Albert cried. "What sort of a hotel is this? You've brought no pigs' pettitoes, no Kingdom of Fife, no limpet stovies or dressmaker tripe! Get it here at once! How dare you, sir!" He sat down at the table, tucked a large napkin into his collar and began to move food onto his plate indiscriminately. "They make a wonderful Gooseberry Fool here," he said, recovering his good spirits, "if you need a sound sweet."

"Your breakfasts are about as real as your films."

"They are only movies, aren't they? But do you really think they're unreal?"

"What kind of a question is that?"

"What is unreal about any film? Where in life do you get such attention to detail?"

"The stories are real, too, I suppose?"

"Indeed they are. If Shakespeare were writing today he'd be writing for the movies."

"Instead we have Goldberg."

"But it's a real art form! Is there anything more real than a murder mystery or a war film?"

"Yes."

"What?"

"Any cop or any soldier."

"But reality in life is a bore, isn't that true? And just because it's one long bone-cracking yawn, does that make it more real than films? Is life scored with music? Are the colors of life as brilliant as ours?"

"Is life *scored*, Alfred? When a man asks for his room key at the desk downstairs, are you saying that an orchestra should be concealed behind the rubber plants laying down a music track?"

"I would if he were asking for a key which was not the key to his room. Or if it is for his room, and three assassins are waiting up there for him."

"Assassins?"

"Music heightens reality! Proper color heightens reality! Cosmetics on women, false bosoms, eyelashes! But they can't have precisely the right music with them when they walk—though I have noticed that one out of three young people in big cities have a transistor playing full blast glued to their ears. But no one can retake their scenes; they can't ask their husbands to please turn off the lights over and over again to get exactly the right movements and mood. Films can do that, and that's why they are more real. Out there"—Albert waved his hand impatiently—"there is no form—no beginning, no middle, no end in the proper order or porportion. When climaxes and denouements occur they are utterly wasted—people don't even recognize them when they occur. There is no selectivity, only chance piled amateurishly upon happenstance. Is that the sort of reality you want? Because if it is, why aren't *you* out there instead of careening around the world with a hundred and thirty pieces of luggage? Why aren't you behind some counter in a department store instead of tying up the ladies' john on a flight from Tokyo to Los Angeles while you wash your diamonds? Is your money any more real than my films? Reality is bred from reality, and whatever reality you possess is due to my films."

"Let's get really real. What about the film I'm here to make?"

"What about it?"

"Who will I be working with?"

"Goldberg has been talking to Sinatra and Michael Caine."

"How many changes do I have?"

"Forty-six. Two more than the last Doris Day film."

"Lovely. And guess what? O'Gorman told me he saw Ty in New York."

"I suppose for the *Ships* opening. I think he's in Europe now. I seem to have heard that he plans to bathe in serenity at Bürgenstock."

"Switzerland?"

"Yes."

"He hates the Swiss! He's said again and again that he would never set foot in Switzerland after their reviews of *Jefferson*."

"By that yardstick where could he go? The only people who didn't attack the film were the Filipinos, and have you ever tasted their food?" McCobb leaned across the table and patted her hand. "Never mind. We start our work tomorrow, and there's the première of *Ghastly* tonight. We were told that Walter Lippmann was in Bonn yesterday, so he might be here."

At this moment three waiters sped in with the missing dishes and McCobb's round, drooping face became ecstatic.

One floor above the carnage of McCobb's breakfast, Carrie-Ann Blongett was writing to her agent. She wrote slowly because she preferred to dot her *i*'s with full circles and make cute little faces inside her *o*'s, and this took time.

. . . and you would flip over the prices for cameras and liverwurst. I am having them make a special gag liverwurst

for Chuck Moses, to get laughs from the broads. I haven't
seen T.B. (you know) yet. The bell captain says *she* is in
this picture!! Wha'? The bell captain is a sensational-look-
ing kid, name of Carl. He speaks English with a nice accent. I mean a great accent—like Turhan Bey. But definitely not like Sig Ruman or Lyndon Johnson. The kid
could be very big, Harry, if you could like set something
for him. Should I send some art on him? If Largo is going
to be in this picture, they could kill each other. Or somebody might kill me. I'm going to wait until after the big
premeer tonight before I make my move. They are having a
big opening, but nobody sends me a ticket. Since T.B. (you
know) got this one for me I should let him do the fighting
for me, right? Listen, Harry, I need to know about my billing. After all, if McCobb is going to cash in because she
named me corespondent in the third divorce, and now he's
in the picture with me, I should get very good billing,
right? See what you can find out about her being in the
picture. I mean, but like even then I wouldn't believe it.
Write also if you want me to bring you a camera or a gag
liverwurst. You can make a two-fifty mark-up on the
camera easy. Come to think of it, maybe you better cable
me if you find out she is in this picture—an impossibility,
believe me. When she walked in on T.B. (you know) and
me in Leonard Shannon's personal Turkish bath, I am telling you I don't know how those guys held her back. She
hates sex for him, you know what I mean? And she hates
me worse, so if you hear anything, please pick up the
phone and let me know, you hear?

8

THE FRONT of the UFA-Palast cinema proclaimed the great-
ness of the night. Four-story-high illuminated banners
shouted the names of TYNAN BRYSON, CATERINA LARGO and
ALBERT McCOBB. Hamburg had become Hollywood-on-the-
Alster, and the word *Ghastly* was on everyone's lips.

On the small traffic triangle facing the theater a bandstand had been erected, and tubas and trumpets were sending out their commanding sounds over the surging mass. Several hundred German Beatle trainees chanted and strained against the linked arms of the police. The crowd went wild when Fräulein Schmeckle stepped down from the long, lewd limousine; it had been rumored that Jacqueline was in town, and Fräulein Schmeckle had dark hair, two eyes and a nose. From bitter experience Tynan Bryson followed her; had he emerged first and then turned to assist her out of the car, he would have had his back to the crowd. He was wearing a black tuxedo with scarlet lapels and a narrow, scarlet four-in-hand tie designed by Le Corbusier, and the crowd roared out its love to the murky skies in one hoarse voice. A fiercely mustached photographer lay on the pavement to get a close shot of the famous Reyes ruby studs Ty was wearing, which gave the effect of spilled ketchup on his shirt front. Basil and Gallagher stepped on the recumbent photographer to take Ty by each arm, knowing that the star could not bring himself to leave such adoration and would have to be dragged into the theater.

Once inside, Ty gripped Basil's arm tightly and whispered intensely, "What were they chanting at me, luv?"

"They were singing—and they meant it from the bottom of their hearts, Ty—'A Mighty Fortress Is Our God.'"

Ty wrenched himself away and tore through the incoming ticket holders to greet those dear people once again, determined to thank them for thanking him in their humble way for all the happiness he had brought them. But quick action by Basil, Gallagher and Fräulein Schmeckle headed him off, and in a flying wedge they propelled him into the theater a few seconds before Largo's car arrived.

The uproar over Caterina's arrival was so great that it could be heard even inside the noisy auditorium. "Who's that?" Ty asked apprehensively.

"It could be Kiesinger," Basil said grimly. "Or perhaps Lippmann."

"Kurt George! Walter!" Ty cried and tried to surge up the aisle, but Fräulein Schmeckle deftly applied a judo hold to his wrist and Basil pressed with all his force on his shoulder. Reluctantly he remained seated.

"Relax, please, Ty," Basil said. "The film is about to start."

He disappeared, but when Ty tried to turn around and crane his neck to find out what was causing all the commotion at the back of the theater, Fräulein Schmeckle stabbed the back of his hand with a long hatpin, going in so deep that she had difficulty in retrieving the weapon.

"What the hell was that for?" Ty screamed.

"Basil told me to make a diversion," she said in German. "I had to do it or I'll never get into films."

Ty couldn't understand German and he had to know what was happening back there; he tried to turn again, and the hatpin stabbed him again. The sound of his scream was almost drowned out by the thunder of the film's musical theme as the lights dimmed and the famous McCobb trademark—a corpse face down in a gutter—loomed under the main title.

The applause was deafening when his name appeared on the screen, but to Ty's distaste and irritation it swelled even louder for the words CATERINA LARGO. His first image, seventeen feet tall, pulled him forward in his seat. Ty was a real movie fan, the most devoted fan that Tynan Bryson had. Though he had proclaimed publicly for many years that he never saw any of his films, there was a print of each of them, along with a small movie theater, in every house and apartment he owned, as well as an ingenious portable projector so that he could run them on the door of the loo. In a moment of particular insecurity, he had once spent an afternoon in the men's room at Grand Central in New York, studying his work in *Torture*.

Now, in the UFA-Palast, surrounded by a thousand fans, his absorption in himself was so great that he was totally unaware of his surroundings. As usual, the film ran its course all too quickly. He had forgotten—in fact, he had never been told—how the picture ended. Because he worked with a more or less permanent stock company, McCobb frequently shot parts of future films with the casts of the current one; as a result Ty was confused and enthralled when the final chase began.

The screen shimmered with the blazing color of a crowded street in an Oriental city. From an alley a rickshaw careered out into the crowd. He was pulling the rickshaw! When had Albert shot this? It almost seemed that the action must be taking place right now, until he remembered making the shot more than four years before while they were working on *East*, in the East. Even though one might memorize Albert's scripts, none ever seemed to resemble the plot they were working on, for the simple reason that usually it was two other pictures. Only Albert could keep it all straight in his head.

A beautiful Eurasian girl was in the rickshaw, seated next to a sleeping Chinese in rich native dress. Ty gaped and

65

sobbed aloud as a pang of longing shot through him. It was Caterina, and he never knew how terribly he missed her until each time he saw her again. It was Caterina just before she had soured, just before the second divorce.

The crowd extras were yelling outraged complaints as the rickshaw raced among them. Ty grinned at the droll costume —a lampshade strawhat and a burlap poncho; trousers rolled up above his knees and socks helped up by Western garters over alligator loafers—which immediately identified him as the traditionally comic CIA man of American films.

Then the camera zoomed in close on the Chinese passenger to show an oozing bullet hole in his forehead. Across the theater Largo stifled a yawn. Ty gripped the arms of his seat tensely. Night was settling fast. Caterina's make-up was terrible, Ty thought, and remembered that O'Gorman had been making the St. James pilgrimage to Santiago de Compostela that year.

Aiee! Five uniformed police were charging down the street. Then four evil-looking civilians with guns came rushing out of an alley. The rickshaw stopped so short that the dead man pitched forward and landed face up on the pavement. He and Caterina stared down at the body and she yelled "Run!" They raced downhill through the growing darkness. Ty threw away his lampshade hat as he ran; it landed on a camera which an American tourist was focusing and everyone laughed.

Some extremely pleasurable memory was trying to get through to Ty, and finally it surfaced. Baby Tolliver was somewhere in that crowd. A tiny archeologist who occasionally worked in pictures to make new friends, she knew more about Indonesian executive copulation rituals than anyone alive. Oh, Baby Tolliver, he thought as he gripped Fräulein Schmeckle's thigh, where are you now?

But his life was in danger up there in glorious Technicolor and to the tune of music. Now Caterina was dragging him into a car, a large black sedan; she was holding the spike heel of her shoe against the back of the driver's head so that he would think it was a pistol. Caterina had all the good bits in this one, Ty thought suddenly. She had told him to run; he was not only the man but the senior star, and he should have been the one to say it. Now she was intimidating the driver; that was his job too. What was McCobb doing to him? She had even commandeered the car. Was it possible that in Red China the women actually dominated the men? But he had the billing.

A car was following them and shooting at them. It was

night, and suddenly he took charge just as everyone expected. He told Caterina to instruct the driver to take the first right, then drive about five hundred yards through the forest. As she spoke to the driver in a strange Oriental tongue, he realized that of course she had been forced to take charge earlier because he couldn't speak Chinese.

A bullet smashed the car's side mirror as they made a reckless racing turn. From the great screen Ty said, "I've been enough trouble, baby. I'll get off now." What he was about to do took guts, and Caterina pleaded with him not to leave. They had a chance in the car, she said, clinging to him, but if he left he would be tracked down and killed.

He tapped the driver on the shoulder to stop, then asked Caterina the Chinese words for "boat," "need" and "now." He would make it to the waterfront, he said, and beat them at their own game. Then he kissed her magnificently, and Albert had used his best profile, the left one, so that the audience would have something to take home with them when the kiss was over. That was the acid test of where an actor stood. Now he slipped out of the car into the night, the car shot away, and he was lying in the underbrush until their pursuers hurtled past. Then he ran like a shot down the dark road to a shack where he found a bike and pedaled away.

Ty the spectator was biting his lips with excitement. He looked furtively from right to left in the darkened theater; everyone seemed tense and moved. Someone up there was a master of suspense, and he was not entirely sure it was Albert. Beside him Fräulein Schmeckle was shredding her handkerchief with her teeth.

Caterina would be safe. The pursuers had forced her car off the road and surrounded it with drawn pistols. But they only wanted him; no man east of Suez would harm a hair on the head of Caterina. He watched himself cycle to the door of a ramshackle riverside café and pound on the door. At last it opened, and as the proprietor peered out he could see Baby Tolliver standing on the stairs in the background. Ty waved money in the man's face and repeated the words "boat" . . . "need" . . . "now" in Chinese while the powerful headlights of the car following him lit up the café. As the Chinese waved him to the back of the house, Ty was pinnned by the headlights of the onrushing car. Shots broke out. He leaped across black space at the end of the dock into the only boat and shoved off into the night. There were more shots, but he had won. The Western world had been saved and a world conflagration had been avoided until the beast in the hearts of men was unleashed again. Softly the closing-theme music,

67

"To the Shores of Tripoli," sounded—Goldberg had wanted to try something new, and so Ty had been cast as a Marine Corps secret agent—and the lights came up slowly in the theater.

There was tremendous applause from a tremendously moved audience. Ty prepared to stand up solemnly and turn slowly to receive the acclamation, but Basil had appeared at his side and was sitting on his shoulder again. The the crowd rose, forming a thick screen all around him, and Basil and Fräulein Schmeckle were lifting him to his feet. Dozens of strangers—but who could call anyone who had shared this moving experience a stranger?—were pleading to be allowed to shake his hand. He wanted to sanctify them all with a firm handshake for the men and a warm copulation for the women, but he was being moved inexorably toward the lobby.

Albert was standing at the head of the aisle, wearing full evening dress like a vaudeville magician, his hands folded over his stomach like a stole.

"Albert, whatever happened to Baby Tolliver?" Ty cried as he was hustled by.

The spacious lobby was filled with people, but a broad aisle ran down its middle between hairy clusters of Beatle trainees with pointed, black-noodle shoes. Ty felt a stab of nostalgia for the World Cup days of his youth as a winkle-picker. Inside the theater Gallagher and Von Klarnet moved Largo up the far aisle, thrusting her through the crowd toward the lobby. She tried to stop and speak to Albert, who resembled a penguin in evening dress, about Ty's mastery of the Ben Turpin acting style, but she was catapulted past him. As she reached the top of the aisle, where she had a fine view of the lobby, a demented-looking girl in the dense crowd broke through the police guard and leaped on the back of a tall man with a beautiful young woman on his arm. The creature wrapped her incredibly long legs around the man's chest and back, clutched him around the throat and shrieked in German, "I'm touching him! I'm touching!" Her impact almost felled the man; staggering heavily, he spun around and looked directly into Caterina's eyes. It was Ty! She gasped with horror as he reeled again, totally out of control.

Caterina beamed disgust as Ty's beautiful companion tried to drag the wild girl off him, screaming for police help, as a cruelty of photographers, working furiously, surrounded them. Made weak by his nearness, dizzy at the thought of enduring again the frieze of women climbing all over him, Caterina regally drew herself up and strode directly through the noise and blur of flailing arms and exploding flash bulbs,

68

ignoring Ty, while the police pulled the fan off his back and his companion patted his cheek and straightened his tie.

Basil dragged Ty along in Largo's wake and traitorously left him standing directly beside her while the TV cameras turned and the press shouted at them in three languages.

"Caterina, baby—I mean, what are *you* doing here?" Ty asked with nausea.

"Are you and Mr. Bryson reconciling, Miss Largo?"

"No! Print anything like that and I sue!"

"Are you and Miss Largo going to marry again, Mr. Bryson?"

"No! Boys, please, this is crazy, a horrible mistake."

"Are you co-starring in the new McCobb film?"

"No!" they shouted in unison while Ty looked frantically across the weedy lawn of newspaper faces, trying to find Walter Lippmann in hopes that he could change the subject to a debate on the State Department's position on the Oder-Neisse boundary. Beside him Caterina was shouting hoarsely, "I did not know this man was here. I was tricked into this! This is a cheap movie-company publicity gimmick, and you'll be dupes if you run a line of it. I did not know he was here!" She repeated this in German, Italian and French, and then hit the line of journalists with the force of an N.F.L. fullback. She was not a tiny woman, and after a lifetime of pasta her moves had authority. The sea of weeds parted and she disappeared.

Instantly Basil and Fräulein Schmeckle were pulling and pushing Ty in the opposite direction. The Beatle trainees had begun to sing "A Mighty Fortress Is Our God" again and the crowd of thousands was swaying hypnotically. With Ty in front, the human wedge splintered the dazed mob, and pushed like the prow of a snowplow through the drifts of human bodies. Ty was flung to the floor of a limousine which moved off at once, with Fräulein Schmeckle on top of him and Basil running alongside shouting instructions in German at the driver. He pulled himself up, feebly fighting off Fräulein Schmeckle, who was trying to swallow the lower half of his face with vacuum-kisses.

"Albert and Baz knew she was in that theater," Ty gasped when he finally retrieved his face. "Why didn't they warn me? How did she get there? She must have had tickets. It was a benefit, and they always control the tickets."

"Basil just told me they didn't know she was coming!" Fräulein Schmeckle said loudly and nervously. "We were trying to rush you out of the theater, and if that crazed girl hadn't thrown herself at you we'd have been gone before she came out. Prince von Klarnet got the tickets; Basil didn't know. Oh, how we tried to spare you this anguish."

"Anguish?" Ty moaned. "You don't know what anguish is, luv. Tomorrow morning I will be totally humiliated all over the world before a hundred million TV watchers. Did you hear what she said into those cameras? This is the worst single moment in my whole destructive, humiliating career, I tell you. I've got to get back to the hotel. I've got to call Dr. Weiler. I'm ready to collapse, I tell you." He leaned back on the seat, breathing heavily.

In front of the UFA-Palast, Albert McCobb was introducing Miss Carrie-Ann Blongett to the press of Europe. He explained also that whereas Miss Largo and Mr. Bryson did *seem* to agitate each other, they really were very good friends. In any case, they would be true professionals when they began work the next morning on their newest film, *Nowhere*.

"Jesus, McCobb, will Blongett be in the movie?" the tall Texan reporter with the bizarre accent shouted.

"We must have a confirmation here, please," Ludwig Berg of the *Hamburger Zeitung* said loudly. "Is this Miss Blongett the same Miss Blongett who was named corespondent by Miss Largo in their last divorce?"

"Wal, y'all gotta unnerstan' that was a misunnerstanin' on Caterina's part," Carrie-Ann said, pushing her foam-rubber bosom at them threateningly and displaying all twenty-six hundred dollars' worth of porcelain caps and six thousand three hundred and ninety-one dollars' worth of plastic surgery on her jaw line, upper lip and eyelids. At that moment she felt as though she had fallen in love with every one of them, and she wished with all her little heart that, one at a time, each of them would accompany her to the manager's office because she felt real sweet and sexy, the way her drama coach had taught her. "Tah an' Ah were nevah annathin' but gud fraynds," she said, again slipping into her induced Dixie accent.

When he realized that they were doing a considerable amount of fast driving, Ty opened his eyes and looked out, expecting to see the hotel looming up on the right. But they seemed to be far out in the country. "Where are we?" he demanded indignantly, sitting up stiffly. "Doesn't the driver know where he's going?"

"Oh!" Fräulein Schmeckle said. "I just thought you would insist on taking me home."

70

"Home? You live in Frankfurt."

"I'm staying with a sick aunt in Sachsenwald, and I thought—"

"But I took a sweet little suite for you. Right next to mine."

"Oh, Tynie! Aunt Eunie was so sick, and my mother pleaded with me. I couldn't say no to her . . ."

"But this is terrible. I mean, I was assuming that no matter what else happened, I would still have your compassion and comfort in this wilderness. Surely you didn't fly all the way from New York to Hamburg just to go to a movie?"

"But I love the movies," Fräulein Schmeckle sobbed. Suddenly there was the sound of firing, coming from a distance, and over his shoulder the driver yelled at them in hoarse German.

"What's happening, for God's sake?" Ty yelled.

Fräulein Schmeckle stared out the rear window, and then turned her ashen face to him. "He says there is a car following us and shooting at us." Two rapid shots sounded. "And he is right!"

"The threat. The telephoned threat from New York," Ty quavered, and he whipped around to stare out the rear window. A long, low car was racing about seventy yards behind them, winking orange blasts; a bullet shattered the side mirror next to the driver. Everything in the movie was happening all over again. Ty screamed and pushed the girl to the floor of the car. Gripping her shoulders, he spoke directly into her ear, exactly the way he had held that Eurasian girl in *Ghastly*.

"Tell the driver to take the first turn off the main road," he said, and a sense of peace and safety began to descend on him, "then to continue along it without lights for about five hundred yards through the forest."

"They must be trying to kidnap you," Fräulein Schmeckle said breathlessly.

"They won't harm you, my darling," Ty sang.

"But what are we going to do?"

"For heaven's sake, will you please tell the driver what I said!"

Fräulein Schmeckle barked out the instructions; almost instantly the car rounded a curve, made a hairpin turn and they were thrown like mice into a pile on the floor.

"Honey, please," Ty said in agony. "Your knee, please!"

Fräulein Schmeckle moved. "What are we going to do? Do you have a gun? Give me a gun and I'll shoot them. Give me a gun!" Her voice was hysterical.

"I've been enough trouble, baby," Ty said. "I'll get off now." The car came to a sudden stop, crushing them like opera hats against the front seat.

"You aren't going to leave me?" It was Caterina's line in the movie, Ty remembered vaguely. "They're after *me*, baby, not you. You'll be okay."

He was halfway out of the car, slithering on his stomach. His suit would be ruined. Schmeckle pounded on his shoulders.

"You coward, leaving me in this car to be shot and maybe raped even, while you run away in the dark!"

"Coward? Run away?" Ty was shocked to his core. This was one of the biggest scenes in a tremendous hit film. Where did she think she was? "Will you *please* let go of me, Fräulein Schmeckle? They'll be coming up that road any second, and already you've cut my head start in half. I assure you, the only way I can save us is to get out of this car." He slid all the way out. "Coward?" he said from his knees in the grass. "You should be ashamed."

"In every movie I've ever seen, the man and woman escape together."

"Did it happen at the UFA-Palast tonight?" he answered scornfully. "Besides, you aren't a star. How far is the river?"

"I don't know."

"Ask the driver!" After an interminable amount of chitchat the driver revealed that the Outer Alster was about half a mile away across the main road.

"What are the words in German for 'boat' . . . 'need' . . . 'now'?"

"Boot . . . brauche . . . jetzt."

"Good-bye, baby."

"No, no!" Fräulein Schmeckle screamed, but Ty slammed the door shut and thumped on the fender. The car shot away and he was alone. He lay on his stomach on the wet grass, waiting. The crickets chirped, and in fifty-eight seconds the pursuing car went roaring past. He leaped to his feet and ran. *There it was!* Twenty yards away he saw the shanty, and when he reached it he was gargling to get his breath. A Vespa, already headed in the right direction, stood where he had expected to find the exhausting bicycle. He climbed aboard, and with a great noise the Vespa darted off toward the main road.

The sign hanging over the darkened waterfront café said: "NASI GORENG."

He knocked like thunder on the door and heard shuffling footsteps approach from the back of the house. The door opened, and a mahogany man wearing a fez stared out at him.

"*Ja, bitte?*"

Ty extended cash. "*Boot,*" he said, "*brauche, jetzt.*" Thank heaven he was a quick study. He prayed that Fräulein Schmeckle had not gotten the words wrong; so far it was all exactly like *Ghastly*.

"*Amerikanische Express Karte, bitte?*" the man asked. Ty started to fumble for his credit-card case, but he realized he certainly would not be able to wait while the forms were filled out in triplicate.

Far off in the distance he could hear the thrum of the approaching car. "Cash!" he said, waving the money, "*Geld!*" Over the Indonesian's shoulder, far in the back of the café, he saw the tiny figure of a woman walking toward him. She stopped under the full light at the foot of the stairs. It was Baby Tolliver!

"Baby!" he cried out. She turned as she climbed the stairs and smiled back at him. The sound of the car was louder now, and when he turned he could see its lights moving up to the crest of the hill. As he ran toward the river, he was caught in the lights of the car and rapid gunfire rang out. He sprinted. There was only one boat moored in the slip behind the house. It had an outboard motor, and its starter gleamed in the headlights. He heard running footsteps, and then people were firing at the sound of the boat through the darkness. They missed. He had won again. He and the screenplay had won again.

9

FRÄULEIN SCHMECKLE sat, drained and exhausted, in a large chair in McCobb's living room. Basil stood beside her, patting her shoulder and talking softly as he stared across the room at Albert, who was pacing back and forth in front of a short, dapper man seated in a straight-backed chair.

"Inspector Heller," McCobb said with an elaborate gesture

indicating that he above all men wished to co-operate with the Hamburg police, "we are deeply grateful that you have consented to comb the city with your splendid patrol cars to find Mr. Bryson, but I suggest that this is something more than the usual wretched kidnap plan and that you appeal for troops—a thousand men, five thousand if necessary—to knock on every door and explore every cranny of this whole region. It must be done. Otherwise you will face the censure and wrath of the entire world."

"We must first establish that such action is necessary," Inspector Heller said coolly. Basil could not shake the feeling that the man had been made up by O'Gorman to resemble the late Heinrich Müller, head of the Gestapo. Heller was not sinister; he did not recall the bad old days; he was simply the most compact, dapper and metal-eyed man Basil had seen since World War II.

"I realize that you are exhausted, Fräulein Schmeckle, and I thank you for the co-operation you have given us," Heller said. "Now, please try once again to describe the men who stopped your car and who then pursued Mr. Bryson."

"I don't know. They were just very, very big men. They were exactly the same size. They spoke English. American, like the gangsters in the movies. They had guns, and they struck the driver in the face because they were angry that Mr. Bryson had got away."

"You could not see their faces?"

"It was very dark."

"You noticed nothing else?"

"*Ja*, I did. I noticed—and so did Mr. Bryson—that what was happening was exactly what happened at the end in the film we had just seen—it was just the same. Ty said the same lines. Mr. Bryson told me to tell the driver to turn down just the way he did in the film, and everything else was the same, too."

Heller looked at McCobb. "Is that possible?"

"How could it be possible?"

"I mean, the actor. Did he . . ."

"It is possible that Mr. Bryson believed it," Basil said. "He relates everything to his films, and—"

"But *I* don't!" Fräulein Schmeckle said. "I saw the film, and then I was in that car, and I swear to you that it was just like in the film."

"Then I would like to see the chase scene in this film," Inspector Heller said to McCobb.

"And so you shall. Basil—tomorrow morning?"

"Yes, sir."

"Inspector, I say this to you with all the earnestness I can command," McCobb pleaded. "There must be no publicity. Can you guarantee that there will be no information given to the press by the police department?"

"Well . . . I will do my best, sir."

"I want a guarantee. I will not have the public think that anyone in my company would seek this sort of cheap, dangerous publicity. Tynan Bryson, who is my friend, who is the greatest, grandest film star in this world, has had his life threatened"—McCobb swallowed hard—"and has, for all we know, been kidnaped. At this moment he is missing and he may be dead, but I must protect his reputation—and my own —for professional impeccability."

"We have been informed that his wife, who is in Hamburg, hates him and would do anything to destroy him."

"No, no, no. Impossible in this context."

"Our information is wrong?"

"Your information is distorted," Basil said.

"These are actors," McCobb exploded. "Everything is larger than life for them. Miss Largo married the man three times, Inspector—or do you wish to consider that destroying him?"

"May I speak with her?"

"Tomorrow?"

"If you insist."

"At the studio. One o'clock? We should break for lunch then."

"Thank you." Inspector Heller paused delicately. "Do you feel it would be correct if I asked her for an autograph for my boy Maxl?"

"Perfectly correct—unless you have arrested her."

"Of course. I would be certain to ask her first." Heller coughed. "In regard to the threat which was received by Mr. Bryson from New York yesterday?"

"Yes?"

"Our information tells us that Miss Largo arrived from New York yesterday. In other words, she was in New York yesterday morning."

"So was I," Basil said. "I was with her."

"Every moment?"

"Of course not!"

"Then she could have made the threatening call from New York?"

"Only theoretically," Basil said sharply as the telephone rang. McCobb picked it up hastily, listened for a minute and then gave a sigh of relief that seemed to deflate him like a

75

balloon. He hung up without a word, then turned and said, "Mr. Bryson is back in the hotel, thank heaven. He is safe." He sank into the nearest chair and passed his hand across his forehead, leaning back with his eyes closed.

"When may I talk with him?" Inspector Heller asked.

"He must be terribly tired," McCobb said. "Perhaps to-morrow when you come to the studio to see Miss Largo?"

"With Ty safe and sound I see absolutely no reason for the inspector bothering Caterina," Basil said.

"Only about the telephone threat," the inspector said. "And although Mr. Bryson is said to be safe, an attempt was made."

"How would noon suit you, Inspector?" McCobb asked.

"Noon will be fine." Heller shook hands all around and left them.

"What I want to find out," Albert said, "is why anyone would want to hurt Ty Bryson."

"Yeughh!" Basil answered.

McCobb rose to his feet and walked over to Fräulein Schmeckle, all graciousness. "We are terribly grateful to you for the way you kept your head tonight, and for the way you faced danger to help Ty and us. To show our gratitude I have decided on the name Dane Ponder for you. It has an excellent aura for an actress. Hamlet was a pondering Dane, and you are a northerner."

"Actress?"

"You were sadly duped by me—and by Basil here—in our attempt to promote friction between Ty and Miss Largo to-night. It was all because I thought it would help Ty's per-formance. There will be no more such tricks, I can assure you. I quiver when I think how close to harm you may have come. In partial recompense I am going to give you a part in this film."

"Rise, Dane Ponder," Basil said.

Fräulein Schmeckle was speechless and could only stare at McCobb with awe. At last she was able to stand up, and in a formal German manner she shook their hands, then sobbed and laughed and fled from the room.

"What a smashing name," Basil said. "But what do we have for her? Have you written in another character? I don't remember anything remotely resembling her in the script."

"All that will be revealed at about eleven-forty tomorrow morning," Albert said. "Right now I must telephone Gold-berg to inform him of his near-disaster. Please allow Ty an extra hour of sleep in the morning. Heaven knows he will need it badly after everything that happened to him tonight."

"I'm afraid he won't get much sleep tonight, sir."

"And why not?"

"As I time it, sir, that phone call came sixteen minutes ago. Thus, he's been in his suite for at least a quarter-hour, and the fact that we haven't heard from him is very odd, considering his adventures tonight."

"Yes, that is odd," Albert answered. He moved toward the telephone, but Basil stopped him.

"If you remember, sir, we hadn't quite finished with the hazing we have just now repudiated."

"I don't understand."

"That weird Beatle trainee? The girl who threw herself on him in the theater lobby?"

Then Albert remembered. "Oh, my God," he said and sat down weakly.

"Yes, sir. You instructed me to plant her in his clothes closet, to leap out on him when he opened it." Basil looked at his watch again. "It has now been nineteen minutes, and there is still no outcry. Knowing Ty, he's solving the problem in his own way—and that can be hell on sleep, sir."

Basil wandered wearily down the long corridor toward his room on the same floor. When he opened the door the newly invested Dane Ponder had invested herself in his large double bed. She was quite naked. He wasn't wholly surprised; it was the sort of banal thing that happened more often than not in his business. But each time it happened, for a fraction of an instant when he saw the glint of bare shoulder and the fling of soft hair across a pillow, Basil's heart would soar because he could imagine that it might be Largo. But when, as always, it was just another ambitious, amorous young woman, it increased his melancholia. As this was always mistaken for indifference, it drove the young ladies to even wilder abandon.

Dane Ponder's hair wasn't flung across the pillow, however. She was sitting up in bed reading a memorial issue of the *Völkischer Beobachter*. Her tidily packed breasts, marked with pink bull's-eyes, beamed at him hospitably from the top of the coverlet. "I was too excited to go to bed alone, Bazzie," she said, and gave him such a fetching smile that for once he didn't sink into disappointment and despond. In fact, he removed his clothes with commendable dispatch, pausing only to leave a five-fifteen call for the morning.

10

UNDER his long, shaggy mod hair, and dressed as though he had just led a raid on Carnaby Street, Basil approached Bryson's front door at the head of a procession at a quarter to six in the morning. He was followed by a bellboy with passkey, two masseurs, a barber and a room-service waiter with a crowded tray. Each man carried a bucket filled with ice cubes. Basil knocked, waited twenty seconds and then motioned to the bellboy to unlock the door.

Ty was spread out on his back across two beds which had been pushed together. He was alone, and Basil wondered whether the girl had retired to the closet for the day. Looking extremely spent after two hours' sleep and an exhausting and exacting night, he was wearing gold pajamas but had neglected to put on his hair net, eye-shade or chin strap. He was snoring a weird D-7 chord which bubbled out of him like chains dragged across cobblestones.

While the masseurs filled the tub with cold water and the contents of the ice buckets, the bellboy pulled back the curtains and opened the blinds, the barber stropped his razor, the waiter tested the temperature of the coffee on the inside of his wrist, and Basil felt Ty's pulse, nodding his satisfaction. When all was ready, the masseurs lifted the body, shucked off its golden robes and carried it to the tub while it slept on. When they slipped it gently into the ice water, it continued to snore for about four seconds before it screamed with the force of a lunch whistle.

Staring directly at Basil, Ty said in an extremely high voice, "Thanks awfully, luv. I would never have awakened otherwise."

"Would you like a benny or a dexter, Ty?"

"No, thank you, luv. Perhaps a stripey. They're next to my bed."

Basil fetched the anti-dread pills while the two masseurs lifted a now rigid Ty out of the water and dried him on a large folding table while the waiter held a cup of coffee to his blue lips. As the masseurs began to knead, Ty tried to sort things out in his mind.

Item One: How did that strange, exaltingly contortionistic girl manage to leap off a film out of his closet and into his bed? He realized that he had never understood the biological definition of the word "ectomorph" until last night.

Item Two: Albert had been standing at the head of the aisle at the theater when he entered the lobby after the showing. From there he had apparently stepped into the last reel of *Ghastly*—just as Alice stepped through the looking-glass. How had he done it? Then he had stepped out of the film at its conclusion and shortly thereafter he was in his shorts and opening the closet door, to release an ectomorphic child who had sprung upon him with loud cries and toppled him backward upon the bed.

Item Three: It was day and he had awakened sitting in a tub of ice water as though Albert had made too abrupt a cut.

Conclusion: He must telephone Dr. Weiler.

Basil entered with a stripey and a glass of water. "What time is it in California, luv?" Ty asked.

"Too late, I'm afraid. But we have booked a call for eight o'clock this evening. I say, aren't these awfully strong little pills?"

"Oh, yes. Very dangerous, really. One a day is all. Safe enough at one a day, but after that, one has an entire menagerie on one's back."

Ty relaxed into the massage after swallowing the pill. He was exalted by his new power to move from life directly into the plot of his films. He weighed the advantages and disadvantages. Obviously he was not yet able to control which films he could return to, and there was a danger that he could find himself back in Virginia, wearing that damn rotten fit of a powdered wig. But the advantages were overwhelming; those films were where he really belonged. There was nothing out here, now that Caterina was gone forever. He was miserable, loveless and unloved. It was an insanely humiliating world filled with constant disappointments. If he could live as he chose for the rest of his days, it would be in one of those old films with Caterina in which she loved him helplessly and in which, no matter what the obstacles, he always won. Only then was his health always glowingly fit; only then were all threats of murder and degradation immediately dealt with by a team of top screen writers.

"I have five pages for you this morning, Ty," Basil said. "Very few lines. Rumpled business suit. Abrasions-and-contusions make-up."

"What's the plot of this one, luv?"

Basil shrugged. "A secret-agent film, I suppose."

"Oh, no, Baz. But don't you *know?*"

"Difficult to tell from just five pages, isn't it?" Basil was barely able to talk to Ty and keep control of his resentment. He sought to remain as objective as a distant Indian sending smoke signals from a mountain top. "The master of suspense himself will be waiting for you downstairs and will drive you to the studio in his usual first-day ritual."

Although it was just after dawn, over two hundred fans were waiting as Ty came out of the hotel. Fortunately, Basil had asked six of Goldberg's men to stand by. They grappled, fought, threw, hit, wrestled, bit and struck at the mass of wild screamers, not one under thirty years of age, until Ty managed to make a dash for the huge car in which McCobb was ensconced in the back. As he landed in the seat and the electric lock of the door clicked safely shut, a ballyhoo truck with enormous posters advertising *Ghastly* trundled past, its loudspeaker singing "I'll Be Glad When You're Dead, You Rascal You."

"That bunch is up early," Albert said as the car sped off toward the studio.

"Sometimes I think you hire them to mob us," Ty answered stiffly.

"Not when our people hit them," Albert answered serenely. "That's how you can tell. If we hire them and then hit them, they simply refuse to work for us again. Did you sleep well?"

"I don't know, really. I dream so much. This week I am dreaming old comedies and action films."

"What was on the bill last night?"

"Double feature—both yours, by the way. First the theater-lobby sequence of—what was it called?—where the girl jumps on my back and—"

"You are losing your grip, old thing," Albert said. "That wasn't a film; that was a happening."

"When?"

"Last night."

"Caterina is in Hamburg?"

"She was."

"You didn't run *Ghastly* twice last night?"

80

"No."

"The chase at the end happened to me twice."

"Really?"

"Albert, was Baby Tolliver in *Ghastly?*"

"Yes. The chase seems like a dream because of the terrible strain and your exhaustion. But it really happened, Ty. It was not a dream."

"It *happened?*"

"Yes. Fräulein Schmeckle was with you most of the way. First the threat; now this murder attempt. I have called in the Hamburg police, because last night, for the first time, I saw with my own eyes that these murder threats are heinously real."

"But why was Baby Tolliver in that river-front café if it all actually happened? Why would she be standing exactly where she was in the film?"

For a moment Albert looked at him with sad affection and then turned away. "Baby Tolliver died in Los Angeles two months ago," he said, "while you were in that Italian clinic."

"Albert!" The outcry was for Baby. "Albert!" And this time it was for himself.

"I understand, lad. We're both in this maze together. Sometimes life is more real than film, but mostly the film is more real than life."

"But one should be able to tell them apart," Ty said pathetically.

"Ah, there's the rub," Albert said, and picked up the Paris *Herald-Tribune.* "I don't think we want to." He opened the front page and scanned the headlines; then his eyes dropped to a large photograph of Largo spread over three columns. Ty saw it at the same time and peered at the story over Albert's right arm.

"Biography of Three Husbands? That's my title!" He snatched the paper from Albert's hands. "Garlic apples! Emotional cripple! Oh, this is too much, Albert. I am going to sue this wop bitch for five million dollars, because that is where her heart is."

Albert peered over Ty's left arm, murmuring, "I say, has she been married four times?" He squinted. "Or more?"

"Four times or more?" Ty's eyes followed Albert's finger, and then he bunched the newspaper into a ball, opened the window wide and threw it out. "What kind of a life is this?" he yelled to everybody within earshot, as Goldberg would the following morning when the recording tapes beneath the seat reached him by air express, "when people go around dedicating themselves to upsetting other people?"

"I feel somewhat the same way after your peremptory handling of my newspaper," Albert said, his pendulous lips hanging downward in acute aciniform. "I hadn't even read Buchwald yet."

After helping to fight the fans and get Ty into McCobb's car, Basil telephoned Largo from the lobby. "I have to talk to you," he said.

"Ride out to work with me."

"No. I don't want Goldberg's drivers leaning backward."

"Come on, Baz, you aren't getting that old feeling?"

"No. And if I am it won't show."

"You may as well come up then, I suppose."

Caterina was alone and ready to leave, wearing a wolf coat over a blouse and blue jeans, when Basil entered. "Did you know Ty has been getting threatening letters?" he asked abruptly.

"Well, as they say about Goldberg, if letters like that hadn't existed for Ty, it would have been necessary to invent them."

"It isn't a joke. Someone tried to shoot him down last night, and Albert said something about someone trying to murder him in Rome."

Largo blinked, and her mind rejected what he had said. "Goldberg?" she asked.

"Ty."

"Shoot *Ty?* What kind of a stunt is that?"

"It was no stunt."

She grabbed his lapels. "Is he . . . are you trying to tell me that—"

"They missed him."

She sat down unsteadily.

"Are you listening?" he asked.

"Yes."

"An inspector of the Hamburg police said he thought you might have done it."

She snorted.

"He was dead serious. Ty was threatened by telephone from New York when you were there."

She looked contemptuous.

"Caterina, the police are coming out to interrogate you at one o'clock today."

"Nobody even knew Ty was in Hamburg."

"I knew. Albert knew. The hotel in New York and the airline knew. Goldberg knew. Is that enough to start?" Basil paused and took a deep breath. "Don't make this picture, Caterina."

"Why not?"

"It just doesn't seem safe to me."

"You think I'm afraid to make seven hundred and fifty thousand dollars—or afraid to work with Ty again?" She leaped out of the chair, suddenly aware of what she had said, suddenly able to see the truth plainly. "Is Ty on this picture?"

"I have been trying to tell you that, my darling."

"How could he?"

"A little joke of Albert's." Basil sighed. "And I am betraying Albert by telling you."

"A joke?" she said harshly. "What kind of a joke is that?" Her heart had begun to pound unmercifully, and though she was snarling, she was feeling the old ecstasy. She would be near him and time had passed and maybe he had changed.

"Albert thinks Ty works better when he's harried. As usual, Albert is right."

"Does Ty know I am on this picture?"

"No."

Largo clasped her hands and spun gracefully all the way around. "Then I will break his back this morning!"

"What do you mean?"

"I know, but he doesn't. When he sees me on that set he will scream like a trapped rabbit, and I will gaze down at him with multo cool. A perfect lady. He'll be dying, and I will say, 'Good morning, Ty, so happy to have you aboard,' and he'll feel like a fool again because he will realize that everybody but him knew about me being on the picture. Harried? If he works best when he is harried, then he will get the Nobel Prize for sure on this one." She threw back her head and laughed raucously. "All thanks to Albert. I'll have to buy him a gold watch."

"Don't get bitter at Albert," Basil said, receiving well on all antennae. "It is just that Albert understands—"

"Don't tell me about Albert," Largo said grimly. "I know all about Albert."

11

Ty WAS getting into his costume in the luxuriously fitted trailer truck which was his dressing room. His dresser and make-up man fussed over him. As he finished reading the five pages of script Albert hoped to shoot that day, Basil knocked on the door and said, "Ready when you are, Ty."

"Thank you, Baz," he said, and mentally went on duty. He was the Gent, the totally unflappable professional. He checked the bruised and swollen cheekbone which the make-up man had just finished, admired the finest tailoring on the most splendid male figure in the civilized world and descended the steps of the trailer to the floor of the sound stage. He walked with a sense of peace, threading his way carefully over the thick cables and zigzagging between set walls toward a vast and golden glow of light at the far end of the cavernous, dark regions of the great sound stage. The ceiling was so high and so devoid of light that it could not be seen, but ahead of him, around the lit area, men were peering down from high catwalks and pulling heavy ropes to adjust huge floodlights. Emerging from the ring of shadow, Ty found his chair next to Albert's broad canvas one where sat the master of suspense himself, as phlegmatic as a six-day-old jury, his arms and hands folded neatly over his large stomach.

"It is always so reassuring to find you so serene on the first day of shooting while all around you there is chaos," Ty said.

"It is only a movie, my boy. Basil!"

"Yes, sir?"

"Our star is here. Assemble the rest of the cast, please."

From the other side of the sound stage and behind Ty, Largo picked her way through the shadows into the constellation of lights. She looked extraordinarily beautiful in some revealing lingerie, her thick red hair falling down below her shoulders. When she was three feet away she said, "Good morning, Albert. Good morning, Ty."

Ty turned very slowly, reddening rapidly, tilting his face

84

upward like a gun turret at this indigestible fact. Each of the forty-two people on the set stood quietly, watching him with complete attention as his expression changed by the square inch. He rose slowly to his feet as his head made a full arc to face her, then the voice fired. "Just who the hell were you married to before me?"

"What kind of a dumb-ox greeting is that?" Largo asked.

"And why are you standing around in your underwear, you lumpy peasant?" It was dawning on him that she had known he would be there, that everyone on the set had known she would be there, had known that he did not know, and that once again he was the patsy to be humiliated.

"These are my working clothes," she answered calmly. "We are here to make a picture."

Ty turned to Albert. His hand snaked downward, grasped his necktie and pulled him to his feet. "When did you sign her, you fat little bastard?"

Albert was standing on tiptoe, but he lost no dignity. "Can you, who own one hundred percent of the gross, think of better casting for the box office?"

Ty released him. "And I become the laughingstock of this business," he cried out bitterly.

"But haven't you always been?" Largo asked sweetly.

Ty pushed Albert backward into his chair. "Sue me, you grotesque little monster," he yelled. "Go tell Goldberg you have no picture," and he began the long stalk toward his trailer. Electricians on the catwalks stared down at him, chewing gum. The script girl buffed her nails, studying them with elaborate care.

Basil stopped Ty's progress by standing in front of him. Albert straightened his necktie and then stepped over the cables and made his way toward Ty. In a low voice which did not carry he asked, "Would you rather have one hundred percent of the gross playing opposite Carrie-Ann Blongett? And if you walk out, what happens to your cherished reputation? The greatest pro in the business—hah! Largo is the biggest woman in show business, but you are billed above her, you have four times more to do in this picture and you are the total beneficiary of all the receipts. What is this moment? A bubble. *It is only a movie.* Which of you will be the more humiliated when the picture is released? You with your billing? You with total domination of the script? You with your unprecedented contract? Or Caterina, who has one crude joke on the first day of shooting?"

"It isn't that!" Ty whispered hotly but falling under Albert's spell, as he had so often before. "How can she remain so calm after all she has done to me?" Injustices raced through his mind like bulls in the narrow streets of Pamplona, and he could not restrain himself from shouting at Largo over McCobb's shoulder. "You stole the title of my book, you guinea bitch, and you and your publishers are going to pay with every cent you have for what you said about me in the newspapers this morning."

"Calm. We must be calm," Albert murmured soothingly while Basil stroked his arm the way a groom rubs down a nervous horse. "What can we gain with threats and shouts?"

"Shall we send for a chaplain?" Largo yelled raucously, causing the company to titter involuntarily. This maddened Ty more than what she had said, and he lunged at her while McCobb and Basil restrained him.

"You pitiable rejected cow!" he yelled. She turned pale. "How can your pride allow you to hang around me like this? Why do you keep crawling after me?"

Largo closed her eyes and fought for control. Regaining it, she maintained her dignity, and was about to launch a cool but massive counterattack when Carrie-Ann Blongett walked on the set behind her.

"Gud mawnin', evuhbody!" Carrie-Ann sang out. She was wearing a simple kilt of Russian sable with matching jacket, a Bohan blouse and a two-hundred-dollar hat. Her costume seemed to have been planned to make Largo look like a slattern who had just been picked out of a sailor's bed on the morning after.

"Mawnin', Mistuh Mac, mawnin', Tah dollin', mawnin'—" She stopped in midstep and midsentence, as though she had hit an electrified fence, when she saw the terrible expression on Largo's face.

Caterina threw her head back between her shoulder blades and let out such a scream that it knocked a man from the overhead catwalk. He lay where he had fallen, still staring at her, and no one moved.

Largo seemed to have swollen into something twice her size. She let the words go at hurricane force. "What is this hooker doing on my picture?" All her exemplary cool had vanished.

"Hooker?" Carrie-Ann shrilled. "I grossed eighty-six thousand dollars last year!"

"Out, bum! Off! Go!" Largo rushed her like a mad rhino. Carrie-Ann screamed in terror, but Largo zoomed past her and grabbed Albert McCobb by both lapels. Towering above him, she swept him like a broom back and forth across the floor, shouting, *Ributtante farabutto puzzolente! You*

86

planted her, you rotten, publicity-sick little monster. You fat rat. *Mostro informe!*"

Basil and two grips finally pulled her away from McCobb. Ty strolled casually into view, smoking a cigarette in a long black holder which heightened the effect of indifference.

"You are behaving *very* badly for an alleged professional actress, Caterina," he said, looking more poised than the Washington Monument. "I should have expected just a little more pluck from you—just a little better show of good manners."

A valet with a pressing iron had rushed out from the large audience of crew and had begun to press McCobb's cravat and the lapels of his jacket when Largo threw off the three men who were holding her, and charged Ty and Albert. There was a sickening noise as she clapped their heads together, and the small valet was smashed between them as they went down. Then she stood over the pile of bodies, kicking Ty and Albert alternately with her pointed shoes until six large men pulled her off.

Later, out of gratitude, they refused to accept any pay for the first week of the production, and it soon became noticeable that they had decided not to wash for at least that length of time. As her wonderfully supple body in the briefest of undergarments struggled in their hands, each of them blessed providence for guiding them into such rewarding work.

While Largo struggled, Basil stood in front of her and spoke steadily as she was dragged, inch by inch, away from the set toward her dressing room. "Stop being such an utter fool," he said. "You are behaving just as they wanted you to behave; you're making them very happy." Breathing like a fireboat, she gradually calmed down and became aware of what was being done to her. *"Stop that!"* she yelled at two men grasping her from behind, and she tore herself free to lambaste one of them across the side of the head for the assistance he was rendering. He fell over the base of the boom, but looked up ecstatically and said, "Any time, Miss Largo," as Basil pushed her into the dressing room and shut the door.

Carrie-Ann had run off the set sobbing, to call her agent and the Associated Press. Four men helped Albert to his feet and the valet immediately began again to press his suit. Ty had to pick himself up.

"What a high-spirited girl Caterina is," Albert said.

"If I were you, Albert," Ty said, rubbing his head, "I would cancel this picture by cable from some safe place such as the Union of South Africa. I know her. She will not rest until she has marked you badly."

"No, no, lad," Albert replied as they settled into their canvas chairs. "As Frederic X. Goldberg has written: 'The show must go on,'—and he means every word of it, because money costs eight percent."

A hairdresser was brushing and smoothing the hair of the great director as he, hands on stomach and round red lips hanging downward, stared at Basil coming toward them from Largo's dressing room. When he came up to them he said crisply, "Miss Largo wishes to apologize. However, before she continues, she demands that the fur suit, the hat, the Bohan blouse and the Ferragamo shoes be removed from Miss Blongett, that Miss Blongett be discharged without notice, that Miss Blongett not be permitted to return to the hotel but that she be taken directly to the airport and put aboard the first plane leaving Hamburg, regardless of destination."

"Rather severe terms," Albert said. "Settling Miss Blongett's contract will cost forty thousand dollars."

"Quieter, please," Basil said. "I have said it would cost you ninety thousand dollars."

"Just don't add the forty thousand dollars to the cost of the picture," Ty added.

"Caterina understands, of course, that she will ultimately have to face Goldberg as a result of this ultimatum?"

Basil shrugged. "She's a spunky kid."

"However, there is publicity value here, and Goldberg will switch Blongett and her contract directly into another picture. In the end she will sell many tickets for both films and we will lose only her plane fare. Send her to Paris, I think, Basil."

"Yes, sir."

"The publicity line Blongett must give out is that she is the woman Largo fears."

"And where will all of us hide when Caterina reads that?" Ty asked.

"We will tell her that Ty made the announcement. You'd like that, wouldn't you, Ty?"

"Yes, I would."

"But you will replace Blongett?" Basil asked.

"I think I'll try for that new German actress, Dane Ponder," Albert answered.

"Who?"

"Dane Ponder, Ty. Extremely beautiful. Very big in the north of Europe, and a deft actress."

88

"Do I know her?"

"I shouldn't think so."

"But 'Dane Ponder' has a very familiar ring."

"I suspect you may have heard of her father, Henry Ponder, the great Walloon star."

"Ah, yes."

"The police will be here within ten minutes, Ty. Be kind about autographs. Then, after you have your session with Dr. Weiler, why not finish up with Wardrobe? Obviously we won't be able to work any more today."

"Albert, what sort of character am I playing in this film? I must get that settled."

"You will be playing, essentially, *you*, Ty. The suavest, most sophisticated man in the world. Gracious, considerate, graceful, charming—in the nonpejorative sense, of course. Just as in real life, you truly like people, and since you fear nothing in this world, you are able to give everyone you meet —as you do in real life—some of your great power."

"I see."

"Real, simple goodness."

"What sort of a film is it?"

Albert seemed startled by the question. "It's a secret-agent film, of course."

"Another?"

"That is all Goldberg will allow, as you know. At least until he takes another worldwide poll next spring. Be patient, Ty. It won't be much longer."

"It's been eight years!"

"I think I can say without betraying a confidence that four comedies are being shot in London right now. That is, four different casts are shooting roughly the same story. And if these hit, I have it on very good authority that Goldberg will permit us to abandon the secret-agent cycle for a few years."

"What's the damn thing about?"

"I can say frankly that I believe we will top everything ever done in the field, Ty. We open with you frozen into an ice cake holding a tub of caviar which is being delivered to the dread headquarters of SMERSH in Moscow. In that first scene alone you wipe out over a dozen high Soviet officials."

"Do we have a big closer?"

"Hah! You are sent by experimental mail rocket from Geneva to Johannesburg, where you destroy Dr. Henri Emmet and eleven very high Soviet and Red Chinese scientists with live steam."

Ty stood up, looking thoughtful. "It sounds like money," he said. "That rocket idea is very good indeed." He walked slowly to his dressing room to begin work on the shadings of his part. He thought he might try a red-and-white checked stalking cap in this one. Would an ascot go? Once again he was an artist soaring above the world of enchained man.

12

CHIEF INSPECTOR HELLER was concerned, alert and respectful, as was his assistant, *Polizeiunterwachtmeister* Skutch. Heller asked for and received an autograph for his boy Maxl, and then went over the entire ground thoroughly.

"Had it occured to you that you might have been deliberately infected with hepatitis in Italy?"

"Is that possible?"

"The disease is contracted by droplet infection. It would be fairly simple. Someone could have used a common spray on you while you slept."

Ty stared. "Why would anyone want to do such a thing?"

"Have you not been extremely depressed? Haven't you had such melancholia that your life seemed worthless? Have you been able to make a single decision with anything like your former ease? Has your life now any song to it?"

"But what a sadistic thing to do! Anyone who would do that should be thrashed! I've gone through hell since the day they threw me in that hospital."

"But very cunning from a murderer's point of view. It makes you—psychologically—an easier victim. May I see the death threats, please?"

Ty handed him the letters, and described the plaque with the Roman script at the Goldberg *palazzo*.

"These closing lines are a Yeats quotation."

"They are?"

"Oh yes. There are many people who believe Yeats was a German. Lovely lines, isn't it? 'The visible world is no longer a reality, and the unseen world is no longer a dream.' "

"*I* don't think so."

90

"Can you describe the voice which threatened you on the telephone from New York?"

"It was like a whispered shriek covered with icy fur."

"Who are your prime suspects?"

"I . . . I haven't any," Ty answered shakily. "This has been a terrible blow to my *amour-propre*. I mean, outside of a few thousand exhibitors who played *Jefferson*."

"What about your former wife?"

Ty answered gravely, "Things with us are not what they seem, Inspector. The only person she could conceivably kill would be someone who tried to harm me."

The California call to Dr. Weiler came five minutes after the police had left. Ty adjusted the tape recorder, waited with his hand on the starting button and pressed it as he heard the psychoanalyst's voice.

"Hello, Doctor? Abe, please . . ."

Dr. Weiler was chewing something. "Listen," he said, "you'll think I'm orally fixated because no matter what time you call—and four o'clock in the morning is a pretty crazy time—I always happen to be eating. But in my own didactic I was certified as being absolutely *average* orally, which is pretty oral, and I think you'll agree that this checks out with my body weight and the fact that I never chew on the ends of pencils. So, how are things in Germany? Slightly paranoid. no doubt? No, I take that back. That is practically a racial joke. Besides, it is a comment which you could interpret as a belief that I thought you yourself had paranoid tendencies. So what's new?"

"Someone is trying to kill me."

"Hey, watch it, that's pretty paranoid." Weiler swallowed. "Are you lying down, Ty? Which way are you facing?"

"West."

"Do you have your striped pills there?"

"I think so."

"Take two. I'll wait."

"Two? At one time?"

"Am I a doctor or am I a pusher?"

"But you said . . ."

"That was then. Now is now. I want you to take two in the morning and two at night."

"But, Abe, isn't it true that—"

"Please, Ty. This is an overseas call."

Ty found the vial of stripeys and took two. "Okay. I did it," he said. "Now, as I was saying, last night someone shot at me and tried to kill me."

"How did you react to such aggression?"

Ty held the telephone away from his face and stared at it as though it were a thing possessed; the stripeys were working very fast. He had never taken two stripeys before and it was like going up in a cloud of steam with nude blondes.

"I was scared," he answered gaily.

"Excellent. A good reaction."

"At *first*."

"Only at first?"

"After that I began to believe I had escaped into the safety of one of my films. I mean, I could feel, as I am beginning to feel right now, that I had actually entered the film and that I was immune from harm because everything was controlled by the screen writers."

"Well now, that's a very interesting conclusion."

"Thank you. But it turns out that the woman who was in the original film and who I saw in the film I escaped into, has been dead for two months."

"That isn't serious. For you, I mean. Kraepelin records many similar cases."

"I'm very glad to hear that—though very sorry to hear about the death."

"A good pattern. You are giving me a very normal, good pattern. There is nothing here for you to worry about. If you take the striped pills—two in the morning and two at night —everything will be fine." Ty felt like a mighty river which could be deflected by the weight of a pebble or a handful of sand. Abe's voice was low and soothing. "You must be proud of this new power, Ty. You must be proud and grateful that you have the power to return to your old films, to the safety and glory and comfort of your great films. There you are safe from threats. There you are important. There the world depends entirely on you and you cannot be harmed. Do you agree? Tell me that you agree. Do you understand what I am saying to you? Do you comprehend me?" The voice was hypnotic. The stripeys were the keys to the great door of the promised land.

While Ty talked and listened to Dr. Weiler, Inspector Heller was being very tactful with Largo. She ignored his diplomacy. "You told McCobb last night that I was suspect," she said, "so let's talk about that."

"That was last night, dear lady. We have since chatted with Prince von Klarnet and the maître d' at your hotel and we know that you were drinking a milk punch while someone was shooting at Mr. Bryson many miles away."

"So now, you suspect the hired bentnoses shot him?"

Heller shrugged. "It happens every day. Who do you think is trying to kill your ex-husband?"

"I don't think anybody is trying to kill him. I think he stages these things to get attention. He gets desperate when people think about objects besides himself."

"No, I don't think so. I spoke with him today. He is very frightened."

Largo's eyes filled with tears. "He is? You know, that's just rotten. I mean, how could—why would anyone want to harm Ty except me? That's *ours*. We have that together . . . Listen, Inspector, I'll pay your boys ten thousand dollars—that's forty-two thousand deutschmarks; to hell with it, make it fifty thousand marks—if they stop this man before he can hurt Bryson. Okay?"

Heller cleared his throat. "Well, uh, a reward is always interesting, but of course you would have to offer it formally —by a letter today perhaps?—to the *Polizeipräsident*."

"Write down his name and address right here, buster," Largo said. "It's as good as done."

13

Ty got got back to the hotel just before seven o'clock. As he came into the main hall of the hotel, struggling through a throng of fans on the sidewalk, Colonel Adler's Midgets were being registered at the reception desk. Seven of them, who got into the elevator with him, introduced themselves deferentially as fellow members of show biz. As always, the warm admiration cheered Ty, and there was a lilt to his step as he entered his apartment.

A heavy white envelope lay on the silver tray in the foyer, and he opened it. It was a letter from Caterina which apologized! He could hardly believe this incredible *virtu*. He turned the letter over and upside down, and then read it again. It said how sorry she was that their first day together had gotten off to a bad start, how happy she was that they

93

would be working together again, and it was signed "Always warmly and affectionately."

Ty felt as though the sun had suddenly come out after months of rain. He sailed his jacket across the room, ripped off his tie, stepped out of his trousers and pulled off his shirt. Then, in a corner of the living room, he noticed eleven mail bags of fan letters, and this made him feel even better. Skipping into his bedroom, he opened the closet door for his pajamas, and once again the tall, thin, wild-eyed girl catapulted out and knocked him over backward on the bed.

In the bedroom directly below, a four-hundred-and-twelve-pound fat lady winced under the crash above her and telephoned to complain to the management for the second time.

It took Ty well over two hours and a half to persuade the young lady to dress and leave, and when he finally got into his pajamas he was exhausted. The maid had drawn his bath as ordered, but by now it was tepid and in any case he was too tired.

He put on his hair net and chin strap, got into bed, swallowed two stripeys, pulled the sequined eyeshade over his eyes and fell asleep.

Caterina got back to the hotel at seven-forty after a long bout with Wardrobe. When she opened the door to her apartment she found the rooms filled with carnations of every known color; many of them had even been sprayed in wonderful colors carnations had never known. There was only one man who knew she adored paint-sprayed carnations! She ran into the salon to search for the card and found it on the floor in the center of the room in a large envelope. Reading the message, she felt like crying; Ty was apologizing for that terrible morning! He had never apologized before in all the years they had known each other. She hugged the letter to her lovely bosom and bathed with it propped on the ledge of the tub.

Afterward Caterina ate one apple, a green salad and a hard-boiled egg. Then she called her art brokers in New York and bought a Wouwerman, a José Muñoz, a Turner and some Rosso sculpture. This was followed by a conference call connecting an architect and a lawyer in Lisbon with a banker in London, in which she agreed to put up forty-two percent of the investment for an underground garage in Paris. At last she got into bed, read Ty's note for the eighth time and fell asleep smiling.

In the dark a telephone shrilled horribly. Bedclothes stirred, and there was a crash as a water jug, a glass and the telephone hit the floor. There was the sound of muffled cursing, and a hand reached out to grope for the telephone. After some moments a light went on, and Ty, still blinded by his eyeshade, managed to sit up. Tugging it off, he found the phone, but when he picked it up he couldn't talk because his chin strap held his mouth closed.

The telephone beside Caterina's bed rang. She turned on the light and picked up the receiver sleepily to hear gargling noises.

"Ty?"

"Who?"

"Is that you, Ty?"

"Now, listen, I left a 'Do Not Disturb' on here."

"Why do you sound so funny?"

He unloosed his chin strap. "Caterina?"

"Your flowers are wonderful."

Ty peered all around the room and then looked under the bed. "What flowers?"

"And your sweet card."

"Caterina, I don't have any flowers."

"My flowers, you nit! You know, you really ought to change those sleeping pills."

Ty surfaced for an instant. "Thank you for your wonderful letter."

"Please, you are still asleep."

"No, no, don't say this is a dream."

"Good night, baby." She hung up.

Ty tottered into the living room. It *had all* been a dream; there were no flowers there, or in the bathroom or even the closet. He went back to bed.

The man operating the bug on Bryson's telephone took off his earphone and shut off the tape machine. Then he picked up the telephone and asked for a number in New York.

"Hello, Mr. Goldberg? Hamburg here." He nodded respectfully. "Yes, sir. They are friends again, which is a miracle after what happened here this morning. She thinks he sent her the flowers and the note and he thinks she sent him the apology. Yes, sir. Thank *you,* Mr. Goldberg. Good night, sir."

14

THERE WAS a four-day delay while they got Dane Ponder ready. Albert was so busy designing her hair style and conferring with the dressmaker he had flown from Paris that he had little time for his boats. He told Fräulein Schmeckle over and over again that she was not to think about acting but only of doing what he told her.

"Pick up that ashtray. No, no. Don't empty it. Please do only exactly what I tell you. I photograph only one action at a time, and all the little pieces are what make up the performance. When I tell you to smile, don't think of why you are smiling; motivations only put actors asleep on their feet. When I tell you to open the door, simply walk to the door, grasp the knob, turn it and pull. And when you have learned to do exactly as I say, we will have a splendid performance and the critics will think you are an actress. The camera is the real actor, and I am its mind and soul. Actors are only the motor. This is for films, you must remember. The director is the story, the storyteller, the cast, the sets and, most of all, the gross. That is what films are about: the *gross*. He acts best who acts in the biggest grosser. Now, please pick up that pretty dress and hold it up to you as though you were looking at it in a full-length mirror. In three parts, please. You pick it up. Good. You hold it to yourself. Fine. Now you look. Excellent. Speak the same way. Each speech is so many sentences, said in sequence. Each sentence is so many words, spoken in order. A speech is not a mass of words; it is one word at a time, and though I have written only a small part for you, when you do speak you will follow my rules and speak one word at a time, one sentence at a time.

"Then the critics will say that you have excellent elocution, which is said to be important for an actor. Perhaps it is—on the stage. When you move, when you speak, when you do exactly as I tell you, you will be independent of me in only one detail. You must concentrate on what it is you lust for most in life; think of nothing else. Each star has one nuance. With Bryson it is a little-boy-lost quality in the body of a handsome, mature man. With Largo it is an earthy avarice. The screen actor must have this one nuance; they call it personality, and he squirts it from the screen. In the theater, actors have to think while they rehearse, then add to that their technique. In screen acting we also think while we work, but not about what we are doing; it is the director who thinks about technique and movement. To be a great star, then, like Bryson or Largo, the actor must think about his most burning secret goal; he must lust for that dream. Then the proles in the darkness, the seekers of the dream, will see the actor stripped bare, and they will worship him because that dream is a living thing, a pure mirror of lust in which they may see themselves. That, dear girl, is where worship begins and worship ends."

While Albert worked with Dane Ponder, Largo spent her days with Wardrobe and her nights on her investments. She and the Parsee wizard overhauled her portfolio because she had a "feeling." They earned a net paper profit of two hundred and seventy-four thousand three hundred and seventy two dollars in four very daring, quick short sales, and invested it all in electronics and aerospace. Then she teamed up with a California real estate operator named Ketcham, and they made a deal with a savings and loan association to prepay the interest on an apartment mortgage of a million two, at fifty thousand a year for five years, after which they would take over the management. This would give her a tax credit off the top of her gross, and an additional depreciation allowance for the ensuing ten years, at which time she would sell the apartment house, take a capital gain and from the management group running the house would get twenty percent of the profits.

While Largo gilded lilies, gold and telephones, Ty caught up on his correspondence with his mother, who was sailing down the east coast of Java. He also worked hard on his stamp album, which was brought up from the hotel safe by a room-service waiter, concealed under a napkin so that there would be no question of its being discovered by Caterina and appropriated under California community-property law. Thanks to the accelerated intake of stripeys, he spent much of his days in a trance, and when he wasn't sleeping, writing to his mama or pasting stamps, he played back his better tapes to gain insight.

"I think it is extremely significant that in my one encounter with LSD, my response was social rather than self-concerned. As layers of me were stripped away by this mystical powerful drug which can quote take one out of one's self close quotation, I saw myself fighting for the rights of my Negro brethren—marching at the side of Martin Luther King, Sonny Liston, Ralph Bunche and other Negro leaders on a crusade which would convince the Congress of the

United States that all men must be truly free. Our march made headlines for days in my LSD revelation, and if called when I am between pictures and in the United States, I think my Negro friends know that they can count on a march or a check from me. LSD confirmed to me that I am a true liberal." This was Tape 207 BR, which had been recorded early in Ty's first analysis, shortly after he had read a *Reader's Digest* article on Booker T. Washington.

Whenever he could, considering the effects of the stripeys, Ty read the script Albert had given him with the explanation that it was on the rough side, in fact just a draft. At eight-fifteen one evening Caterina telephoned about the script. "Ty," she said, "I'm a little confused. What is the setting of your script?"

"Why, we open in Moscow at SMERSH, then switch to a hidden Chinese naval base on Staten Island."

"Yes, I heard it was another foreign-agent gargle, so I don't understand my part at all."

"Why, what does your script say?"

"That's why I'm calling. The one he's handed me to study is the same script he gave me in Honolulu six years ago. I'm supposed to be a girl in a department store who is in love with the floorwalker, except she doesn't know that he's a Ruritanian prince and he doesn't know that she's actually the daughter of the owner of the store."

"I think you'd better call Albert."

When Largo stated her complaint to Albert, he replied, "You will remember that first I gave you that script to study while we were making the beachcomber picture. You will admit that the beachcomber picture was extremely successful, will you not?"

"Albert, I am not questioning the hits! I am saying I have to know what to do when I get in front of the camera!"

"Have I ever failed to suggest what you should do? Are you suddenly going to turn into one of those motivated actors who read Proust and ride motorcycles? Is it your hope that when you step down as an actress, you will direct films by Camus and Kafka? Do you give Little Readings in your home to worthwhile friends against the day when you return to Broadway in *Medea*? What is this unseemly stress on the content of these ridiculous scripts? They are only for the front office in case the banks ask what a director is shooting. Scripts keep writers employed; these people breed like rabbits and face enormous bills. But they have nothing to do with us, Caterina; we are the working stiffs and we have to bring in a big hit every time. I am ashamed of you, at this stage of our long association together, for grumbling over which story we

98

are going to shoot. As it was in the beginning, when you were just a poor avid little actress, I will provide everything. You can be sure that Ty would never think of asking such silly questions."

"I'm sorry, Albert."

"Well, it *is* disappointing, Caterina."

"I *am* sorry, Albert."

Each night, because she had to relax somehow from all the discipline and tension, Dane Ponder persuaded Basil to take her to dinner at a secluded outdoor restaurant overlooking the Alster. Afterward, when the action had begun, they moved on to the Reeperbahn, which had the wildest night life in Western Europe.

Fräulein Schmeckle would light a stick of marijuana and smoke it as they strolled through the cottony spring air; it was not so much the funny grass that helped her to relax, she explained, as the defiance. "Everybody owns wonderful things except me," she said, "and now that I am a movie star, my director—what's his name—thinks he owns me. I have to banish that feeling or I will get all tensed up and do bad things."

"You are a movie star?" Basil would answer, smoking a sixty-cent cigar. "How very interesting."

Fräulein Schmeckle liked to walk in the Herbertstrasse, where the big union whores worked, because since it excited her, she thought it excited Basil. It was a broad street, sealed off at one end and closed to all but foot traffic at the other. The whores sat in well-illuminated store windows, as though they were merchandise such as mechanical pianos; each of them wore the costume and props which made clear her specialty. There were little crones wearing children's satin party dresses, windmill hair ribbons erect on their gray hairs; in fact, there were three of these in one display window, scabby triplets presumably offering to pick over any client in tandem. There were muscular blondes in black tie and tails like headwaiters; small, high-busted women wearing barbed wire around their jackboots, sitting in a red spotlight to make them look menacing and bloody. There were women menageries of monkeys, donkeys and fluffy little dogs: there were bearded girls in stuffed bikinis. But Schmeckle always stood longest in front of the window featuring a saber-toothed woman with eyebrows like John L. Lewis who wore the white uniform of hospital nurse and displayed electric probes and oddly shaped massaging gear.

"It is so bizarre, don't you think?" she would say breathlessly. "I mean, it is either evil in an innocent way or innocent in an evil way. That must be why it excites me so. Does it excite you?"

"No, but you excite me when you get excited."

"Ooooooh, Bazzie, good, good. That I love. Look! Look at the great police dog with the long red tongue. What must she do with him? Oh, Bazzie, could we go in and pay her and see?"

"No, we could not."

Each night Fräulein Schmeckle would plead with him, but he would only pack her into a taxi and hurry her off to the hotel and bed. They sat in darkened Reeperbahn bars and strip joints when Basil felt he could not endure the Herbert-strasse one more time. They watched strippers work together behind white sheets, throwing silhouettes; the men who went there had come to prefer the illusion of nakedness to the real thing. They watched motion pictures in looped reels which ran endlessly over and over again, twelve hours at a stretch, showing banal hordes of nudes cavorting on a Baltic beach. They watched barmaids leap out from behind stacked steins of beer, jump up on the stage, strip to the buff, grind, bump, run off stage and reappear fully dressed behind the beer again.

"If I didn't love you I would like to strip for men," Fräulein Schmeckle said. "Look at them sitting and staring so blankly. Look at their lips move silently. See what their hands are doing!"

"Who are you, anyway?" Basil asked one night.

"What do you mean?"

"Where do you come from? What kind of people are your parents?"

"I have no parents. They went to South America and never came back."

"When?"

"When I was about two."

"Did they just abandon you?"

"No, no, they were very respectable Nazis, I am sure. My father left English pounds and American dollars to pay for me. With a wonderful lady. I never missed them. She loved me, and they didn't. She was Frau Schmeckle; I don't know and don't care what their name was, I hate them. They must have been Nazis. They must have been bad. Except for the money—they were nice to leave the money. I had nice dresses and I went to the university, and when I am famous as Dane Ponder I am going to tell all the newspapers that my real name is Schmeckle."

Each night when they returned to bed she became more and more obsessed and he became more and more worried.

She was too much. She was more than slightly mad, and he had nightmares about being involved with her for life. But he was fond of her because she was unwholesomely unexpected.

They didn't need much sleep. When they weren't making love, they talked.

"These people I spend my life with," Basil said, "I simply do not dare to know them more than casually because they confuse me and have the power to distort what is real."

"Ah," Dane Ponder sighed, "I can help you there. I was once a surgical nurse."

"What has that got to do with anything?"

"It has to do with reality."

"How?"

"To see a scalpel make an incision across the abdomen, that is reality."

"I meant a different kind of reality."

"When I was a stewardess, we crashed in a big jet. I was the only survivor, and I was all smashed up and I remember every second. That is reality."

"Not really."

"What is, then?"

"What other people do, I suspect. Making do with less. Pushing one's self beyond one's powers. Honor. Hope. Refusing to take no when there is no yes. And whatever it is poor people do with their lives. That must be reality."

"Who wants that? They don't want it."

"I do, sometimes, I think it's this damn money they pay me. It's so much more than I could earn anywhere else that it has made me a damn slave. But maybe it's money that is the reality."

"Death is reality, and perhaps when we are making love?"

"Perhaps least of all then."

"That isn't nice."

"When we make love, after all, you are just a mirror in which I admire myself."

"You will hurt my feelings."

"Please, no! What I mean is, I don't know you well enough yet—or rather, myself well enough yet—to call it love. Any two people can make love, but this is taking, not giving, and surely taking can't be reality."

When he felt Dane Ponder was ready, Albert instructed her the night before shooting began on how she must identify herself to Ty, who might be confused because he had known her under a different name. She knocked timidly on his door and he opened it at once. He was wearing eyeglasses, but when he saw who it was he snatched them off and put them in his breast pocket, saying too heartily, "Well! Good evening, Miss Schmeckle." She smiled. "Uh, won't you come in, Miss Schmeckle?"

She entered and moved into the living room. Ty shut the door. "This is quite a surprise," he said. "Tomorrow is such an early call that I assumed everyone must be fast asleep."

"After what we did on that plane, how can you still call me Miss Schmeckle?" She giggled, looking very beautiful.

"I don't think I know your first name."

"It doesn't matter now."

"Why not?"

"Because I am not really an airline stewardess and my name is not Schmeckle."

"I don't understand."

"I am an actress. You see, my father lent Stanislavsky money once, and after Stanislavsky began to teach, my father called Konny and—"

"Konny?"

"Konstantin Sergeyevich Alekseyev Stanislavsky."

"Oh."

"And he got me a place in the Moscow Art Theater."

"When were you born?"

"In 1942."

"Stanislavsky died in 1938."

"This was his son. How could I work under the father in 1960 when he died in 1938? Like the father, the son said, 'Do not just look like an old woman; approximate the state of mind of an old woman.' At the time I met you, I was trying very hard for the part of an airline stewardess, and to approximate such a state of mind I decided to become an airline stewardess for one trip—"

"And luckily," Ty said, "your father had once loaned Orville Wright some money, so he telephoned and got you a spot on the airline."

"My father?" she said, blinking. "It is why my name is not Fräulein Schmeckle with no first name. My name is Dane Ponder."

Ty gaped. "Dane Ponder? Our new star?" Immediately he felt the urge to exercise his droit du seigneur over this woman now that she was an actress in his picture. "The daughter of Henry Ponder, the great Walloon star?"

"Yes. How sweet of you to remember Daddy."

Ty moved closer at the same instant Fräulein Schmeckle moved closer. "I can learn so much from you," she said. "Are there . . . will we—will we be playing love scenes together?"

102

"I am sure of it," he said and put his arms around her.

"Then we must approximate that state of mind," she said, opening her mouth to receive his.

15

Ty AWOKE, wonderfully refreshed, at five forty-five, took two stripeys and a cold bath, and dressed himself in a suit of bawneen. He gazed at the contents of the breakfast tray with pleasure, drank the triple orange juice for instant energy, and while he devoured the small steak, read the label on the ketchup bottle carefully. When he had read the front side four times, he turned to the back, all this while carefully chewing each mouthful twenty times. Instead of the label ordinarily reading: *"Shake Well"* and *"Guaranteed Free from All Artificial Preservatives or Colouring Matters . . . Made from Tomatoes, Sugar, Spirit Vinegar, Salt, Spices & Flavourings,"* the print read, in the usual typeface:

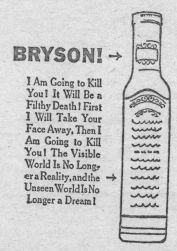

BRYSON! →

I Am Going to Kill You! It Will Be a Filthy Death! First I Will Take Your Face Away, Then I Am Going to Kill You! The Visible World Is No Longer a Reality, and the → Unseen World Is No Longer a Dream!

103

The two stripeys were so effective that Ty read the threat several times before looking dreamily at the waiter. "Where did this bottle of ketchup come from?" he asked mildly.

"From the pantry, sir."

"Did you set this tray?"

"No, sir—that is, I don't know, sir. We all set trays early, and then as the orders come down we pick them up at random. Is anything wrong, sir?"

"I don't know," Ty answered. "Please call Mr. McCobb on the telephone." He went back to his steak. Someone was beginning to push him too far, he thought hazily from behind the veil produced by the stripeys. The anxious waiter handed him the telephone.

"Albert? I have another threat here. Yes, brand-new. It just came in. It is printed this time on the back of a ketchup bottle."

"An outrage! How vulgar!"

"I thought so, too."

"You don't sound a bit concerned."

"Don't I?"

"We'd better get you a taster. Remember in *Awful* how you foiled the poisoner by changing tasters?"

"Why tasters, luv?"

"Well, this threatener does seem to have access to your food, doesn't he?"

"To my ketchup, yes."

"It's an awful death, poison."

"I don't think poison is intended. The threat keeps saying"
—he reached for the ketchup bottle—"*First I will take your face away.*"

"My dear fella! You should see someone's face after a good poisoning. Mere half-grain of strychnine causes such convulsions that *any* face becomes *quite* unrecognizable. The body is bent backward until the soles of the feet touch the top of the head, the limbs tremble violently, the neck stiffens and the face becomes grotesquely contorted in *risus sardonicus.*"

"Albert, please. Not while I'm eating."

"Still, think of silver nitrate. Or plain gasoline. And what's better for convulsions than a few jiggers of insect spray?"

"Nonetheless, employing a taster would be cruel and cowardly. Besides, the press would be certain to find out."

"Nonsense," Albert replied. "It could provide work for some eager hypochondriac."

"But the food would get cold."

"You haven't handled the bottle, I hope?"

"Well, I had to. Oh damn, fingerprints!"

"Pity. Still, I'll have Basil come by with a laundry bag. There just may be prints. Ty?"

"Yes, luv?"

"Would you mind having one or two male nurses share the room with you? Some bruisers who could provide real protection."

"You're goddamn right I'd mind."

"Well, we'll have to do something. Your security is quite awry."

16

ON THE huge sound stage all lights were trained on a set which seemed to be a precise copy of Ty's apartment at the hotel. Caterina, in a flame-colored knitted dress, battered trench coat and heavy tortoise-shell glasses, walked listlessly back and forth across the set reading a script absorbedly. McCobb sat beside the camera, just beyond the invisible line where the fourth wall would have been, his hands and arms folded neatly over his stomach, his polished shoes barely touching the floor. Wearing a red dinner jacket with a large black boutonniere to match his famous mustache, Ty ambled slowly to and fro through the door of the mock bathroom, reading his pages woozily through the veil of the stripeys. Neither he nor Caterina looked up, but they never collided as their paths crossed. Occasionally he stopped on floor marks, and a man would stretch a tape measure from the lens of the camera to his nose. Finally he strolled to the edge of the brilliantly lit set and peered into the darkness to address McCobb. "I'm as ready as I'll ever be," he said, "but I'd like to check my interpretation of the character, Albert. As I see it, he is blithe and suave even when under extraordinary pressure. Right?"

"Right."

The cameraman shouted changes in the lighting to the electricians overhead. O'Gorman had propped Largo against a wall on an angle board, and while she continued to read her pages he was improving the line of her right eyebrow.

"What would be the operative words, then, to describe my attitude in this scene?" Ty asked.

"Blithe and suave."

"Thank you." Two carpenters began hammering simultaneously, and three more large lights were shifted overhead.

"Albert, how am *I* motivated?" Largo yelled.

"By greed, darling."

"I mean the character, you son of a bitch."

"Anxiety growing slowly into fear, darling. You fear something dreadful is going to happen. Shall we walk through it?"

The script girl took out her stopwatch, and Caterina walked off the set through the door which led to the hotel corridor while Ty watched at the bathroom entrance, still clutching his pages. "There is something terribly familiar about this room," he said vaguely.

"Is he right for you, Eustace?" Albert asked the cameraman.

"Yeah, yeah, yeah. But the lighting is still wrong."

"Not to worry. Let's run it, everybody. Caterina you may begin."

" 'She knocks on the door,' " Largo read from the page. She knocked. " 'And she hears his voice.' "

"One moment," Ty read, walking toward the door. *"Coming."*

"Albert? Would I really be able to hear his voice through the door?"

"No matter. We'll be shooting from Ty's side."

"Actually, there should be a bell, luv," Ty said.

"Is there a bell at the entrance to your suite?"

"Indeed, yes."

"Basil!"

"Sir?"

"We'll want a bell for that door immediately after lunch."

"Yes, sir."

"Continue, please."

Largo knocked again.

" 'He opens the door,' " Ty read. " 'He is very suave.' "

"Close on Caterina, then close on Ty, then a two-shot. Go on, please."

Caterina walked in, followed by a small man with a large pincushion attached to his shoulder, and by a tall woman. Whenever she stopped they hovered by, measuring her shoulders and back and the diagonals from hip to shoulder. Caterina ignored them. *"You are Ames Monde,"* she read. *"I think you know who sent me."*

"The door is opening slowly behind her, Ty."

"Which door?"

"The same door."

"But we haven't closed it yet. We must establish a closed door before it can be opened again."

"You're quite right. I agree."

" 'The door opens noiselessly behind her,' " Largo read tonelessly, " 'and a cleated triple-bulb bomb comes rolling into the room and stops at their feet.' "

" 'He looks down,' " Ty read, " 'as the bomb hisses and sputters. He is very suave, very blithe. Frightened, the girl leaps into his arms.' " Ty appealed to Albert. "If she is frightened, she would run away, wouldn't she? If she clings to me, she'll hamper me."

"If you aren't running out of the shot, I'm not either," Largo said sharply.

"Why must every line present a problem?" Albert yelled. "Let us run this scene properly. *Please.*"

" '*It's only a bomb,* he says, and he leans over suavely and picks it up.' " Ty bent over and scooped at the floor.

"No, no," Largo read.

Ty stepped away from her, holding the nonexistent bomb in his cupped hand and still reading aloud. " 'He strolls to the doorway of the bathroom and tosses the bomb with a blithe underhand pitch into the filled bathtub.' " He simulated this and then exclaimed, "What am I doing in this dinner suit? I should be in a dressing gown and pajamas if my bath is ready."

"Would he receive a strange woman that way?"

"Monde? Besides, she's an enemy agent."

"Ty, for heaven's sake——"

"Albert, the man did not know she was coming. Why would the bathtub be full after he's finished dressing? Does he bottle his used bath water?"

"I see your point. Basil!"

"Sir?"

"Immediately after lunch we'll want a silver dressing gown and the white T&A pajamas with the slightly padded shoulders."

"Yes, sir."

"I had no idea one could neutralize a bomb by dropping it in water," Ty said. "How thrilling it is to learn a new fact a day."

They finished rehearsing at seven-twenty and got back to the hotel at half past eight. Although Largo and Ty left the studio separately, they arrived in the lobby of the hotel simultaneously and could not avoid riding up in the elevator together. To Ty, Caterina seemed particularly beautiful. She wore a white-and-ginger pony-skin coat and a cloth headband spotted with emeralds. It was the first time they had been alone together for fifteen months.

Ty blurted, "How is the book doing?"

"They tell me that as of last Monday they've sold one hundred and eighty-seven thousand four hundred and twelve, but the computer is running behind. Congratulations on winning the Rudolph Valentino Award," she added, tactfully changing the subject.

"I didn't get it, really. Ten minutes before the ceremony, the Tourism Minister asked me where in Italy I was born; he said he needed to know for his speech. When I told him I was born in Wales he nearly dropped. It was pitiable. The press had come all the way to the south of Italy, and the rules insist that the award be only for Italian-born actors. So I told him that you were born in Italy and that I could stand in for you. That relieved everyone, and you won the award. Really, someone should have told you; it was in all the papers."

"I was at Indian Head, Saskatchewan," Largo said, "and our only news came through on shortwave." She was blushing. "That was a very sweet gesture on your part."

"I went directly into the hospital at Castellaneta after that. I've never had a chance to congratulate you." The lift opened. "Congratulations. You really deserved it." He trailed her awkwardly into the corridor. "Valentino's real name was Guglielmi. Exotic, isn't it?"

Largo shrugged. "It's about equivalent to Rudy Williams in English." She stopped and faced him. "Are you on junk?"

"Junk? Me?"

"Then what the hell is it? You've been walking around like you were packed in excelsior all day."

"Well, uh, it's a new prescription that Abe Weiler insists I take. But you know damn well Abe wouldn't give me—" They stopped in front of her door and she unlocked and opened it.

"Take care, baby," was all she said.

"Caterina, can we talk for a little bit, luv?"

"I have four overseas calls coming in, honey."

"Later?"

"And play a few hours of your thrilling tapes?" she said

108

over her shoulder as she entered the room. "If it gets un-
bearable in here without you I'll scream." The door closed
behind her, and he was still staring at it when she opened it
again ten seconds later.

"What's the matter, Ty?"

"Someone is trying to kill me. I'm scared."

She pulled him into her apartment. "I want to hear about
that," she said.

They sat facing each other in the large living room. "It's
all so disgusting," he said slowly. "And what is worse is that
everyone—even Abe—thinks that all actors always overdra-
matize everything to get more attention."

"What happened?"

"Someone has tried to kill me four times."

"Ty!"

"In Rome, in Castellaneta, on the *Queen Mary* and in
Hamburg. This morning the fifth threat was delivered. The
first four attempts missed only because of the most unfore-
seen circumstances." He told her the story of the Japanese
plane launcher attached to the diving board at Goldberg's
palazzo.

"My God, Ty," Caterina gasped. "That Gertrude! What a
gallant little broad!"

"When the second threat came I could not have been less
ready for it," Ty said earnestly. "I was ill in Castellaneta—re-
cuperating but very miserable—and I was trying to learn Italian by one of those amplifying devices one slips under the
pillow—you know, the kind that teaches all night."

"You were studying Italian?"

"I thought it would please you. You must remember that I
was in a diseased state." He blinked at her and looked away.
"I was counting sheep in company with the machine—*sedici,
diciassette, diciotto, diciannove*—when the strange voice
which has now become so familiar, a weird voice covered
with icy fur, broke into the counting from inside the machine. It said it was going to kill me, and that it would be a
filthy death."

She stared at him with numb horror.

"The nuns found an asp in my bedpan the next morning."

"A what?"

"A deadly adder." He shuddered. "It would have bitten me
on—"

"No, Ty, no!"

"The third threat came by coded cable aboard the *Queen
Mary*. It made no sense, but I can still remember it." Ty had

begun to sweat in recollection; he wiped his face with a large handkerchief.

"What did it say?"

"It said: 'PEPPERDOG WALKS BENOIT KOENIG AND PEPPER-DOG WEARS AN IRIS TO SEVILLE. BUROTEL WINS BRUXELLES FOR TWO KINGS.' "

"How did you know what it meant?"

"Ten minutes after it arrived the key to the code was delivered by a bellboy. He later told detectives that a policeman had handed it to him on the pier in Southamptom and had told him to give it to me at six minutes after six in the evening on the third day out. When I decoded the cable it was the same threat, in the same words."

"How long did you have to wait?"

"No time at all. I had returned to my cabin rather badly bruised from having played squash during the hurricane—a tricky game at best at sea, unless one has a lower center of gravity—and had phoned ahead to the cabin steward to have a good hot bath drawn, to forestall stiffness. After I had decoded I undressed. On my way to the bathtub all the lights on the ship suddenly went off, but I groped my way into the bathroom and"—his mustache seemed to grow limp with the remembered terror—"just as I was about to climb into the tub"—Caterina had stuffed a fist into her mouth—"and I assure you that my right foot was within an inch of entering that water—the lights came on miraculously. The tub was filled with thrashing snakes which later investigation proved to be pit vipers. Four feet long and as deadly as a bullet in the heart."

"Excuse me, baby. I have to be sick." Caterina ran into the bathroom, slamming the door. A few minutes later she emerged, whiter than cut milk, and said weakly, "What is Abe Weiler's new prescription?"

"The fourth threat was telephoned from New York in the same voice. Then someone tried to shoot me after the *Ghastly* opening, so they are getting cruder and more direct." Ty sat gripping his knees, his knuckles white. "Then the threat was printed on the back of a ketchup bottle at breakfast this morning, which means that the fifth attempt can't be far away."

"The threats are always in the same words?"

"Yes."

"All four murder attempts were—"

"Exotic?"

"No, flashy. Show-bizzy. Three threats were printed—marble, teletype and ketchup label—and two were spoken, and the wording has that same show-biz flash. What else do they have in common?"

"Well, it sounds wild, but—"

"Honey, nothing is wilder than what's been happening to you."

"They all remind me of movies we've made. I mean, in *Murder* I saved the fleet but lost my life by launching myself from the deck of that Jap submarine to the U.S. admiral's bridge and moaning out the enemy's battle order with my dying breath, receiving the Congressional Medal of Honor posthumously in what Albert actually told the AP was a coda. The asp got you in *Nile,* and it was brought to you in what certainly *looked* like an Italian bedpan."

"My God, was that an asp?"

"Do you remember *Wind*—and there's no reason why you should—in which Albert cast me as Dan'l Boone? Well, the chief of the Shawnees ordered that I be thrown into the Pool of the Deadly Snakes—"

"And I saved you."

"Yes, thank you. Well, those were water moccasins, Albert said, and water moccasins are another way of saying pit vipers. And that chase here in Hamburg was precisely out of *Ghastly.* I mean, foot for foot."

"Then the killer must be someone who has seen *Ghastly.*"

"Honey, it did eight million five in the States."

"Who do you suspect?"

"Nobody. Everybody. Albert? You? Basil? O'Gorman? Who? Albert has had the same crew and department heads for twenty years. They're all my friends. In a way, I feel like weeping."

"Well, Goldberg has to get you some bodyguards. I'll take care of that. But if Abe knows you've been threatened, why would he prescribe stuff which has you walking around like a dope fiend? What kind of stuff is it?"

"The same old stuff," Ty answered listlessly. "Stripeys."

"Stripeys?"

"Two in the morning. One before I call him. Two at night."

"I don't believe it."

Ty blinked.

"There are kindly family doctors around Hollywood who would be happy to hook you on Demerol or stripeys," Largo said, "but not Abe. Abe is no pusher, and he has a revulsion for junkies."

"You don't believe it? Wait here," Ty said, and walked out of the apartment like a sleepwalker. Caterina reached for her private telephone, dialed the overseas operator and placed a call to Weiler in California.

When Ty came back he was carrying his portable tape player. For Caterina he ran the tape recorded on the telephone in which Abe increased the stripeys. After the third playback she said, "That's not Abe."

He gaped at her.

"You wouldn't know, because you never listen closely. You're so busy examining your navel that—"

"If that isn't Abe Weiler, then his wife is living with the greatest mimic in the business."

"Ty, I'm a foreigner, and linguistics is one of the reasons I got to the top in this business. I hear differently than you because I still have to keep breaking the sounds down. Those sounds are not Abe."

"Then who is it? I call his number in Encino every day at a quarter to two. I'm in Hamburg and he's five thousand-odd miles away and he's there every time I call, sitting and talking in Abe Weiler's house."

Largo's telephone rang. "Hello? . . . Thanks, I'll hold." To Ty she said, "Pick up the other extension by the bed and listen. Abe is coming on. Listen carefully— Hello, Abe? This is Caterina."

"Caterina?" a worried voice said. "Where are you?"

"In Hamburg with Ty."

"But what's happened to Ty? He called me once and arranged to call me every day at the same time, and since then I haven't heard a word from him."

Ty spoke into the other telephone. "Abe," he said hoarsely, "I *have* called you every day for the past week, and until this instant I thought that I had been talking to you for an hour a day."

"You talked to *me*? Maerose," Abe said in an excited voice to his wife, "did I talk to Tynan Bryson since a whole week? No, of course not. Ty, listen. Are you hallucinating?"

Caterina spoke up again. "Abe, whoever he talked to told him he had to take five stripeys a day. You hear? Five. And *stripeys*."

"Stripeys? Five. My God, he didn't take them?"

By the time the conversation ended, Ty was shaking violently. Caterina set him down in a padded chair and began to massage the back of his neck. "You'll be okay, baby," she said. "Six days is nothing to kick."

"It's not that. To hell with that. I'm so scared I could kick eating. It's just— Who was I talking to for six hours last week?"

112

"The killer."

"The rotten sadistic bastard."

"Go take a nice hot bath and flush every stripey you have down the john." She pulled him to his feet and walked him to the door. "And in the meantime I'm going to get you some protection. We have to take this big. Whoever this guy is, he's a real nut who wants to kill you." She walked him down the corridor to his door. As they reached it a chambermaid came out, curtsied as though she were on camera and told Ty that his bath was ready.

"Is anyone in there?" Caterina asked.

"No, madam."

Caterina took Ty inside, threw away all the stripeys herself and ordered him to lock the door behind her when she left. "And don't open it unless someone gives three slow and three quick knocks."

Back in her room Caterina stared at the carpet abstractedly as she paced up and down. Finally, her mind made up, she put on her coat and left the hotel. Downstairs she got into a cab and told the driver to take her to police headquarters. She didn't trust telephones any more.

At the station house she was sent to the second floor, where she opened a door marked

Polizeibezirksobermeisterbüro

Franz Heller

One of two police clerks was gazing dreamily at the door as it opened. As he saw who was entering he fainted, falling over sideways noisily. His co-worker leaped to his feet. "Pardon, Fräulein Largo! *Polizeienwarter* Mudi is the president of your North German Fan Club, and evidently the shock of seeing you here was too much for him."

"May I see Chief Inspector Heller, please?" Largo asked.

"He will be honored. This way, please." She had to step over Mudi to enter the inner office. The clerk announced her and then withdrew. She found herself facing a bulky, white-haired man behind a small desk, busily eating an ice-cream cone. He had off-black pouches under his eyes and was wearing country tweeds. She had never seen him before.

"Oh, I am so sorry," she said, "I came to the wrong office."

"Whom do you seek, dear lady?"

"I must see Inspector Heller."

"I am Inspector Heller."

113

"But our case has been handled by a different Inspector Heller."

"In the *Hamburg* police?"

"Yes. He is a dark, small, very carefully dressed man of about thirty-five."

The man smiled. "That certainly does not fit me, but I have been on the police force here for over thirty years and I am the only one of that name."

"But he conducted an investigation for us. He interrogated me for over a half-hour," Largo said patiently but firmly.

"Then we must deal with first things first," the inspector responded. He beckoned Caterina to the window. "Look at the two men walking below, please," he said. "In uniform is *Polizeihauptkommissar* Hanfman. The civilian is *Polizeipräsident* Frankenheimer. Which one would you prefer to identify me?"

"The man in uniform," she said uncertainly. The inspector opened the window. "Friedrich!" he shouted. The two men stopped and looked upward. "Yes, Franz?" the man in the uniform yelled back.

"Will you please identify me for this lady?"

The man below shrugged, then said, "You are *Polizeibezirksobermeister* Franz Heller."

"Is there anyone else of that name and rank in the Hamburg police?"

The man laughed. "Not yet," he shouted back.

"Thank you, Friedrich," Inspector Heller said and closed the window. "Please sit down and explain why you were being interrogated by a man claiming to be *Polizeibezirksobermeister* Heller."

Caterina collapsed into the chair behind her. "Someone is trying to kill my husband—my ex-husband—and we called the police for help. This impostor came to see me at the studio after having questioned all the others."

"You are a painter?"

"No."

"Your husband?"

"A painter?"

"You mentioned a studio."

"Oh. We are actors—film actors."

"You are from Hollywood?" Heller seemed delighted.

"Yes."

"You know, this is marvelous," the inspector said expansively. "You are the first person from Hollywood I have met in twenty-six years, and you bring back very happy memo-

114

ries." He snapped a switch on the intercom. "One maple walnut, please, Mudi."

"You've been to Hollywood?"

Heller nodded happily. "On my honeymoon. We were driving from Dublin to Cork. We passed through your charming little village and it was so irresistible that we stayed the night." He wagged his head with nostalgia. "And they make films in such a tiny place. It must be north of the village, yes? On the right?"

"I—I don't think I understand."

"No matter. To business. You have made serious charges. Attempted murder and a man who impersonates a police officer, thus denying you protection." He leaned across the desk to fill in a word on a crossword puzzle as Mudi entered with another ice-cream cone. Looking only at Largo, he almost took a bad fall.

"Tell me the entire story, omitting nothing," Heller said, and Caterina began to talk rapidly, beginning with the first murder attempt in Rome and finishing with the horrifying account of the false Dr. Weiler.

"Did the false inspector speak English?" Heller asked.

She nodded.

"Then I will speak in English, too," he said, in an accent reminiscent of that used by vaudevillians for comic effect.

"That's funny," Caterina said. "In English you have a New Jersey accent."

17

TY UNDRESSED slowly, thinking what a bother it would be if he had difficulty in weaning himself from stripeys. He remembered horrible scenes in *Hooked*, in which he had rolled screaming in agony on the floor, ruining two suits. He was unbuttoning his shirt when he heard the front door open. His first thought was that this was impossible; Caterina had insisted that he lock the front door and he remembered doing so. He peered through the door of the bedroom at the entrance hall. The front door was opening slowly and silently, and as he stared, a fused, triple-bulb cleated bomb just like the one described in the new script rolled across the carpet toward him, sputtering as it came.

Ty went dizzy with fright: strangling sounds like those of a low comic came from his throat as he forced himself to remember the instructions from Albert. "You are suave, you are blithe," he told himself. He tried to bend over to pick up the bomb, but his legs had locked. With incredible effort he projected himself into the fantasy of the screenplay where he would be safe because the script had already been written, and his legs relaxed.

"I am very suave," he said aloud in a quavering voice. "I am blithe, I scoop up the bomb and with a graceful underhand pitch I toss it across the room into the filled bathtub."

Like a robot he bent down, picked up the bomb and tossed it through the open door into the water of the huge tub. The bomb's destructiveness was nullified. He swayed and clung to the door for support, thanking heaven that he had been given a short course in bomb-neutralizing that very morning, and blessing Emma, the chambermaid who had filled the tub. He would buy her a set of flashy green velvet garters to show his appreciation. He was at least twenty years younger than she was, and that wasn't young by a long shot, but by heaven, if she indicated her desire he would even tumble her in bed to show his appreciation.

In the tub the bomb exploded with a tremendous roar, almost bursting his eardrums and sending a geyser of water to the ceiling. Ty stared dumfounded as it tore an enormous hole in the floor, revealing the bathroom below.

Directly below, the fat lady was eating triple-dipped chocolates with brandy-immersed cherry centers as she creamed her face in front of the dressing table while waiting for her bath to fill. The two remaining charges of the bomb descended with great noise and such a flood of water that she was knocked off her chair. A geyser of water from the contents of the combined tubs rose two floors to dash itself, before Ty's glazed eyes, upon the ceiling of Ty's bathroom.

Two floors below, six of the midgets were standing on a long bench in front of the bathroom mirror, shaving together before they bathed together in their enormous tub. They paused as they heard the first explosion two floors above, and stared at one another in consternation at the sound of the second explosion. But before they could react they were awash, sent sprawling by great waves of water into bidets, washbasins and toilets by the force of the last remaining

116

charge. The third geyser soared three floors, just missing Ty who was standing at the edge of the open crater looking downward.

Herr Wimpfheimer, the hotel's chief receptionist, was at that moment sneering to an arriving guest in the main hall, "You insist on a bath, sir? There is not a room in this hotel without a bath," when the ceiling opened like thunder and nearly a half ton of water fell upon the two men, knocking them across the lobby and causing a visiting Texan dining in the grill room one hundred feet away to compliment the maître d'hôtel upon the "attractive waterfall effect."

Basil got to Ty's room first. He found him clutching shards of the shattered tub and staring into space. "I've definitely kicked the stripeys, Baz," he said dully. "Is my hair quite gray? Have I aged terribly?"

"But what *happened*, Ty?"

"It isn't true that water neutralizes bombs, Baz," Ty said. "Albert will have to change the script."

Herr Zendt, the manager of the hotel, and McCobb rushed into the room together. As they stared downward through the great holes in the three bathtubs to the waterlogged lobby, Herr Zendt stifled a choking sound and then covered his face with a handkerchief. Below could be seen the fat lady's pink legs moored in deep water, and on the floor below her a half-drowned litter of midgets.

Herr Zendt took the handkerchief off his face and walked to the mirror. He was pale but was recovering control. "Zendt," he ordered the mirror's reflection, *"benimm dich wie ein Mensch!"* and then he fled from the wreckage.

18

MUDI banged into Inspector Heller's office, almost disregarding the door. "There has been a serious explosion at the Pacific Seasons Hotel, sir," he said breathlessly.

"Ty!" Caterina screamed.

"Was anyone killed?"

"No, sir."

"Anyone hurt?"

"No, sir. Just bruises and shock, sir, but the bathrooms of three floors and the reception area in the lobby have been destroyed."

"Mr. Bryson is still safe." Inspector Heller said to Caterina. "And I intend that he shall remain that way. Let's go." Donning a tweed hat and accepting a blackberry ice-cream cone from one of the clerks, he took her by the arm and they hurried out of the office.

Forty minutes later, after a minute examination of the scenes of the crime, conferences with the bomb squad and the issuance of instructions to his assistant, Sergeant Skutch, Heller gathered the principal members of the film company in Tynan Bryson's living room. As he conferred with the sergeant, they waited near the broad windows overlooking the Inner Alster. Caterina and Dane Ponder sat on the sofa, Ty between them; Basil and McCobb faced each other in chairs on either side.

Albert was full of admiration for Herr Zendt's behavior. "I accepted total responsibility," he said, his arms folded across his stomach. "I insisted that it was not the hotel's fault that someone was trying to murder Ty, and that I felt it was Goldberg's duty to fully recompense the hotel for damages. He wouldn't hear of it. He actually said to me, 'After all, what is it but a few holes in a few ceilings?' He said I should have seen the place after the British occupation, when the hotel was an officers' club. And I had to say to him, 'Herr Zendt, I must say you are being awfully chic about this whole affair.'"

Inspector Heller, eating a double lemon ice-cream cone, came over and sat down facing them, and Albert turned to him. "If I had thought about it at all, you know," he said, "that bogus police inspector wouldn't have fooled me for a moment. He was too sleekly dressed to be a policeman. And what busy policeman would keep pestering suspects for their autographs?"

"The Hamburg police department won second place on the Ten Best-Dressed Police Departments list in *Interpol Magazine*. We are all pretty nifty dressers. The police president designs his own neckties, for instance. As for the autographs, what more discreet way could one find to collect fingerprints?"

"I see," Albert said thoughtfully. "I stand corrected."

"Now, about this aspiring killer. He is a show-off, so I can assure you that he will be apprehended. Such people always need to add one extra flourish when they should be escaping on a plane to Hong Kong. However, that compulsion to show off is also his greatest weapon because it means unmitigated boldness. With his nerve, he has been manipulating all of you and warping your imaginations. Obviously, killing means nothing to him; today he used a sledge hammer to try to kill a fly, and it is a miracle—an absolute miracle—that many people aren't dead as a result. We also know that he employs confederates, which is very dangerous for a murderer. The false police inspector and the false police sergeant are probably not the killers because Mr. Bryson has never seen either one of them before and the pattern and psychology of these crimes indicates that the killer is probably someone he knows.

"Also, a telephone operator in this hotel has deliberately switched calls placed to police headquarters here and to Dr. Abraham Weiler in California. Incidentally, the telephoned threat which supposedly came from New York probably emanated from here, thanks to this operator. We will have that solved before I leave.

"Now, what are the other possibilities? Well, this could all be a series of elaborate suicide attempts by Mr. Bryson in which he lost his nerve each time."

Everyone laughed. "Except that actors do not kill themselves while they are working," Basil said. "They wait for the notices."

"This man survived *Jefferson*, Inspector," Albert said, "and life will be ever sweet to him because of that."

"What is *Jefferson?*"

"Please, Inspector," Ty said, "not while you're eating."

"*Jefferson* is a film which Mr. Bryson both wrote and starred in a few years ago, Inspector, which focused on a little-known fact of the statesman—his experiences as the first importer of spaghetti into the United States," Albert explained.

Heller shuddered. "I saw it." He turned to Ty, trying to control his distaste. "My wife was a great advocate of the democratic process and a life-long admirer of the Sage of Monticello. Her library of Jeffersoniana was one of the finest in Europe. She persuaded me to take her to see your film. We have never seen a motion picture since, and she became a neo-Fascist and burned every book and pamphlet in the library."

"It was that goddamn director!" Ty shouted.

Heller shrugged and abruptly changed the subject. "Then

119

we are all in agreement," he asked everyone, "that this is not Mr. Bryson's plot against himself?"

"You might as well accuse Goldberg," Largo said.

"Who is Goldberg?"

"Who is Goldberg?" McCobb asked incredulously. "Frederic X. Goldberg is said to control the world's film industry."

"Which explains why there are so many lousy movies," Largo said.

"He also owns his own international airline so that none of us ever have to be wait-listed," Basil added.

"Goldberg is so clever with figures," Ty said, "that he is finance chairman of the Republican National Committee *and* the Mafia."

"Is he in Hamburg now?"

They all looked blank.

"Don't any of you know him?"

McCobb cleared his throat. "Uh . . . well, not actually. He is very much the private sort of family person, you see. I chat on the telephone with him from time to time, but I don't believe that anyone—outside of Mrs. Goldberg and perhaps his children—has seen him for more than twenty years."

"From what you say, he might very well have the power to hire fake police, manipulate telephone calls and engineer murder from a distance," Heller mused.

"I don't think he's all that interested in me," Ty said.

"He loves Ty," Caterina insisted. "Ty is his biggest single grosser."

"Then what *could* be his motive—just speculating, of course, that our man is Mr. Goldberg?" Heller asked.

McCobb's reply was subdued. "If Goldberg is responsible," he said slowly, "and I, for one, cannot accept such a heinous thought, it could be because Mr. Bryson is the first star in history to demand—and get—a hundred percent of the gross at the box office as a fee for his services."

Caterina stood up so violently that she knocked over a vase of flowers on the table in front of her. "A hundred percent of the gross?" she yelled. "He's paying me a lousy seven hundred and fifty thousand dollars!"

Ty smiled beatifically.

Albert approached Largo from the front and Basil from the rear, and together they managed to get her back on the sofa and hold her there until the tantrum subsided.

"As you can see, Inspector, the contract has established a dangerous precedent for Goldberg," Albert said, still breathing heavily from his exertion a few minutes before. "However"—he took a deep breath and exhaled slowly—"there is

120

something I must get off my chest because it bothers me very much."

"Of course. You must tell me everything," Heller said soothingly.

"Uh, Basil?" Albert addressed his assistant.

"Sir?" Basil was still holding Largo, but she had been reduced to muttering under her breath.

"Since you took the ketchup bottle with the label threatening Ty to police headquarters this morning, how is it that you did not discover that the policeman was an impostor?"

"I didn't take the bottle to the police," Basil said. "I rang police headquarters and talked to the man. He said he would send for the bottle, so I left it in a laundry bag with the hall porter and rushed to the studio."

"But you told me you had a receipt."

"That's right. He left the receipt with the hall porter."

"Did you call police headquarters from a hotel telephone?" Heller asked.

"Yes, sir. From the lobby."

"Did you give your name and room number when you called?"

"Yes, as is required."

Heller beamed his appreciation at one of his police secretaries who entered bearing a strawberry ice-cream cone. He licked the cone with relish and said, "I must ask each one of you to tell me your whereabouts while Mr. Bryson was in that clinic in Italy. Miss Ponder?"

"I don't understand. What clinic?"

"Miss Ponder is new," Basil said. "In fact, she joined the company just a little more than a week ago."

"Ah. Miss Largo?"

"Miss Largo was in Canada and Mr. Schute and I were in London," Albert answered crisply.

"Basil did visit me during the first week," Ty said nervously.

"That is true. To deliver the calf's-foot jelly from me," Albert said modestly.

"Did any of you visit Mr. Bryson while he was aboard the *Queen Mary?*" Heller asked. "That is, before the sailing?"

"Mr. Bryson was quite weakened by his illness. I was in Hamburg at the time, preparing this film," Albert said, "and I asked Basil to accompany him to Southampton and to see him aboard comfortably."

"And you were in New York, Mr. Schute, when Mr. Bryson received the telephoned threat which ostensibly came from that city?"

"Yes, I was, as a matter of actual fact," Basil said stiffly, "and I am not at all sure that I appreciate the turn this conversation is taking."

The inspector shrugged. "There have been four murder attempts, Mr. Schute." He stared at the production manager.

Everyone became very quiet; even Largo stopped muttering about money.

Sergeant Skutch entered. "We have the telephone operator, Herr Chief Inspector," he announced. "She has admitted everything."

Heller stood up. "You must excuse me," he said. "First things first. We will continue this conversation at a later date. You will please keep yourselves at the disposal of the police." He bowed and left the room with the sergeant.

The telephone operator was a tall, heavy, sad-looking blonde whose make-up had been streaked by the tears she had earned. Herr Zendt was staring at her as though she were a leper.

"This is Frau Margo Fringl, Herr Chief Inspector," Skutch said. "She has been employed by this hotel for nine years, and has been chief operator for two years."

"Why did you do it, Frau Fringl?" Heller asked sadly.

"He tempted me with money."

"Who is he?"

"I don't know."

"You want to protect a murderer?"

"Please, sir. I tell you always the truth. To my house a letter came. I keep it in my purse. Here, look." She fumbled with the purse as she wept. "There was five hundred marks in it, the envelope, when it came." Heller read the printed circular she handed him as Herr Zendt peered over his shoulder. It said:

Put some sunshine in your life;
win a trip to sunny climes; play the new, easy
telephone game. Call Center 35980 and five
hundred more big, easy deutschmarks will enter
your mailbox. Put some sunshine in your life.
Win a wonderful trip.

"Maybe the killer is a travel agent?" Herr Zendt asked.

"To whom did you speak, Frau Fringl, when you called this number?"

"A voice. It said that it was a recording. It told me that I must tell the other operators that all calls from the film people were to be referred to me. All I had to do was to transfer these calls to Center 35980. Oh," she wailed suddenly, "what will happen to my job?" Herr Zendt turned away without speaking and left the room.

"Take her to headquarters," Heller said, and a policeman led Frau Fringl away.

"What did you find at the Center number?" Heller asked Skutch.

"A recording machine with a very ingenious transmitting apparatus. When Frau Fringl rang the number, the call was automatically transferred to another telephone, which could be anywhere within a half-mile radius of the transmitter. Presumably whoever answered assumed various identities, depending on who the caller was trying to reach. Otherwise the room at that number is empty. The rent was paid for three months in advance."

"Get the rental agreement. I want the starting date."

"Yes, sir. Also, I have talked with Mudi at the office. He reports that a used bottle of ketchup has arrived by mail, addressed to you."

"Good. Call him and tell him I want the identities of every fingerprint on that bottle."

19

FOR THE next three days McCobb kept everyone busy shooting the bomb sequence. At two o'clock each day Ty re-established comforting contact with Dr. Weiler; all that marred their rapport was that Weiler had developed the irritating habit of answering the telephone in California by chanting, "The real Dr. Weiler is now standing up. Will the real Tynan Bryson please lie down?"

The terror stayed with Ty, but he kept himself going by

imagining that he was creating a performance in which nonchalance and easy charm were required. For a while Caterina was grim and somber on the set but within a few hours he had teased her out of it, and the others were either too busy or too indifferent to dwell on the fact that somewhere beyond the rim of light a man was waiting to kill him. On the third day they broke early, and it was only six o'clock when Ty got back to the hotel. He had been moved down the corridor to a large apartment directly adjoining Caterina's, and at night he would imagine he was able to feel her presence through the walls. But even sex had been changed by the terror; death had become a constant preoccupation and he thought very little about women. His own fate was far more absorbing.

Bolts had been put on the doors; he never passed near the windows, where his silhouette might be seen, and refused to accept any mail until it had been carefully examined. This evening he fidgeted around the room for a while after bathing, read some of the accumulated fan mail and wrote to his mother. Then, bored, lonely and desperately missing the only one in the world he could bear, he took a deep breath, picked up the telephone and asked for Miss Largo.

Raddatz, the butch Latvian hairdresser, answered. She had a voice like a tuba encased in Orson Welles's stomach, and was tattooed with crossed anchors on each forearm. Her hairdress was more of a hairsuit. Three years before, right after the second divorce while they were making a film about the life of Simón Bolívar called *High*, in the Andes above Bogotá, Raddatz had taken a singular objection to Ty after having read the stenographer's transcript of both divorce proceedings. He had been forced to fight her in the rarefied oxygen of the 9300-foot altitude with bare knuckles before knocking her down and kicking her unconscious. But the loathing was mutual. There was no hanky-panky between Largo and Raddatz—not even Caterina's worst enemies claimed that—and she never talked to Raddatz.

Clara Raddatz simply was a superb hair stylist who had gotten her job by threatening to throw herself into the polar-bear cage at the Bronx Zoo if Largo didn't give her a chance to prove that she was the best in the world. She was also a dauntless bodyguard; she had once beaten up three drunken Bulgarian sailors because they had whistled at Largo. She tasted dubious food under dubious circumstances, traveled a day ahead to test conveyances, building elevators and airplane ramps, and even investigated the health records of all airline pilots and ships' captains who were to transport her

124

idol on her worldwide missions. Consequently Largo had raised the art of self-preservation to a very high level.

"Get off the phone, you dyke moron," Ty yelled. "Put Miss Largo on."

"Bryson? You twit, step out into the hotel corridor and I'll break your goddamn arms."

"You want me to have Goldberg make you wear taffeta and lace in the street? Get Largo, you degenerate monster."

Raddatz sobbed; Ty always knew how to break her. Though she had spent two years as an infantryman with Wingate in Burma, where she had learned karate from Japanese prisoners, and fourteen months as regimental sergeant major in Thailand's royal bodyguard battalion, where she had mastered the lightning art of Thai footfighting, Bryson always mopped the deck with her. The last time she had charged him was during the shooting of a sheep-rancher idyll in the Australian Outback, and he had beaten her even though she had an extra edge of sexual impetus because he was playing his part in a kilt. By now she was resigned to Bryson and to Largo's feeling about him; though she still cried herself to sleep in beer joints.

"Ty?" It was Caterina. *"Shut up, Raddatz!"*

"Hi, luv."

"Just a minute, honey. *Get the hell out of here, Raddatz, goddammit!"*

"What is it doing?"

"She's crying like a basso banshee and ramming her head into the wall. *Out, Raddatz, out!"*

"How about dinner?"

"I thought that after ten years you finally understood that we shouldn't even have dinner with each other."

"That's crazy."

"All right. Dinner. What time?"

"Twenty minutes?"

"Okay. And after dinner? What happens then?"

"Well, this town has a weird night life. The Reeperbahn has as much action as Tokyo."

"Aaaaaah."

"No, it's special stuff. They have women who wrestle in mud, and . . ."

"Excuse me, baby, Raddatz is hysterical, and I don't want her going out and hitting a cop. *Raddatz!* Straighten up and get out of here. Listen to me! They have a club somewhere where women wrestle in mud. That's like an evening of Mozart for you." There was a pause before Caterina spoke again. "You made her happy, Ty. She perked up so at the news that

125

she didn't slam the door. What else happens in Hamburg?"

"They have a bar where you can buy drinks for alcoholic horses, and tattooists who can reproduce a stained-glass window from the Cologne cathedral across your stomach."

"Now you're talking. We'll start with dinner in here."

"Thank you, luv. Thank you very much."

He was so exhilarated that he rang for room service, tipped the waiter twenty marks and told him to take a chilled magnum of Dom Pérignon to Caterina's room. Then, arranging the mirror so that he could not see his face, he tried on his white silk pajamas with the slightly padded shoulders, and an ivory, blue-piped dressing gown. He stared at the effect but decided he couldn't get away with it; Caterina might bar him at the threshold.

When the doorbell buzzed he approached it warily and asked loudly who was there. Albert answered. Ty opened the door and flinched at the size of the two blank-faced men who were standing behind the director. Albert slipped into the room while the two men remained in the corridor.

"You are under my protection now, Ty," Albert said with a certain majesty, "so we may consider that all the nonsense is over. Going to bed so early?"

"Who are those golem, luv?"

"They are your bodyguards. Built of pressed steel by Krupp. Masters in every art of self-defense and attack. Brothers: Moni and Schorschl Gänzenmüller. Their mother was a Percheron."

"Which is which?"

"It doesn't matter. They have names only for legal reasons. They are deaf-and-dumb and they don't know which is which. But why are you in pajamas? Tomorrow is Sunday; there's no call."

"I'm taking Caterina to dinner."

"Great Wellington, Ty, you aren't going to start all that up again?"

"What can these bucentaurs do for me?"

"They will guard you."

"But they can't yell for help, luv."

"They have never needed help."

"They are not to interfere—please make that very clear. I don't want bodyguards tagging after me. There is nothing which annoys the public more than that, luv. How does one tell them they are not to interfere?"

"They have been instructed."

"Good. Please see that they stay ten yards behind. We'll be dining at Caterina's, and then we may go for a walk. It should be clearly understood that they are not to belt fans tugging on our threads for autographs."

"Count on it."

"And thank you, Albert. I've been picky, but I am most grateful. This is a very touching thing you've done." Ty produced his most sincere smile, his dazzling white caps gritting together brilliantly like Teddy Roosevelt's.

"Goldberg isn't paying for this, you know."

"You're paying?"

"No, you are. It's a legitimate business expense."

After Albert left, Ty tried on a café-au-lait jacket with a cocoa-colored ascot and a pair of beige vicuna trousers, but the combination didn't seem to work. Dressing in a violet dinner jacket, he studied his body movements in the foreshortened mirror while humming "Yellow Submarine" and doing the watusi. But when the telephone rang he had changed into full dress and was fussing with the white tie.

"What the hell happened to you, hon?" Caterina asked.

"What do you mean?"

"You said twenty minutes. It's been an hour and ten minutes and the waiters are getting mutinous."

"Over an hour? That damn Albert. He arrived with some damn bodyguards, and—"

"Bodyguards? Oh, Ty that's wonderful. But please hurry or the champagne will be flat."

On a final impulse Ty changed into a dark-gray flannel suit with a maroon tie, started to equivocate about the tie and then bravely decided to take a chance. Hurrying to leave the room before he lost the nerve, he opened the door and ran into a solid wall of flesh. The two bodyguards stood shoulder to shoulder to protect him from the possibility of an attack by mice in the corridor. Bewildered, he tried to move around them, but they kept blocking his way.

"What is this? What are you *doing?*" he said, pushing against their chests with both hands and almost snapping his wrists. They stared back at him without expression or sound. "Moni! Schorschl! I am only going in *there,*" and he pointed to Caterina's door.

It was useless. "Goddammit," he snarled, "wait till Mc-Cobb gets through with you."

He slammed the door, ran back to the living room, picked up the telephone and told the operator to get Albert Mc-Cobb. After a long delay he rattled the telephone frantically. "What is happening down there?" he shrilled. "Get me Albert McCobb."

"Mr. McCobb's room telephone does not answer," the

voice sang, "but we are paging him in the Dulles Room, the Basilisk Room and the Logarithm Bar." Ty slammed down the phone and sprinted back to the front door. Moni and Schorschl still stood like Dublin temperance cadets on duty in front of a saloon, as immovable as bronze.

"Boys, listen." He knew that they couldn't hear, but perhaps they had been schooled in lip reading. "McCobb just stepped out for a second." He mouthed the words like a man who is chewing too much peanut butter, then pantomimed eating motions daintily lest imaginary sauce fall on his tie. There was no response, and in a sudden tantrum he hammered rapidly on their chests.

The telephone rang, and again he slammed the door and ran back to it, ready to rip Albert in half.

"Listen, Ty," Largo's voice said. "I don't know what kind of a rotten, neurotic trick you are trying to pull, but let's forget the whole thing. I mean the whole thing. The entire, whole, complete, rotten, neurotic, goddamn thing that you're trying to start up again. You hear me?"

"They won't let me out!" he wailed. "They are deaf-and-dumb and I can't explain to them and Albert didn't tell me who owns them and he's left the hotel."

"The bodyguards won't let you out?"

"Luv, you never saw such big men."

Caterina began to laugh like a mad macaw, in spasm after spasm. At last she was able to say, "Just a minute, hold on. I have to look." In a minute she returned to the phone. "My God, they're bigger than Duke Wayne's horse. I'm sorry about laughing, hon, but I can't help it, it's so funny."

"All right, dammit. Pour the champagne. I'm coming in." He hung up and went to the window. It was narrow, and he had difficulty working his way out on the ledge. It took exactly three and a half minutes for the impetuosity of his act to wear off, and he was nearly halfway to Caterina's window when he made the mistake of looking down.

He froze; his conviction that he was going to fall off the ledge locked his arms and legs in a pinwheel position. A light rain was falling, and out of the corner of his eye he could see a large crowd collecting on the sidewalk far below him.

Then he heard Herr Zendt's voice close by, calling from his window. With a sickening effort he managed to turn his head in that direction, his whole frame trembling and filled with nausea.

"*Bonsoir*, good evening, Herr Bryson," Herr Zendt said cheerily. "I am not here to curtail your privileges or to interfere with your plans, let me assure you. As a guest of this

128

hotel, I wish you to enjoy your stay in whatever manner is fitting. But—and it is an important but—the police has telephoned, you see. This will automatically involve the press, and the press would be ever ready to misunderstand your exercises out on this ledge. Surely, Herr Bryson, that would be regrettable, particularly if the firemen have to come."

"Herr Zendt! I cannot move! My knees have locked!"

"You mean you want to come in?"

"Want to come in? Have you gone mad, Herr Zendt? I have to get in."

"You are not attempting suicide?"

"Dammit, man!" Ty was near tears. "I was only trying to visit my wife."

"Ah, so. I see. Then we must use the mind. Become one with the religious of the East. We think easy thoughts. We breathe easily. We free the diaphragm. We breathe, we relax. We teach ourselves to move with the greatest of ease."

"Yes, I see. I see now. Yes." Ty projected himself back into reel eight of *Quail*, the first secret-agent picture of the current eight-year series, in which, using only his fingers and toes, he had made his way down the face of the Empire State Building during a sleet hurricane, from the tower to the seventy-first floor. He imagined he could feel the wind machines at his back and hear Albert's running instructions. Suddenly he was back in the film, high over New York, clinging to the ice-smooth side of the building. Everything became simple, and a moment later he was inside the warm hotel beside Herr Zendt and his staff, shaking like a tuning fork.

He lay down on the sofa and tried to explain. "The two men standing outside that door," he said, gesturing widely from his reclining position, "prevented me three times from leaving this suite. I want them removed from the building as quickly as possible. But take a strong force; they are as big as houses."

Herr Zendt exchanged glances with the house detective and chambermaid. "But there are no men outside the door, sir," he replied. Ty leaped up, ran to the door and threw it open. Moni and Schorschl were gone. He sprang out into the corridor, looking in each direction, but they had vanished. Nearly purple with humiliation, he turned to Herr Zendt and his staff and said, "I deeply regret all the trouble I've caused you this evening, Herr Zendt, and I can only assure you that it will not happen again."

"We will deny everything, of course. Good night, dear sir." The hotel manager shook Ty's hand warmly, gently ushered him back into the suite and shut the door.

Ty called Caterina. "Caterina?"

"My God, hon, were you out on that ledge? There must be five hundred people down there."

"It's all right. It's okay. I won't be coming in that way," he said. "The two monsters have gone. But I've ruined a suit, luv, and it will take a few seconds to change." He hung up, raced to the closet, grabbed the first suit of clothes his hands fell upon and re-dressed without even thinking about changing his tie. He slipped a lavender carnation into his buttonhole, glided through the living room as though he were on roller skates, and opened the front door to bump squarely into the iron wall which was Moni and Schorschl.

"No!" he yelled in frustration and fury. "I will not stand for this." He was running back to telephone Herr Zendt when through the wall which separated him from Caterina he heard a weird clatter, as though someone were gargling with diamonds. Then Caterina screamed his name twice, and the word *"Help!"* Ty spun around, sprinted for the front door, flung it open, hit Moni with the Japanese knee kick called a *hittsui-geri,* followed it instantly with a full-force back-snap kick into Schorschl's Adam's apple—a flawlessly executed *ushiro-geri-kaege* from *Gagged,* which he had made in Tokyo two years before—dropped to both knees with his full weight upon Moni's solar plexus, rolled to his feet like a tumbler and raced to the door of Caterina's room, leaving the two blank-faced giants unconscious on the floor.

When he burst into the room Caterina was huddled on top of the mantelpiece, staring with sick horror at a grotesquely large whip scorpion directly beneath her on the carpet. Ty picked up the thick volume of J. C. Cohn's *Precious Stones and Gems* with which Caterina always traveled, and crushed the loathsome thing. He found himself wondering vaguely whether Herr Zendt, when he saw the stain, would continue to be chic.

Caterina dropped her exquisite legs over the edge of the mantel, leaped lightly to the floor and stared at Ty in wonderment and love. He took her in his arms and moved weakly to kiss her but fainted dead away.

20

INSPECTOR HELLER faced them in Largo's salon the following morning as the church bells in the five great steeples of the city could be heard ringing. Albert sat between Dane Ponder and Caterina on the sofa, while Ty and Basil occupied chairs at either end. Sergeant Skutch took shorthand notes while Heller was striding back and forth, stern and preoccupied.

"What is particularly horrible," he said, "is that according to our laboratory tests the scorpion had been nurtured for several months on tubocurarine and the bark of the Strychnos and Chondrodendron tomentosum. As you all know, these are the principal alkaloid components of the dreaded poison of the Orinocan Indians. Have you ever made a film in the Brazilian jungle?"

"Why, yes," Albert said. "We made *Swamp* in 1961!"

"I see. Had the scorpion struck Miss Largo, the poison would have been transmitted neuromuscularly. The muscles of her eyelids would have failed, loss of speech would have followed, the neck and spinal muscles would have become paralyzed, and finally the muscles of the diaphragm would cease to function. Death would have been caused by respiratory failure." His eyes moved from face to face as he spoke to them. "Who wants to kill you, Miss Largo?"

Caterina was very pale. Her dark eyes seemed enormous, and she gripped her lip between her even white teeth and stared at him.

"Don't be afraid," Heller said. "It is a lovely sunny morning. There is a normal world out there. No one will be harmed."

"You have to know who he is before you can stop him," Caterina answered dully.

"But I know who he is," Heller said. Their collective gasp sounded like an air brake. "Tell me what you know about a man named Carl Waldenfon."

"No! Please!"

131

"Who is Waldenfon?" Albert asked Heller in a gallant effort to give Caterina a chance to recover herself.

"His fingerprints were on the base of the ketchup bottle and on fragments of the bomb. During the war he achieved the dubious distinction of becoming a double war criminal, wanted by both sides. The SS tried to track him down for the mass murder of SS troops, and the Allies wanted him for the machine-gunning of Italian civilians." His voice suddenly lost its gentleness. "Do you care, Miss Largo?"

"I don't know anything. That name frightened me, but I can't remember anything else."

"It's no use, Inspector," Ty said. "You have to know Miss Largo. She is a scientist at self-preservation; she will survive at all costs. She knows that—don't you, Caterina?"

"I can't help it!" She buried her face in her hands.

"She really *can't* remember, you know," Ty told Heller. "There's nothing evil about it; she just can't help it"—and his voice had the sadness of all those who see and understand weakness in the one they love.

Caterina sat erect and held her head high. "I want to help if you can show me how," she said, looking at Ty. "I am afraid. I have never been so afraid, and I don't know why that man is trying to murder us."

Ty's heart soared.

"Will you consent to hypnosis?" Heller asked gently.

"Inspector, really, I don't think—" McCobb said with concern, but Caterina interrupted him. "Yes. But do it now before I can change my mind." She was obviously terrified of what might be uncovered but desperate to protect Ty from any danger.

At a sign from Heller, Skutch opened a small satchel and began to set up its contents on a table. Heller drew the blinds, then helped Caterina to her feet and led her across the room to the table which held a pair of binaural earphones plugged into a box and a small circular mirror attached to a motorized pivot. "This is an American contribution," Heller said, "an externally induced psychedelic experience which is known as Mason's Effect and which is very efficient. It consists of a three-second loop of stereophonically recorded audio tape. On the left channel we have recorded six notes from a Bach violin partita. On the right channel is recorded the ticking of an ordinary alarm clock. The sounds are extremes of wave shape: a pulse and a transient. Put these on, please, Miss Largo." He offered Caterina the earphones. She clasped them over her head. "The two loops will be repeated again and again over the two specially modified channels

132

which were chosen for optimum high-frequency and transient response, dropping to progressively lower levels. Twenty seconds is all we will require. Mason's Effect is standard issue for our department now. The sergeant brings it along at the interviewing stage of all of our cases."

Caterina listened to the sounds inside her head and watched the illuminated mirror as it spun, breaking the light into thousands of shining splinters which seemed to fly into her great eyes. Suddenly Heller leaned forward and stopped the two mechanisms. He removed the earphones from Caterina's head. Skutch sat beside her with an open notebook while the four others watched tensely.

"What is your real name?" Heller asked.

"Maria Aguzzo."

"Where were you born?"

"Perugia, Italia."

"Do you know Carl Waldenfon?"

"Yes."

"When did you meet him?"

"The day he killed my mother and sister. He made me watch what he did and he told me that if I ever told about it he would kill me in the same way. He will kill me now. He told me I was not to remember him until he said it was safe to. He said he would kill me if I remembered him."

"He will not kill you. You are safe. Who was he when he killed your mother and your sister?"

"He was SS—an SS surgeon. They were retreating to the north. He tied me to his wrist after killing my mother and sister. He took me with him, always moving at night. He used me to steal food and as a guide to talk to people while he hid. His own people were after him. Something had happened to his head and he had been killing for days before he murdered my family."

"Where did he take you?"

"He paid a boat to take us to Yugoslavia. He killed the crew before we landed. He took their papers and their clothes."

"How old were you?"

"Fourteen."

"Why didn't he kill you in Yugoslavia?"

"He got sick. He had fever, and when he got better he was different."

"Why didn't you run away when he got sick?"

"I was afraid, and still am, since the day he killed my mother and sister. He would find me—I knew it." She shuddered.

"What did he look like?"

"I don't remember."

"Try. You must try to remember."

"I can't, I can't, I can't."

"What happened after he recovered from his fever in Yugoslavia?"

"We got aboard a refugee train to Vienna. By then the war was over, and we were sent back to Italy. He took me to Firenze."

"Where is he now?"

"In Hamburg."

"How do you know?"

"He telephoned me last night. He told me to go to the armoire. I was to open the present wrapped in pink ribbon for me and tell him how I liked it. The scorpion was in the box."

"When did you last see him?"

"In Firenze, one year after we came back from Vienna. He put me in a convent school. He said I must study languages and work very hard and that he would come back for me, but that if I remembered him or anything about him and told anyone, he would come back sooner and kill me the way he had killed my mother and sister. For weeks before he left, he would put me to sleep every day. He would say the same things over and over, but I can't remember what they were."

"Did he ever come back?"

"No."

"What did you do?"

"When I was eighteen years old the nuns gave me an envelope. In it were five hundred English pounds and instructions that I was to be sent to Munich to see a man named Otto Floen who was a film producer."

"Where is Floen now?"

"He is dead."

"Why were you sent to him?"

"I don't know, but he gave me parts in three pictures. After the third part I was starred in a French picture, and then I was signed by Goldberg and McCobb."

"If Carl Waldenfon told you today that you must go with him, what would you do?"

"I would go with him. He would kill me."

"Why does he want to kill Mr. Bryson?"

There was a long silence while Caterina breathed heavily. Finally her face contorted and she said, "Perhaps because I married him."

"Have you ever been married to anyone else?"

"Yes. For a short time I was married to the assistant director on my first picture. But it was a secret. No one knew."

"What was his name?"

"Basil Schute."

There was a second of silence, and then Ty jumped out of his chair and hit Basil, knocking him over in his chair. Heller snapped his fingers, bringing Caterina out of her trance, and then he and Skutch and Albert pulled Ty off Basil.

"What is happening?" Caterina screamed.

"They're trying to kill Bazzie, you bitch," Dane Ponder yelled, interrupting her keening over Basil. "How could he marry a silly bitch like you?"

Caterina clapped a hand over her mouth.

"Are you Carl Waldenfon?" Heller asked Basil grimly. Basil merely glared with dripping contempt at Ty and said, "You ridiculous *actor*," and Ty had the sickening realization that Basil had never liked him.

"One moment, Inspector," Albert said loudly. "There can be no question that Basil is this man Waldenfon. His father, Sir Martin Schute, is so English that even Wales and Scotland are foreign countries to him. Basil is from the best public schools and the right regiments; besides, what German could wear clothes like that?"

"Nevertheless, for many reasons, I think Mr. Schute and I will go to headquarters for a chat."

"No need to protect me, Inspector," said Basil. "I can take care of myself. Waldenfon is either Goldberg or—"

"*Goldberg?*" Everyone but the two policemen responded with one voice.

"Please say nothing more," Heller said.

Basil shook the inspector's hand off his arm. "He could also be the false Inspector Heller. But you could be Waldenfon, too, Albert. You claim you don't speak German, but I know you do. And there has never lived a man so immersed in total grisliness, and who conveniently is able to sublimate such an omniverous appetite for murder and violence as yours."

"And make a fairly steady one million six hundred thousand dollars a year net, while so doing," Albert replied tartly.

"But I haven't mentioned my prime suspect," Basil continued. "Bryson could be Waldenfon."

"Oh, Basil, for Chrissake!" Largo shouted.

"I'm too young to have been made a major in 1945," Ty said calmly.

"He's never *quite* been murdered," Basil said hotly to Largo. "Several painfully theatrical attempts have been made

135

to kill him, all drawing more attention to him, but he always escapes, doesn't he? Until he really kills whoever it is he has decided to kill. Like Caterina, perhaps, with that scorpion."

"Don't be such a total twit, you twit," Largo said contemptuously.

"That car he rode in? The night someone was supposed to be shooting at him? Not one bullet hole. Not *one.*"

"They shot away the side mirror, you clot."

"I looked at that," Basil shouted back. "It was rigged by a special-effects man and was blown up from inside the car. Did you know that, Inspector? As for the asp in the bedpan and the Enid Blyton adventure about the snakes in the bathtub and the bomb which he just happened to intercept . . . it's rot, all of it pure rot."

"Why would he do all that, you creep?"

"To win himself a hunting license. To kill you for all the rotten things you've done to him. And now to kill me because he knows I'm in love with you."

"You are watching the world's most rotten loser," Caterina said to Inspector Heller. "He's been playing this self-pity scene ever since I told him to get out of my life twenty years ago. He is a nut. Every man who walks past a movie poster of me he suspects of plotting to run off with me. He's been sick with jealousy from the instant I met him—it's a wonder we stayed married even two months. And now I'd like to ask a question, Baz, if you'll shut up for a minute. Did Ty plant that thing in my room, then knock down two muscle men to get in here to save me, then faint after he had saved me?"

"What better cover could he have?" Basil asked.

"He fainted, you ungrateful bastard! He fainted with relief and fright and joy because he had saved me. The way he wept when he found out he could fly from Mexico City to Amsterdam in time to give you a transfusion of that cruddy Z-type blood of yours—weeping like a goddamn schoolgirl in Thomas Cook's because he was happy he could save your life." Basil looked away, and Caterina pressed her advantage. "He was just reacting the way he reacts when he is able to do anything real in his life—which God knows isn't often."

"Oh, Caterina, really," Ty mumbled.

"And all of us here can tell about people who have survived because Ty paid their rent or their hospital bills or put up bail for them. He's the only guy I ever knew who is always around when someone is desperate."

Basil's face was dark and his voice was choked. "All right, let's get everything out into the open." He spoke through clenched teeth, in pain from the flames of the last bridge he

136

was about to burn. "That piebald story about being chained to an SS maniac which she told while pretending to be under hypnosis is merely a bad synopsis of the plot of *Horror,* McCobb's third picture."

Heller spoke gently to Largo. "Were you lying when you told us the story of your time with Carl Waldenfon?"

Largo sat down and put her face into her hands. "I don't know," she said. "I don't know what I said to you."

21

NEITHER the local nor the world press knew about Ty's being chased after the première of *Ghastly* because the only man who might have told about it was Ty's driver, a bonded Goldberg man. Herr Zendt had such a well-disciplined staff that although the headlines everywhere said: "FILM STARS' HOTEL BOMBED," the press did not discover that the explosion had begun in Ty's room.

Then Frau Fringl was arrested and booked. Lugwig Berg of the *Hamburger Zeitung* was having a slow news day and he persuaded the desk sergeant to let him talk to her because it seemed so odd for the chief telephone operator of the Pacific Seasons to be arrested on such a grotesque charge. Luckily for Berg, Frau Fringl had reached that stage of hysteria where she wanted to explain everything to everybody. Besides spouting a great deal of nonsense, she told the reporter she had nothing whatever to do with the bomb going off in Herr Bryson's rooms, and that she had, of course, no idea that she had been hired by a murderer.

Berg's story was picked up on every continent. It brought the press of Britain and Europe, including *Pravda,* plus specialists from all American wire services, into Hamburg. By cable, Goldberg forbade any of the principals to grant interviews because he felt press coverage always lasted longer that way, but he did authorize the issuance of statements. The official line in all of these was that the bomber had mistaken Ty's room for that of a crucial political figure. Eleven Michigan papers immediately printed stories that Governor Romney had been in the hotel while on European tour. Herr Zendt co-operated by refusing to show his guest register for the day of the bombing, and his reception clerk was persuaded to hint to a wire-service man that his employer had been forced by a foreign power to conceal the identity of the political figure who had long since departed.

Unfortunately, on the day of the statements attempting to explain away the bombing, Ty's bonded driver was told by his dentist that all his teeth would have to be extracted. The driver flinched from disturbing his savings, so he telephoned Ludwig Berg and said that for the price of the dentist's bill and the new teeth, he could prove that the bombing was not an isolated miscalculation but one of two attempts made on Bryson's life since he arrived in Hamburg.

Berg's story had incalculable effects. The Hamburg postal service was paralyzed for eighty-one hours trying to cope with the flood of cables, letters and telephone calls to Bryson from fans all over the world. An additional hundred and sixty-four members of the press were flown to the city with orders to talk to Bryson, Largo and McCobb. Seventy-three of these were American, and twenty-three were from *Paris-Match* alone.

The streets around the hotel had to be cordoned off, and the director and cast were transported by armored trucks from the film studio, which was protected by armed police and ferociously trained dogs. The Dow-Jones average dropped 22.3 points, on the theory that if any harm were to come to Tynan Bryson, the English pound would topple.

At a press conference the Premier of Italy expressed his confidence that the West German authorities were taking every precaution to protect Caterina Largo's life. The Benjamin Reyes Girls High School at Iris, Connecticut, abandoned classes and marched on Washington, twenty-four hundred strong, to demonstrate there for the dispatch of NATO forces to protect Bryson's life. Rudy Vallee recorded a song called "We Gotta Stop That Crazy Man."

UPI broke the story that Bryson had been "talked in" from the ledge of his hotel ten stories above the street, before the horrified eyes of over a thousand witnesses, and published the twelve smudgy photos snapped by Dr. Elizabeth Blue of Erwinna, Pennsylvania.

With this, all work literally stopped for ten hours in the United States while the population sat staring at their television sets as the networks canceled all scheduled programs and ran clips flown in from Hamburg in between old movies in a Bryson-Largo-McCobb Film Festival.

Other films made by the three principals were reissued by Goldberg in three hundred and twelve theaters simultaneously, and in its fourth run *Ghastly* became a hard-ticket show. Over a four and a half week period the McCobb comic books sold 12,066,788 copies in the United States and France alone.

At last, as pressure built and David Susskind devoted an entire program to the question of whether or not Tynan Bryson had been attempting suicide on that ledge, Goldberg broke the production company's silence by ordering a single joint press conference. Four hundred and three thousand dollars' worth of additional television equipment had to be sent via air freight from the States for the meeting, which was held from the stage of the UFA-Palast theater with just over six hundred of the working press attending.

Dick Gallagher opened the press meeting on a stage, which was bare except for three chairs against a neutral backdrop, by citing the arbitrary rules imposed for this occasion. Police lined the walls of the auditorium and stood in ranks in the wings of the stage itself. Since the air conditioning had broken down due to the overload of all the electrical equipment, the auditorium was stifling.

"Let's get this straight," Gallagher said grimly. "They will walk out on this stage and read their statements. There will be no questions permitted. Repeat, there will be no questions permitted. Miss Largo will issue her statement in German, Italian and French, and the statements of Mr. Bryson and McCobb will be available in mimeographed form in German. When they have read their statements they will leave the stage."

He paused, and no one spoke; the sound of the television cameras and the flashes of the camera bulbs were the only response. Gallagher looked into the wings, nodded and the three principals filed onstage and sat down.

Gallagher said, "Miss Caterina Largo."

Caterina, arresting in matching lilac suit and shoes, with a band of amethysts across her hair, smiled slowly, looked for the red lights on the television cameras in the first balcony, deliberately crumpled up the statement in her hand, threw it over her shoulder and said, "Hello, boys."

The applause was spontaneous and overwhelming. A hoarse voice from the back of the house bellowed, "Tell us the truth, honey, like you always do."

139

"You think this is a publicity gimmick?" she asked. The cynical audience laughed back at her.

"If it is," she said, "someone is trying to drive us out of The Business, and if it succeeds, Ty Bryson is going out the hard way—in a long box."

"Oh, Jesus," Gallagher moaned. "Why does she ignore the statement?"

"Here are some facts you should have," Caterina said into the microphone. "A maniac—a homicidal maniac—has made five, *not* two, attempts on Tynan Bryson's life. Driving him out on that window ledge to save me was only one of them. He has also been deliberately infected with hepatitis, nearly bitten by a planted asp, nearly rocketed to death in Rome, almost poisoned by snakes aboard the *Queen Mary,* and shot and bombed in Hamburg. Some publicity stunts. Also, and I am proud of this—after all, Ty shouldn't get all this marvelous publicity just for himself—the maniac tried to kill me two nights ago."

That was the end of the press conference. Every newsman in the theater tried to reach the stage, but the police were there to stop them. Only Gallagher's lightning presence of mind in dragging the three out the rear entrance prevented a riot.

Erna Kirschner, aged fifty-seven, a chambermaid who had been in the employ of the Pacific Seasons Hotel for sixteen years, died of heart failure in the corridor on the tenth floor at six forty-seven the following morning when she discovered a pair of shoes left to be polished right by Basil Schute's door. What had evidently upset Frau Kirschner was that a pair of man's legs, in socks and garters and chopped off just below the knees, were still in the shoes. They were Basil's legs. The remainder of his body, at least most of it, was found in the bathtub in his room.

Momentarily distraught by the deaths of a valued chambermaid and a guest, the stain on the carpet made by the whip scorpion, the publicity resulting from Ty's venture onto the tenth-floor ledge, and the total destruction of three bathrooms in his hotel, Herr Zendt lost his chic and ordered the film company to leave the premises at once. But after a long consultation with Inspector Heller he was persuaded to withdraw the banishment so that all suspects in the case could remain together in protective custody.

In addition to the ten thousand dollars offered by Caterina Largo, there was a telephoned offer of twenty-five thousand dollars more from Frederic X. Goldberg for the apprehension and conviction of Basil's killer. But in his private conversation with McCobb, Goldberg was harsh indeed. "Listen, you might think all this is good for your picture, but believe me, if anybody thinks that boy was killed as a publicity stunt, then we're gonna feel a fan backlash. We projected a seventy-million-dollar gross for this picture. Hocus-pocus and threats are good, but I don't like this killing stuff. Also it's gonna get us overexposure."

"F.X., please! Basil was my dear friend and colleague of many years, and you simply cannot talk as though—"

"Shut up. The boy's parents must claim him and—"

"He was no boy. He was forty-three years old."

"Shut up. We gotta have a wonderful, sincere English funeral. But not on the Hamburg location—in London. Even if I have to pay for it. We'll close down the production until the funeral is over just to show them how bad we feel."

"We're closed down as it is. If this keeps up, we'll be so far over budget that—"

"Shut up. The boy was English and so are the insurance companies. Don't worry about it—they owe me a few."

Basil's murder had made Dick Gallagher the busiest man in northern Europe. The California morning papers got him out of bed at six o'clock, and throughout the day and night, people representing the principal newspapers, press associations, magazines and radio and television networks badgered him in person and by mail, phone and cable from every part of the world. Within hours after the brutal murder the circulation departments of the world press had worked themselves into paroxysms of greed. Worse, the writers from thirty-seven fan magazines of the United States, western Europe and Japan who had made their living for twenty years by writing only about Bryson, Largo and McCobb, came to Hamburg by camel, car, plane, ship, rail and on foot, distraught that their bubble was about to burst, meaning that they would either have to bone up on Jacqueline Kennedy or find jobs. Desperate with worry, each of them tried every ruse to get into the hotel. They all failed.

Because Heller refused to let Bryson and Largo appear in crowds, Gallagher conducted all news conferences himself. At first these were held at the rear of the hotel bar, but as coverage grew, they were shifted to the Hamburg Opera House, at 9 A.M. and 3 P.M. every day. In the beginning, when the cramped confines of the bar necessitated a pool arrangement, each conference was attended by a revolving cross-section of the press. These journalists were selected by their peers and changed daily, limiting the newsmen to one medium from each nation concerned. Forty or fifty writers would sit in a compact mass. Gallagher would enter through the dishwashers' restroom, always precisely on time, sodden with fatigue and overwork because each announcement he issued had to be cleared with Goldberg in New York. Goldberg scared hell out of Gallagher and would continue to do so until the company's pension plan went through.

Gallagher would raise his hands wearily to gain silence and say, "Ladies and gentlemen, I have just been informed by Frederic X. Goldberg in New York that the fourth threat was made on the label of a ketchup bottle. The police are processing this item, but at the three o'clock conference I will be permitted, Mr. Goldberg has assured me, to pass among you with enlarged photographs of its message. Any questions?"

"Who made the ketchup?"

"This was your James Beard Autographed Gourmet Ketchup, serial number 31847625. It was manufactured by GantPick Delicacies, St. Mary's Lane, Ticehurst, Wadhurst, Sussex, England, and retails at five shillings."

"Does Mr. Bryson always take a bath at seven-five every evening?" a lady representing the Australian Consolidated Press asked.

"His bath time varies from seven o'clock—that is, nineteen hundred hours—to seven-seven each evening, at slightly below body temperature to prevent dawdling."

Basil's remains were given a memorable funeral; it was the first show of its kind to be carried in color via the Early Bird satellite. Goldberg saw to it that the cathedral was packed with the most dignified people from the arts and from the military, ecclesiastical, financial and political walks of life. Basil's parents were extremely pleased.

22

THOUGH the manhunt was under the overall command of *Polizeibezirksobermeiser* Heller, it was rumored from North

Crescent Drive to Carrolwood in Beverly Hills that Goldberg had persuaded the Sûreté, the CIA and MI5 to send forces to Hamburg to hunt down the killer. Certainly, most of the faces of the staff at the hotel changed overnight. The total reward, including fan-magazine bounties, had swollen to two hundred and nineteen thousand and fifty dollars. Police bodyguards, in three eight-hour shifts, were assigned to Bryson and Largo; stationed across the corridor from their rooms, they escorted them whenever they left the hotel.

Of course, since they had never met her, they didn't notice the absence of Dane Ponder, *née* Fräulein Schmeckle, who had mysteriously disappeared the day after the murder. It was rumored that she was hysterical with grief and had fled back to Frankfurt, where she had been put under intensive psychiatric care.

Inspector Heller had withheld much information behind his screen of amiability. For sixteen hours a day he was in pursuit of Carl Waldenfon, who had submerged in Italy in 1945 but who had surfaced again in Hamburg in 1967. His men searched through the SS archives in Berlin, London, Tel Aviv and Alexandria, Virginia, for a photograph, but apparently the only one ever extant had been torn—no one knew when—from a fingerprint-record card in the Himmler-office dossiers in Berlin. There was no specimen of Waldenfon's handwriting or even a physical description of him, but his background was well documented. He became a member of the Nazi party in 1927, and while studying medicine at the University of Munich, contributed his free time as a supervisor of the *Deutschvölkische Jugendschar* and the *Jungfrontkampfverband*. He graduated with honors as a surgeon in 1933 and was at once permitted to buy his boots and black trousers, the privilege given to volunteers for the SS. He had no police record, and his service record was excellent until late in 1944, when he began to murder casually Italian civilians—women, children and old men. When his arrest was ordered by his war-sick, exhausted commander, Waldenfon ran amok and shot down eleven of his comrades before disappearing. Until its dissolution the Gestapo searched for him throughout Europe, with orders to take him alive, if possible. But he was never found, and except for moldering files and a few isolated individuals with long memories, was soon forgotten in the course of the collapse of the Thousand-Year Reich, nine hundred and eight-eight years before schedule. Perhaps because of the death camps and the existence of such major war criminals as Eichmann and Bormann, no one seemed to

143

attach much importance to one more insane murderer at large in Europe.

But Heller kept working doggedly, intent on finding as many survivors of the SS massacre as possible. To find energy for the task, he consumed two hundred and seven ice-cream cones during the darkest hours of the investigation. He never gave up, and he was always confident. A break finally came eight days after Basil's murder. But what Heller discovered changed everything, thoroughly confused the investigation and brought the case he had slowly but methodically built crashing down about him.

By elimination, he had begun to feel certain of the identity of Basil's killer. A survivor of Waldenfon's battallion, who had been located in Galway, the German-language county in the west of Ireland, was able to give a description of Waldenfon as he had looked twenty-three years before. The composite portrait drawn by the Hamburg police specialist was confirmed by the man, but he could not identify a photograph of Heller's prime suspect.

While Heller was puzzling over this, members of the Swedish Secret Service (which Goldberg had persuaded to take an interest in the case), triumphantly produced Carl Waldenfon's death certificate, dated August 1960 and stating that his battered body had turned up in the River Plate. His murderer had never been found. Also attached was Waldenfon's photograph, and statements from his widow and mother in Argentina. Ironically, it appeared that Waldenfon had worked as an extra in *Moan*, the gaucho epic which McCobb, Ty and Largo had made on the pampas, but no one in the production company could remember him.

Heller began to hit the ice-cream cones heavily. "This is a very clever show-off we are searching for," he said bitterly as he stared at the documents. "He dies in 1960, yet leaves fingerprints in 1967. But when did cleverness get anyone anywhere? Most brilliant people aren't very smart, and this one has made a big mistake because we know something now, don't we?"

"We do?" Skutch said.

"We know that he worked on a McCobb-Bryson-Largo film and that he could have been in contact with any one of the tightly knit McCobb company—including the late Herr Schute. This tells us also that someone who is very patient made a cast of Waldenfon's fingerprints seven years ago, because the SS man died right after working on that foolish picture. Above all, this tells us that the killer has been cherishing these murders for a long time, accumulating a cast of finger-

144

prints, a plane launcher from a Japanese submarine, water moccasins, hepatitis virus and a whip scorpion—all as though he were filling a theatrical-property warehouse for the Grand Guignol."

The inspector paused to stare at an enlargement of Waldenfon's thin, sensitive face while he ate an entire persimmon-flavored ice-cream cone. At last he said, "But why Waldenfon? Our man could only have chosen those fingerprints because he knew Waldenfon's secrets as a war criminal. That's it—he must have served with Waldenfon in the SS. It has to be; there is no other explanation. Therefore he has told us where to look. We are no longer blind. Skutch, I want pictures of every permanent member of the McCobb company. We will take these photographs and search down everyone who ever served with Waldenfon, until eventually one of the pictures is identified." He laughed exultantly. "That is the trouble with brilliant people, Skutch. They are not smart. They always underestimate the genius of routine. Don't you see, Skutch?"

"I see, sir," the young man said. "But it was Waldenfon, not his impersonator, who dragged Largo across Europe in 1944. Because I believe what she said. I know she went under when you hypnotized her."

"Yes. She was under."

"And I am still troubled by the disappearance of the young girl, Dane Ponder. She had no connection whatever with these film people."

23

WHILE Heller stitched away at his morbid tapestry, Caterina and Ty moved through the soft evening air among the crowds along the Jungfernstieg, past the Alsterpavilon. Wearing dark glasses, they walked hand in hand, followed by two policemen who in turn were followed by two policemen.

Caterina was wearing a brunette beehive wig, teased so high and so out-of-date that no one would glance at her, and

Ty had a red Hindenburg mustache and a false chin rigged up for him by O'Gorman. They were warily delighted to be together. As they left the Alsterarkaden at the Gustav-Adolfs-Brücke, the ballyhoo truck with its posters advertising *Ghastly* at the UFA-Palast trundled past them, displaying Ty and Caterina in an intense nine-color clinch. Plastered across the bottom of the billboard was a legend in bold type saying: "LAST DAYS!" and the truck's loudspeaker urged all within earshot to see the movie, in between short bursts of martial music.

They hailed a taxi to go to the Planten un Blomen, and waited courteously until the two sets of bodyguards were able to flag vehicles of their own. They strolled through the park, gasping at the glorious flowers, gaping at the wonderful fountains, then wandered off and had a light dinner at the Ratsweinkeller while the bodyguards bolted huge knuckles of veal behind huge pillars. Afterward they drove to the bar where they could have coffee and brandy with an alcoholic horse. En route, the bodyguard detail changed. The new eight-hour shift was composed of Japanese secret police, a small token force arranged by Goldberg. They were tall men who employed the futile cover of carrying Eastman Kodak cameras.

A bleary-eyed white horse strolled up to Ty and Caterina's table within minutes after they had been seated in the low-ceilinged, smoky bar. He whinnied thickly and raised his pink, thick upper lip to show dinner-plate yellow teeth in a helpless, barfly's smile. They ordered him a bottle of beer, and when it came Caterina held the bottle for him. He staggered away without so much as a hiccup of thanks.

"Horrible sort of fantasy, isn't it?" Ty said.

"I've seen worse."

"Like what?"

"I remember a movie with Rock Hudson as a brain surgeon. Listen, with Goldberg at the helm we may end up seeing Otto Preminger playing a lovable little Irish priest."

"That's The Business. There's no fantasy there—it's the realest thing there is."

"Nothing else is real?"

"You're real, luv."

"Yeah? If I'm real it's because I fight all this opium Goldberg manufactures. If I'm real—and I doubt it—it's because I keep struggling and because I need. I hurt, I need so much. And hurting is real."

"You hurt?"

"If I have to tell you a secret like that—ah, the hell with

146

it. Don't look so confused. Cats don't make sense to mice, only the other way around." She sighed and shook her head. "Come on. Pay the check or we'll have to buy the livestock another round. Let's go and find some music."

They went to Der Schmutzige Kniff in the Reeperbahn, a huge bare hall with hundreds of tables equipped with telephones and identifying numbers, facing a raised stage. The phones were there so that people could call each other from far across the room to request a dance and to carry out unlicensed business. All around them, strange men were talking into their table phones to distant strange women—dreamily, persuasively, aggressively, or with the bland authority of seasoned bucket-shop operators in Wall Street.

"We have stumbled into the Valhalla of all flesh peddlers," Caterina said delightedly.

"Yes. This must be where all agents go when they die. The telephone never stops ringing, and everybody's name is 'sweetheart.' "

"God, it's romantic," Caterina murmured as the room dimmed, stage lights came up and the curtain was raised.

On the platform there was a large tank filled with black gook. Ty noticed that the people nearest to it had covered themselves with sheets provided by waiters. A short, square, extremely muscular woman strode out from the wings, tested the mud, then smeared it stolidly across the stretch of skin between the upper and lower halves of her bikini. Then a tall, slope-shouldered, ham-handed giantess came out from the other side of the stage, picked up a handful of mud and flung it into her opponent's face. "It's Raddatz!" Caterina yelled.

Instantly the two women applied hackenschmidts and hammer locks to each other, slamming and being slammed into the thick, black, viscous mud. "With any luck she'll break Raddatz's back," Ty said, but his enemy won easily in a few minutes and simpered like a soubrette under the crowd's roaring approval. The lights came up again. "I wondered why her fingernails had gotten so black," Caterina said as the phone rang on the table between them.

"Well, at last," she said. "I was beginning to feel like Stella Dallas." She answered, made a wry face and handed the phone to Ty. "I forgot that this is the Coarse Bourse. It's for you."

Ty took the phone with a grin, said hello, and then the grin fell off his face. His hand shook slightly as he quickly replaced the telephone.

"What's the matter?"

"That same voice. It was the same threat." He got to his feet to look around, but there were hundreds of faces, all of them laughing and talking animatedly into telephones. Caterina rose, and instantly the four bodyguards got up. Ty dropped money on the table and they moved to the front door, the bodyguards following them.

On the sidewalk the six of them got into two cabs and drove back to the hotel. As they got out at the entrance, the ballyhoo truck advertising *Ghastly* went by. Suddenly its loudspeaker was switched on and a loud voice blared at them. *"Bryson! I am going to kill you!"* it shouted. *"It will be a filthy death! First I will take your face away, then I am going to kill you! The visible world is no longer a reality, and the unseen world is no longer a dream."*

Caterina screamed. The truck was only fifteen yards away, and Ty began to sprint after it along the rain-shining night street as though in a scene from a Carol Reed movie. Now the truck's loudspeaker began blaring out the mindless lyrics of "I'll Be Glad When You're Dead, You Rascal You."

Ty closed the gap between them until the truck was almost within reach; then it pulled away from him slowly and easily. The music stopped and the maniacal announcement began again: *"Bryson! I am going to kill you—"* Ty ran on heedlessly, as if hoping desperately to grasp the threat in his hands. Then he tripped and fell, and Caterina ran to help him. The truck raced away into the darkness, the sound of its loudspeaker laughing raucously long after it had disappeared from sight.

24

INSPECTOR HELLER was not seen for six days. When he reappeared he looked exhausted, and as though he had been to places where ice-cream cones had never been heard of. During his absence his place was taken by an Inspector Winkler, who checked the bodyguards twice daily, sold a six-page outline for a screen story to McCobb for forty-six hundred deutschmarks, read Largo's palm and spent most evenings listening with apparent zest to Ty's taped accounts of the psychological effect upon him of his dispute with the May Company of Los Angeles over a bill for a garden hose which he claimed had been improperly measured.

There was no detective work to do because no new threat or attempts were made upon anyone's life—except McCobb's, which was threatened by the same voice on his own dictaphone. Albert had placed the machine near the tub, intending to dictate in between naval battles. To say that he remained cool would have been incorrect; he had heated the bath to 115 degrees in order to recreate the frame of mind of the Japanese fleet admiral commanding the enemy forces at the Battle of Leyte Gulf.

Albert telephoned Winkler at once. The inspector arrived tubside within ten minutes, listened to the threat without comment and then slipped the tape into an envelope. In that terrible voice the message was: *"You will die soon too, McCobb. Perhaps before they die. The visible world is no longer a reality, and the unseen world is no longer a dream."*

"I don't like that one bit," Albert said.

Winkler spoke with Inspector Heller on the overseas line that night.

On the morning of Heller's return to Hamburg, everyone was asked to assemble in the living room of McCobb's suite. Largo, Ty and Albert faced Heller, Winkler and Skutch as they all sipped coffee.

"I have been to Buenos Aires," Heller said quietly, licking a blackberry-and-cherry combination. "I have been chatting with Carl Waldenfon's wife and mother—except that they are neither his wife nor his mother. The first is an unfrocked physician and the second is a darling old criminal with a police record as long as Bob Cratchit's scarf."

"What else did you find out?" Ty asked.

"We dug up the Waldenfon coffin. There was no body."

Caterina made a choking sound, grasped Ty's knee tightly and looked ill. Ty produced a bottle of brandy and uncorked it, and she took a long drink.

"But how did you get all of this information?" Albert asked, almost agape.

"We rely on the genius of routine," Heller replied. "Quite a bit has been yielded by digging into the past. Of interesting significance is the fact that Miss Dane Ponder, once Fräulein Schmeckle, was born Wanda Waldenfon, Carl Waldenfon's daughter."

149

No one was able to speak. Largo took another belt at the brandy, then handed it to Ty, who drank and passed it to Albert.

"She has disappeared, as you know," Heller went on, "so I have been unable to question her. But there were things I had to know, and presumably her mother, Waldenfon's wife, was the only one who could tell me."

"We are very patient," Winkler volunteered.

"Yes," Heller said, "each of us is patient, and the sum of the department's patience is greater than that of all of us together." He sighed. "We have found the murderer of Basil Schute."

They sat motionless, waiting to hear the name, to be released from terror, until Albert broke the spell by lifting the brandy bottle to his lips.

"Dane Ponder, *née* Waldenfon, killed him," Heller said. "And she is dead—"

"Dead?" The cry seemed to come from the depth of Albert's heart.

"She was found hanging in a clothes closet in the film studios where you are working, with a note pinned to her blouse. She was dressed in riding clothes."

"Her first scene in the picture," Ty said, tears welling up in his eyes. "This is the worst news I've ever heard."

Albert wept too. "She was such a sweet and willing child," he said, covering his face with a large handkerchief. "At last it is all over," he said, his voice breaking and muffled by the handkerchief.

"I'm afraid not," Heller said. "Schute's murder and her suicide had nothing to do with the attempts on your lives." He took a handwritten letter out of his breast pocket and read it aloud.

"Dear Living,
I have murdered the only man I have ever loved and I do not want to live any more. He deserved to die, of that there is no doubt in my mind, for making love to me and making me love him, when all the time he was concealing his love for someone else."

"Oh, God," Largo said, beginning to weep.

"But I do not hide behind this, nor do I reject the guilt. To clear him, I must write that he regretted that he had made love to me and that he had made me love him. But he could never be mine. I regret having put out his stained shoes to be cleaned, causing the death of an innocent woman who always brought fresh towels quickly, but the shoes *were* stained.

"Please deliver my eyes to the eye bank, my bones to the bone bank. I wish I could have become a great film star. Sincerely yours, Dane Ponder."

Albert picked up the telephone beside him and asked for Martin Keys, Basil's former assistant, who had been promoted. "Mr. Keys? I've just learned we must replace Miss Ponder. I'll call New York and get them to work on it, but we will have to reschedule the next week or ten days of shooting and hold her scenes until the very end."

25

As TY was leaving for the studio the following morning, a Monday, he found a special-delivery letter mailed by his mother from Perth, Australia. He read it at once.

My dear John,

We are coaling here for the voyage to Sydney. I must say I will be happy to board an oil-burning ship again because the wind-borne coal dust from the forward funnels plays havoc with my white corduroy knickers, so fresh and clean each day—you know how personally dainty I am. However, by staying with this line's ships for fourteen months, I have accumulated more shuffleboard points than any passenger in their 114-year history, and when we cross the Equator I will be crowned All-Time Shuffleboard Queen and awarded a ukelele made of tanned pineapple skins.

I do not write this letter to brag, however, but to warn. Your brother Howie's Christmas Club Fund has at last matured, and he and Mimsey will now be able to enjoy their summer in Europe. It saddens me, as you know, that

Howie resents you because you were born in romantic Wales and he in the less musical United States, and because you earn two or three million a year while he will not exert himself to climb over the $4000 level.

But the point is that your brother and sister-in-law are now somewhere in Europe, and Howie has been proclaiming loudly that he is so miffed that the assassin the papers keep writing about has botched the job that he is going to "immobilize" you himself. Of course it is just the beer talking, but I would be dreadfully embarrassed, son, if a silly squabble between my two boys with guns or knives were to appear in the ship's news, so please ask that sweet Mr. McCobb to arrange to have Howie thrown out on his head if he tries to barge into your studio.

To reach me, you had best send mail to Central Uganda, where I plan to attend the opening of the new Hilton on Lake Kivu. I look forward enormously to hearing Bobby Kennedy's campaign speech to the gallant Bahutus of Ruanda-Urundi.

All love, and please have Howie cooled,

Mother

Elated at an excuse to have his brother arrested, Ty decided to stop off at Inspector Heller's office on the way to the studio. There must be some really serious, long-sentence charges they could cook up to hit Howie with. After all he'd been through, Heller owed him a few favors.

26

As CATERINA opened the door of her dressing room, a switch was pulled and lights flooded the new set.

The instant she stared at it, she felt like flying. She drank in its sweetness with her eyes. Then she became frightened. Why was it there? How? Thoughts like the outlines of ferocious animals waiting just beyond the ring of light of a jungle fire flickered menacingly around the edges of her mind. She left the trailer cautiously, and fearfully walked across the sound stage to where Martin Keys was listening to a stills photographer tell a dirty joke.

"Martin?"

"Yes, Miss Largo?"

"Is Mr. Bryson here yet?"

"Not yet."

"Is Mr. Folkes here today?"

"Yes, indeed."

"Will you send him to my trailer immediately?"

"Is something wrong?"

"No, nothing—nothing at all."

Fredd Folkes had designed the sets for every one of Albert's films. An elderly man whose trousers were so baggy that he seemed to be wearing berets on his kneecaps, he always had paint on his hands and was a compulsive yawner.

"Caterina?" he asked at the door to the trailer. He came in yawning like a sleepy old lion and slumped into the nearest chair. "Smells wonderful in here."

"I'll send you a bottle."

"What's up?"

"Well, I opened the door and thought I had never seen such a romantic and beautiful set."

"Now isn't that nice? I've always said you were the nicest girl in pictures."

"Fredd, did you just *imagine* that set?"

"Hell, no." He yawned so widely that it sounded like the lead car at the Indianapolis Speedway and he needed both hands to cover his mouth. "That's a copy of an old inn way up in the Italian Alps. Beautiful place. Way off the track."

"How did you find it?"

"I keep a file. Besides, Albert mentioned it four or five years ago. He was up there when he was thinking about a ski movie. Never made it, but he mentioned the place, so one Christmas I went up there."

When Folkes had left, Caterina stood in the doorway staring at the re-creation of the past. Almost twenty years before she had been brought to Hollywood to play the sensational role of Rifke in *Hopeless*, her first American film, opposite the great Tynan Bryson. Within four days she was in bed with him, and within a week he asked her to marry him. She refused.

"How can you keep saying no, luv?"

"Marriage is serious."

"No more serious than my proposal. I've been around a
153

long time, and I've never been serious enough to ask anyone to marry me."

"You are too old."

"Too old for what?"

"You've been jumping up and down on women too many afternoons for too many years to be able to change."

"Change to what?"

"Change to a husband. To one woman."

"But I can. I will. I swear to you that—"

"Aagh, you are an actor! The invisible audience can reject you—which is what I think you really want—or it can reassure you by applauding. People are saying 'We need you, thank God for you' when they applaud and send letters and swell the grosses. They give you a personality, they let you know you are alive."

"Baby, what does that have—"

"The women in your bed are just the audience in the most intimate proximity." She shrugged. "They try to devour you, but you devour them instead. They cling, and their weight and taste and smell tell you that they need you, and that they thank God for you. They make you need more and more women because you must be sure that what the invisible audience is screaming is true."

"Why me?" He was nettled. "What about you? You're an actress. If I do this because I'm an actor then you must have the same reasons."

"Phooey. I am a woman. I have always been poor. I am in this silly business because there is nothing in the world that pays a woman better, and because I need every penny I can get."

"What do you think I'm in it for—fan letters?"

"Yes. And for women. And for all the attention you can get for as long as you can get it. The most remote Trappist, African pygmies, a lifer in solitary in Lubianka—they all know that the women you have screwed could fill a colosseum and keep a ninety-dollar shoe factory in production for two hundred years. You are the *most* actor of them all, not the best but the most, so you have ten times the anxiety that others do. Only for those few minutes when you're making love do you feel that your audience is responding, really loves you back."

Ty became angry. "What you and I have been doing, my dear woman, happens to take two people. Why are you in this bed?"

Caterina brushed the words away. "I haven't slept with a

man since Germany," she said, "and that was seven months ago. We are not the same, my friend. I cannot marry you."

But she loved him, and she could not train herself to live without him. She could not bear the thought of walking away from him without a backward glance on the day they finished the picture and then seeing him again across a room in London or Rome or Hollywood, or, when they signed for another picture together, either picking up casually where they left off or watching him invite some tart to his dressing room. But she could not marry him because of her pride, even though she knew she was wrong.

Ty nearly became ill with frustration. He could think of nothing else. He began to lose weight, so much that a short pneumonia scene had to be written into *What?*, his next picture. He had achieved his emaciated look by fasting under hypnosis and by some ingenious make-up by O'Gorman, because he had to prove to her that he was serious.

When that didn't work he sent Dr. Weiler to speak to her. "Now look here, Miss Largo," Dr. Weiler began without preamble. "You are responsible for a man's whole art, and perhaps for his life, if you continue to refuse to marry him. To say nothing of a couple of million a year and the livelihood of thousands of people. He is not Van Gogh, you know, who wrote, 'The more I become decomposed, the more sick and fragile I am, the more I become an artist.'" Weiler shook his head firmly. "But we will not slip into the pitfall of identifying creativity with neurosis, *ja?* Or conclude that creativity stems from the only partially successful sublimation of an unresolved Oedipus complex. I can tell you this, however . . ." and he jawed away for a good half-hour.

Caterina didn't understand a word of what Weiler was saying, but she liked him, and after their first meeting she went to the Weilers' for dinner once a week for a cooking bee. Mrs. Weiler would make *tzimmes knaidle* and Caterina would reply with *grazeola*.

Finally someone arranged to have Goldberg call Caterina.

"Miss Largo?"

"Yes."

"Frederic X. Goldberg is calling."

Caterina almost dropped the telephone. Ever since she started in The Business this man, who was said to control the world output of motion pictures and television, had seemed on a par with Dante to her.

"Miss Largo?" It was a Miltown-pitched whisper.

"Yes?"

"May I call you Caterina?"

She became flustered. "Yes, but—what should I call you?"

"Call me Mr. Goldberg. Why don't you marry this boy?"

"Boy?"

"Tynan Bryson. Life isn't as short as they tell us. At the end of the road there could be a little cottage, rosebowered, whitewashed. A man and a woman—Ty and you, older now but straight and proud—stand by a picket fence and hear the happy sounds of little children—little grandchildren—and their minds wander back to their wedding day. Gounod and orange blossoms—the flower, not the cocktail—and the kindly old minister who chuckled and kissed the bride so shyly. The eyelashes on their first baby. Memories cuddling in their arms. Life is full at last, as full as a nest of birds and as soft as the marshmallows with which your bridesmaids will pelt you on that glorious morning when you leave that little church and scamper beside him under the crossed swords of his classmates. Marry the boy, Caterina. Marry that boy of yours."

"No."

The soothing whisper disappeared and the voice became harsh. "Listen, I have six million one tied up in his two unreleased negatives—one in work, and four more lined up. Don't try pushing me around. He's a sick boy because of what you're trying to do to him. I don't want him married. Marriage can be a terrible thing for a star, but it's better than a dying actor. Yes, he could die, this boy, because of what he feels for you. You like The Business? Be nice to me, a little favor, and you won't be sorry. What is he asking you, after all? A little marriage. It could ruin the rest of your life? Marry him. Call him now and tell him you'll marry him."

"No."

"Caterina? All right. You know what I plan to give you kids for a wedding present? Fiesole. Yes. Where you went to school. You like that, hah? A suburb for a wedding present? Plus—I'll tell you what—you can have the Filipino and the Indonesian rights to *Hopeless,* your first picture here. Okay? All set?"

"No."

"*All right,*" Goldberg yelled into the telephone, "then back to the bush leagues!" and he slammed down the receiver.

Caterina was exhausted. She was with Ty all night every night except for the weekly dinner with the Weilers, when Ty took a twenty-four-hour water cure to strengthen the small of his back. She thought about nothing except loving him. She knew that she would end up marrying him, but she refused to find a way to open that door and usher in the humiliation that would inevitably follow. At last she overcame the dilemma by telling herself that if she could be certain that he truly loved her, if she could merely be sure of that, then nothing else mattered. It was a tragic underrating of her jealousy.

After some days of thought she developed her test for true love, and on the last day of shooting *Hopeless* she revealed it to Ty. They were eating pastrami on rye, flown in from The Stage in New York, when she blurted abruptly, to avoid giving herself another chance to think, "Ty, I'll marry you—"

"*What?*"

"—if we can both pass the test."

"Oh, my luv! What test?"

"Have you ever been to a town in the Italian Alps called Arcobaleno?"

"No."

"It is a tiny town, and it has an inn called the Principio. *Principio* means 'the beginning' in Italian, and it is the best word for what I am trying to say."

"Baby! What is the test?"

"I go back to Paris tomorrow, and unless I look like very big money in *Hopeless,* Goldberg will keep me away."

"Why, for heaven's sake?"

"He asked me to marry you and I said no."

"Honey! What is the *test?*"

"All right. I go wherever I have go to for one year from this moment. You go where you have to go. If we still want to marry, then we will meet in Room Number One at the Principio in Arcobaleno a year from today. If we find each other there, then I will marry you."

She had read too many bad scripts.

Now, all these years later, Caterina stood in the doorway of her dressing room and looked across the sound stage at an exact reproduction of Room No. 1 where it had all started. Three marriages, a hundred public disgraces, a thousand shames, ten thousand humiliations and ten years of grief and hated had followed that first night. She could not escape from him and from the emotions which had become her life after she set it all in motion by entering No. 1. She wanted to cry, but she had to go to work in a few minutes and her face had to be serene, so she shut the door of her dressing room and rocked back and forth with her head in her hands, moaning softly to herself.

Heller had assured Ty that he could count on eighteen months at hard labor for his brother if Howie attempted an

157

assault. As he was about to leave Heller's office with the good news, his eye fell on a headline on the inspector's desk. It said: "JETTHROW-GOLDBERG MERGES WITH AMALGATED PIE." He picked up the newspaper with horror. The subhead said: "PIE KING ENVISAGES WRITING FILMS BY COMPUTER." Dazed, he read the story. Goldberg had merged his companies with the world's largest pastry complex, which was not only the biggest manufacturer of fruit and custard pies but also dominated the earth-auger boring field, as well as low-tension wiring, cosmetics and what was left of the whaling industry. Though the merger was described as "the best-kept secret since Mary Pickford decided to marry Doug Fairbanks," Ty sensed that everyone in the industry in New York and Los Angeles had known the secret but had not had the heart to admit it. The new company's name was to be Jetthrow-Goldberg-Pies, he was sure—Goldberg's way of mocking him. He must have come to the end of his rope if Goldberg bothered to mock him.

"Are you all right, Mr. Bryson?" Heller asked. Ty dropped the newspaper on the desk. "Everybody seems to be trying to kill me," he said numbly as he left the room.

He sat brooding between the two bodyguards in the limousine. In his trailer he dressed mechanically. When he walked, preoccupied, onto the set, Caterina's beautiful face was aglow with something more than make-up; and yet she seemed terrified at the same time. "What's the matter, luv?" he asked.

"Look around."

It took several seconds to register; then he said with a beatific smile, "Why, it's Number One at the Principio!"

"Yes!" She hugged him, grinning, but as she did so she whispered, "Why?"

"Whenever you are ready," Albert said loudly from his chair beside the camera, his hands folded across his stomach. Largo wheeled on him, her voice heavy and harsh. "Why *this* set?" she demanded. "What does this have to do with the script we're supposed to be playing?"

"I am delighted that you think you know which script you are playing," Albert said, "because actually we're not playing the same script."

Ty and Caterina both looked baffled.

"It's all rather a compliment to me, actually," Albert replied. "You see, the secret-agent films are finally beginning to flop, not only in the United States and Europe, but in China and Bechuanaland too. Goldberg has asked me if I could switch this picture into a different story, which would establish an intermediate cycle until he can finish his market tests

158

to determine what the next batch should be. Quite a pat on the back, don't you think?"

"I think of it more as an insult," Ty said.

"He's Punch, I'm Judy and you are kindly old Gepetto," Caterina added.

"No, no. This is a *much* better story we're doing now, and you must admit you were weary of secret-agent films. It means the great breakthrough has arrived. He may allow us to make something slightly civilized and non-sadistic."

"Answer the question," Largo snarled. "Why this set?"

"What is wrong with this set?"

"It's a beautiful set. I still want to know how it fits?"

Albert shrugged. "You are a woman who has, to all intents and purposes, married a certain man. Not Ty. He has saved your life, then rebuilt it entirely, making it possible for you to have everything under the sun. Then he goes away. Actually, he goes to prison. You meet Ty. You betray the other man and let Ty make love to you. Then he wants to marry you. Some shred of honor makes you tell him that you cannot, but you are particularly careful not to tell him *why* you cannot. You put it all on his shoulders because before he met you he had many women. You resist him, you make him press his suit. Then, for absolutely rotten reasons—but of course marvelous reasons for the plot and the parts—you tell him that you have devised a test of love for each other. The test —as banal as your avidity can make it—is that if you still love each other one year from that moment, you will both journey from different parts of the world to this room"—Albert waved one fat hand—"in an old inn high up in the Italian Alps, and that you will marry him and let the man who saved you burn in hell. What we will be shooting today is that scene, exactly one year later when you both arrive at the inn."

Caterina's face was as white as the Snow Queen's. "Did you write this story, Albert?"

Albert blinked as though the question were a nonsequitur. "I always write my own scripts."

"Did you write the original story?"

"I . . . I don't know. Let's say so. Artistically it is an extremely impertinent, not to say unethical, question. Of course Goldberg knows I buy little story ideas along the way. He even remembered this one and asked me if I could make it work. I thought of making it five years ago but never got around to it. It wasn't a story, really; I just bought an idea, this basic situation I've been telling you."

"Whom did you buy it from, luv?"

159

"Some fella. But what is all this grim, jut-jawed fuss? You look ready to weep, Caterina, and Ty is as tense as a new scoutmaster. What have I said or done?"

"What is the name of the man who sold you this story?" Largo said tonelessly.

"If I ever knew it, I've forgotten it. But *why?*"

"We have to know who wrote it," Ty said.

"That's easy enought. It was paid for. It will be in my Central files in California."

"Call them."

"We will not call them now. We're making a picture. We'll call them tonight."

"You can't make the picture without us," Caterina said, "and we won't work until you call the Coast and get the name of that writer."

It took thirty-five minutes to get the treasurer of Albert's company. It was four o'clock in Hollywood, and the man was asleep in bed in the San Fernando Valley. It took him forty-five minutes to drive to the McCobb Enterprises Offices, about twenty minutes to find the records and thirty minutes to call McCobb back in Hamburg.

While they waited they played three-handed gin and Caterina won two hundred and four dollars.

At last the call came in. "Yes, Alvin? . . . Whaaaat? . . . Who? . . . My God. Thank you, Alvin." Albert managed to hang up the telephone shakily and turned a whey-colored face to them. "Carl Waldenfon," he said. "He wrote it. Seven years ago."

27

THE TRIPLE-MURDER attempt in the Bavarian Alps happened five days later. For security reasons, as well as for the increased publicity, Goldberg had the company flown from Hamburg to Munich in a chartered 707. The exodus resembled Lyndon Johnson going on a Texas picnic; the plane was followed by two other 707's, chartered on a pro-rata basis by the press, with *Paris-Match* paying the largest share because their coverage had soared to fourteen photographers, eleven reporters, three researchers, a statistics and logistics man, a *capitaine de l'équipage*, a *chef de cuisine* and a patchworker.

In his usual mysterious fashion, Goldberg had pulled certain wires to have Inspector Heller temporarily assigned to the West German Federal Police so that he would have jurisdiction over the case in Bavaria. Each member of the crew worked next to a stand-by who was either a German detective, a CIA or MI5 man, or a representative of the William J. Burns Detective Agency.

The tremendous coverage by the world press, radio, television, and even the more alert supermarket throwaways, attracted twenty-seven thousand four hundred and thirteen rubberneckers to the new location site. The size of this crowd precluded the maximum security precautions instituted by Heller, and the visitors could not be controlled or made to go away. Many of them were just lucky tourists; the others were locals or neighbors from southern Germany, Switzerland, France and Austria. Three charter flights from New York, which had been en route to London for the "Gamble with George Raft Weekend," voted unanimously to fly to Munich instead, where they wagered a total of two hundred and thirty-nine thousand nine hundred and fifty-seven dollars in various combinations and parlays on who would get it, how they would get it, when they would get it, and in what order. A lottery was established, the winner to be the sucker who picked the first victim and came closest to the time of death.

Hotels within a fifty-mile radius of the production were jammed, and the railroads had to lay on special trains from Munich so that the fun-seeking crowds would commute each day to be at the scene of action and yet return to their warm beds each night. Twins, later christened Tynan and Caterina Buechlemüller, were born in a 1956 Volkswagen during a traffic jam leading to the location site, and the wire-service stringer who stumbled on the story got a fifteen-dollar bonus.

"I cannot tell you how all of this has thrilled Goldberg," Albert said on the first morning of shooting. "Not even *Cleopatra* got the steady, engulfing news space this production is getting. We're outpulling them four to one."

A lump formed in Ty's throat as he meditated on such homage. Having had *fegatelli di maiale alla valdarnese* for breakfast because of the cold, Caterina only burped loudly.

"Now," Albert continued briskly. "I will be using four cameras with extremely fine zoomar lenses. These are now in position at different parts of the location, looking down,

161

across or up at the *téléphérique* in which you will be riding."

"That cable car rises rather steeply," Ty said.

"It's not as bad as the climb to Everest," Albert said.

"How high?" Largo asked.

"Oh, at the very most you'll be zipping along at about eleven thousand feet."

"That's a long fall."

"Can't you rig up some kind of net?" Ty asked. "I hate high places if there isn't a net."

"Ty, where would we put it? The ride is two miles long, and there are about one hundred and thirty-eight square miles of open air under the car. But you'll be as safe as if you were in a rowboat."

"A rowboat at eleven thousand feet, that is," Largo said.

"Nonsense! These things are utterly foolproof."

"All right, Albert. I may pass out in the middle of a take, but what's the action?"

"It's a chase. I need some breath-takingly beautiful wide-screen effects, and there is nothing to beat these magnificent Alps and in the foreground that gallant little cable car climbing to reach the top and safety. When you get there, Ty will use a huge cable cutter so that the heavy and his band will plunge eleven thousand feet downward. Special effects, of course," he added hastily.

"Why are we always killing people in our pictures?" Caterina asked irritably.

Albert shrugged. "Darling, you know as well as I do that it's the whole reason for films if they hope ever to be sold to television. Now, dress warmly. Good stout coats, strong gloves."

"Why can't you double this, luv?" Ty asked. "Surely stand-ins could take this tiresome ride?"

"No, it can't be done. This is a very visual moment, which is why we've put all this money into these lenses. As you ascend, the heavies will be shooting at you from the pursuing cable car about five hundred yards behind. The whole point of this is that it won't be just another studio shot; it will be the real thing, seen from the killers' viewpoint, and with real background instead of rear projection."

"Oh, all right," Ty said petulantly.

It was extremely cold. A light snow, which froze as soon as it touched the ground and which put a high shine of ice on the great bowl of mountains, was being driven by the wind. This was strong enough to cause the cable car to sway slightly, a condition which delighted Albert, who had been hoping for just this sort of melodramatic weather. The lead

162

car containing Ty and Caterina had been painted blood-red; the one in which the villains would ride was a mordant green. The course of the cable rose almost 45 degrees for a distance of about a hundred yards, then climbed less steeply for two hundred yards to a steel tower; from there it angled slowly across a widening and deepening valley which fell farther and farther away as the cars neared the summit.

The four cameras were co-ordinated by a walkie-talkie controlled by Albert, who had positioned himself halfway up one mountain beside the master camera. There he sat on a steel-boom seat, with powerful binoculars mounted on stands to his left and right. The master camera's platform had a revolving base, which would turn to follow the car bearing Caterina and Ty. The reel changes had been rehearsed exhaustively.

Far below, in the valley, a great sea of tourists and voyeurs waited like a sea of baby birds with their mouths open. Albert checked the readiness of all the camera crews through his walkie-talkie, and then ordered Keys to begin shooting on the floor of the valley, over a mile below. Two thousand yards away the tiny figures of Caterina and Ty approached the cable car on the run and jumped in. Almost immediately the bright red gondola began its steep ascent.

"Very good, Martin," Albert said through the walkie-talkie, peering down myopically, like a near-sighted deity, through the binoculars to his left. "Now cue the heavies."

A blue car careened across the snow and slid to a dramatic stop next to the green cable car. A man with a large sniper's rifle, followed by one with a drawn pistol, threw himself out of the vehicle and raced to the cable car, which instantly began its climb in pursuit of the stars.

"Count to five, please, in the green cable car, then start sighting and shooting upward at Ty and Caterina. The man with the revolver first. Two shots. *Thaaaaat's* it. Thank you, Beppo. Now the dreaded Dr. Emmet attaches his telescopic sight, pats the stock of the rifle and smiles viciously." There was a pause as Albert watched the action on the closed-circuit monitor screen. "Splendid, Dr. Emmet. Very nice. Camera Four at the ready, please. One and Three will reload now."

"Caterina, darling—you must see that I am a different man now," Ty lied as the cable car passed the quarter mark of the climb. "Perhaps it was the hepatitis, or maybe the exposure to death, but I feel I've matured. I'm different—I know I'm different."

"Different from what?" Caterina asked.

"I'm trying to say that I haven't even been alone with a woman since I entered that clinic in Castellaneta." Since they were all alone, and since it was the first time they had discussed anything personal since the third divorce, Ty almost believed what he was saying. "I am not in any way *incapacitated*, mind you," he added hurriedly. "It's just that—well, I have matured. I . . . I see everything differently. Please believe that and say that you'll marry me, luv."

Albert's voice on the intercom interrupted. "Camera Four on the first car, please. Ty and Caterina? Ready, please. Dr. Emmet is shooting at you. Register fear and frustration, please."

They grasped the wire grating of the traveling cage and stared back along the cable at the pursuing car, tension and fear gnarling their faces photogenically. As the first rifle shot rang out, Ty grasped Caterina roughly around the shoulders and pulled her to him. Seven thousand feet in the air, just past the halfway mark, they glanced anxiously over their shoulders, right on cue, to see how far they had to go. Just as Albert had hoped, the car was now swaying dangerously in the high wind, which drove ice particles through the grating into their faces.

Ty drew a pistol, aimed with suavity and fired downward. In reply the rifle from the green car fired and Ty's tiny Tyrolean hat flew off. "How did Albert get that effect?" Caterina asked admiringly, registering proper terror and desperation for the zoomar lenses of the distant cameras.

"Get down!" Ty yelled. He dropped to the floor and pulled her after him.

"Ty? Caterina? Where are you? Our cameras have lost you."

"That wasn't any special effect," Ty shouted hoarsely into Caterina's ear. "They're firing live ammunition."

"Live ammu—?" Real fright glazed her eyes.

"Waldenfon is down there somewhere with a telescopic sight."

"Ty! Caterina! This is a take, dammit! Get on your feet! Do you want to do this all over again? The weather's closing in." Albert's rage was unmistakable. "Get to your feet and go to work."

"Very funny," Caterina said through chattering teeth as two more bullets ricocheted off the side of the metal cabin. Petrified, they clutched each other on the floor of the cabin as it swayed back and forth in the wind.

Suddenly Caterina screamed.

"What?"

164

She pointed as they began to slide. The floor of the car was slowly separating from the wall at the end farthest away from them. Ty screamed even louder than Caterina, and their twenty fingers clung simultaneously to the grating of the gondola's wall as the floor fell completely away, leaving their legs dangling in the empty air, high wind and driving ice particles, nine thousand feet above the valley floor.

Below them the sea of tiny people gave a great cheer as the floor dropped away, and the binocular concession was cleaned out of its stock within ninety seconds.

"Don't look down!" Ty croaked. "Oh, my God!" he screamed after disobeying his own advice, and promptly vomited into the void.

"Honey, your suit!"

"Don't look down!" he sobbed.

"I can't hold on," she moaned. "The wire is cutting my hands."

"The Method! Use the Method!" Ty shouted. "You're only stretching yourself. You're in your own gymnasium at home, and you're stretching yourself on the bar. You love it, it's good for you, you will not let go. Stanislavsky was right—the Method *can* help an actor. Hold, grip—my God, *land!*" Instead of air beneath them there was snow, just eighteen feet below, then twelve, then eight. Then men were standing there, reaching up for them. Ty dropped heavily into a drift. Caterina, moaning "I am a grabber, I am a grabber," still clung to the wire. Ty got to his feet and grasped her legs. "It's all right, baby. We're safe, you can let go." But they had to climb into the cabin to pry her bleeding fingers loose.

McCobb's collarbone had been fractured by a falling tree, the result of a time-bomb explosion directly under his seat which had disrupted earth and forest on the mountainside in a thirty-foot area around the platform. Had he not leaped away from it, pulling the camera operator with him when the floor of the cable car fell away and he saw their legs dangling, he would have been killed. In his panic he had started to run down the mountain to get help, when the bomb went off. He was pinned under a large fir tree and most painfully crushed. The camera operator escaped injury.

McCobb and the two stars were flown by helicopter to the General Hospital in Munich, and Caterina had to be put under sedation for two days.

Heller sent out a dragnet over the entire region, using NATO troops, Alpine guides, planes and dogs. When the laboratory examination revealed that the bomb meant for Albert had been a time bomb, Heller realized the killer was no longer in the mountains, and the vast dragnet was called off. The single day's operation involving troops, planes, helicopters, trucks, trains, field kitchens, man power and material had cost NATO five hundred and sixty-three thousand four hundred and twenty-eight dollars, but when the expenditure was questioned by the junior senator from New York, over thirty thousand telegrams calling for his immediate impeachment were received in Washington.

As soon as the company returned to Hamburg and was literally sealed into the Pacific Seasons Hotel, which had been ringed with barbed wire and gun emplacements, Ty quit the picture. He apologized for being so unprofessional, but said he could no longer take the chance of seeing Caterina hurt or killed. Albert, resembling Lon Chaney's interpretation of Quasimodo, with a T-shaped splint across his back and his left arm in a sling, pleaded with him to carry on. "Don't do it, Ty. You'll be ruined in The Business."

"*Albert!* Good God, man, try to think straight! We can all be killed making this bloody picture!"

"You have so much to gain, Ty."

"Gain a gold casket? Gain a maudlin funeral like the one Goldberg staged for poor Baz, with doubles of Mao Tse-tung and Archbishop Makarios paying their respects? Thank you, Albert, but no thank you."

"Hear me out, Ty. Of course the trade will understand if you withdraw. No one in The Business, except Goldberg and me, will blame you. But you'll be through with the public, washed up."

"Why?"

"Because they simply do not understand that it is nonsense that the show must go on. They've been brainwashed with that line for over a century; it's one of the most important illusions they cling to. They'll lynch you, Ty. I mean it."

"Albert, which show must go on? This film we've been trying to make, or these murderous attacks?"

"The attacks, of course. You're the king who must die. Caterina is the queen; I am the regent. They want fate to have its due. If you elude the killer, you will continue to be their king. If he kills you, they will mourn you hysterically. But you cannot cheat them by eluding your fate; if you do, they'll destroy you."

"Albert, you're sick. I cannot believe that even you could—"

"You are the focus of the world's blood lust right now, the object of the most authentic emotion they have. Schoolgirls in North Dakota are watching television with bated breath to see which of us will provide the thrill of being murdered first.

166

Gamblers in Macao are making fortunes on us. Gardeners in Surrey and dentists in Helsinki are neglecting their work in the hope of participating vicariously in our violent deaths. This is real for them, Ty! Perhaps the only reality they have! They're spoiled! They're no longer satisfied with fake violence and impersonal wars. Their king must die or save himself. Die and you resurrect them; live and you give them life. They are all Carl Waldenfons. They've paid you a king's ransom for twenty years, and now you must pay that debt. You owe this to them; you cannot quit."

Ty returned to his apartment, called Dr. Weiler and in numbed tones reported this conversation. As usual, Abe was eating something. "He could be right, he could be wrong, Ty," he said. "That's show biz. But to me that kind of thinking is all academic. What's the problem here? Is this fella who wants to kill you all of a sudden going to stop just because you're a job dropout? No, sir. This is an important thing to him, as I hope he has convinced you. This way at least you have Goldberg's protection—which you won't, bubby, I assure you, if you quit the picture.

Ty talked to Caterina, who agreed with both Albert and Abe. "If we quit, or if we stayed sealed up in here, he can't get a shot at us, and if he doesn't, the cops will never catch him. I say we should continue and make him try again. Are you scared or something, Ty?"

"Scared? *Scared?* I shake so hard continuously that I can't get into my pajamas. For heaven's sake, Caterina, aren't *you* scared?"

"How can I be scared? They have me doped to the gills with stripeys."

As a court of last appeal, Ty decided to call Goldberg on Caterina's private line, one of the very few in the hotel which by-passed the switchboard. Ty was one of the three people in the world—the others being Goldberg's wife and mother—who were permitted to call him F.X. All others called him General, Doctor, Professor or plain old democratic Mister.

"F.X.?"

"My boy, my boy! I cannot tell you how worried I am."

"You've got to get us out of this picture," Ty said harshly.

"The show must go on."

"Aaaaaaaah!"

"It *can* be done, of course. We could fake your murder, but it would mean you'd have to accept a plastic job on that wonderful face of yours and retire from public life forever."

"Fake my murder?"

"How else can you quit, my boy? The show must go on—you know that."

"I know. So Albert said—and he told me which show, too."

"Also, we have to finish the picture. We can double you. He's not as talented, but he is your exact image. Only Albert and Caterina and I would know the difference. You want me to double you?"

Ty shivered, thinking of the one hundred percent of the gross the double would win if he got through the picture alive. "But a double could get killed, F.X."

"So could you."

"But at least I'd get killed for being me, which seems more moral than if he is murdered for playing me."

"The fate of phonies. But if he makes it—and a lot of phonies make it—boy oh boy, is he set for life! Like I keep saying, the show must go on. I have a one-hundred-and-thirty-seven-million-dollar gross projected for this picture worldwide, so you know I'm not just being sentimental."

"Isn't anything real?"

"Ty, you have a hunnert percent of the gross on this. I ask you, ain't that worth getting killed for?"

Ty was shaking violently as he held the phone. "I see what you mean, F.X.," he said brokenly. "When you put it that way—yes, I see."

He hung up in a daze and walked over to the house-phone to tell Albert his decision. The line was busy, and he sat gazing dreamily for two minutes before trying again. When McCobb answered, he said, "I have just talked to Goldberg, Albert, and after due reflection I have decided to stay on and see this thing through."

"That's wonderful news, Ty," Albert said. "But when did you talk to him?"

"Just now—two minutes ago."

"Impossible, dear boy. I've been on the phone with Goldbert, apprising him of the possibility you might quit the picture, ever since you left my room."

Within two hours, Heller and his men had traced the tampering with Caterina's phone to another bare room almost exactly like the first and with the same electronic equipment. The sole difference was that the room had only been rented forty-eight hours before, to a Mr. Carl Walden. Since the transaction had taken place over the telephone and by delivery of an anonymous postal order, further investigation was useless.

28

GOLDBERG had ordered a change in the story of the film again. It was now a musical, set in the home of a granddaughter of Jonas Bronck, founder of The Bronx, in the 1890's. Caterina played the little mother of the Bronck family, the world's happiest, singingest, dancingest, muggingest, grinningest, jiggingest, funlovingest, gamin-loaded family, who were so appealing that for once Goldberg had agreed to a long title: *Bronck's Cheer*. In a stiff strawhat and reversible striped blazer, Ty played a taffy-pull concessionaire unable to find a profitable location, and Caterina was the girl who helped him find it—which was the plot in detail. The script, score, sets and costumes were sent by air freight from California.

When the nature of the change became apparent, Albert, who loathed movie musicals, panicked. He spent hours on the overseas telephone with Goldberg or his lieutenant, Leon Roth, complaining bitterly that the picture was not his style. How could the master of suspense, who had become a symbol of fear for a billion people, be asked to direct a mindless movie musical? He pleaded to be replaced, but Goldberg was an unmovable mountain. The trinity of Bryson-Largo-McCobb had more box-office appeal than anything since the embalming of Lenin, and Goldberg was suddenly piqued by the prospect of contrasting the murderous atmosphere surrounding the production in Hamburg with a story and film without a moment of violence or evil.

"Also," he bellowed to Albert thirty-eight hundred miles away, "if this killer wants to be a wise guy, this way we'll make it real tough for him. Let's see what he can do, the momser, with every girl in the chorus a cop and everybody on the production crew backed up by another cop."

"But I simply cannot direct a musical."

"You'll see. It'll be the greatest thing you ever did. The public will demand that you make only musicals."

"No, no, no!"

"We oversold the violence kick, Albert. You'd be dead at the box office anyway if you didn't have this fantastic gift for musicals. The time for total schmaltz is here. I feel it! I know it! Mrs. Goldberg feels it and knows it!" But though Albert lost the war, he won a battle by flatly refusing to cast Phil Silvers as Ty's best friend.

The Kallikakian simple-mindedness of the script, combined with the unfamiliar technical demands imposed by the musical form, drove Albert deeper and deeper into the depression which had started the day Heller announced the suicide of Dane Ponder-Schmeckle, and which was reinforced the day he was hit by the tree, when physical pain and fear had become permanent companions. He began to mumble to himself and neglected to shave. He would stare off into space, silent in the middle of a sentence, and gaze blankly at nothing until Martin Keys tugged at his sleeve. Or he would fly into a rage, which was as foreign to him as the musical film he was making.

The company had been locked in a single compound for security. They lived and worked on one great sound stage; no one was allowed in or out, and would not be until the film was completed. The press was held at bay beyond locked iron gates; beyond that was a second wall, topped with wire, completely around the compound. Huge savage dogs and armed sentries guarded every foot inside the wall, and there were two sets of guards at every outer entrance to the lot itself and to the inner sound stage.

Comfortable apartments had been built for the principals, and dormitories were constructed along the walls for the rest of the cast and crew. Food was cooked and served army style.

Ty and Caterina danced time steps, winging bucks and buffalos-off-to, as though choreography had died on the Keith circuit. Caterina wore obscenely suggestive bathing suits and thick blue eye make-up for the pastel-color camera. In forty-five days a dulled and nearly demented McCobb got almost all the picture into the can, but at a terrible price. His spirit was broken; his nerve had gone; he was a stranger to his friends and his mirror. He could not face anyone because his pride of craft had been so shattered. He would stare at the floor as he mumbled directions, and these would be relayed in a loud voice by Martin Keys to the rest of the company. He could not eat; in the middle of a mouthful he would grind a liverwurst sandwich under his heel, throw his head on the communal table and sob loudly in full view of the company until Martin led him gently off to his quarters.

"A movie musical," he whispered croakingly on the last day of shooting. "I, Albert McCobb, the unchallenged master of suspense about whom the French, the proudly civilized French nation, wrote whole bookshelves, sentenced by his greed—or in penalty for his pride—to make a Hollywood musical with the screen's greatest Hamlet as his hoofer, history's greatest Camille as his soubrette, and plot and lyrics written by computers programmed by a pie baker." He held his head and rocked crookedly back and forth. "How did it happen? Where did I go wrong? Should I be surprised? No, no. Did I flee when told I would henceforth be the employee-partner of a corporation called Jetthrow-Goldberg-Pies?" he wailed, clinging to Ty for support. "Why me? I, who have made the world examine its recesses of evil, its instincts which it did not know existed." He stumbled and sat down heavily, wadding his face with his hands. "I cannot face making the next shot. Goldberg has extracted the reality from my life. He has done me in."

The police car inched through the rain and sullen crowds of newspapermen, photographers and approximately three thousand of the general public who were milling among the lights and television equipment outside the gates. As the car made its way millimeter by millimeter, four fan-magazine writers lay down ostentatiously in its path, forcing it to stop so that their spokesman could demand their rights.

"If those people are not on their feet by the count of ten they will be arrested," Heller said equably.

"What is arrest, even prison, to us, sir?" demanded Dame Maria Van Slyke, chairwoman of the Fan Magazine Circle of the British Commonwealth and famous as the woman who had obtained the first "home sitting" for an English fan magazine with Francis X. Bushman. Her voice was majestic and her mink coat had cost over forty-six hundred dollars wholesale. "You deny us the right of all free men—the right to work," she cried.

"Dear lady, I deny you nothing. That is private property beyond that fence, and they don't want you in there."

"We have to know that they're still alive, don't we? Simply allow us to see them. Let them throw down a few kisses from the roof."

"I'll do my best," Heller answered. "Now get those people up. We're going through." The man from *La Prensa* stuck his head in on the other side of the car to ask if McCobb's fracture permitted him to work; Heller answered that he was working like a man inspired. Four desultory flash pictures

171

were taken of the police car, the fan-magazine writers rose sheepishly from the road and the car rolled through the first of three gates.

In the radio transmission truck, which was linked to Telstar, the chief telegrapher was transmitting directly to Dow-Jones, as a service to the New York financial press. The confirmation that McCobb was at work would mean a heavy fall in the market averages because it presaged an earlier completion of the film and a greater chance of the three principals' escaping assassination. One clean murder would put the entire production back to Go, which would send the market soaring to new season highs. The stasis in production news (Gallagher had been forbidden to make any further announcements for four days so that Goldberg could take a short position in the market and try to recover some of the heavy production losses incurred so far) had caused a nine-teen percent slowdown on world industrial production (Soviet and Chinese figures unavailable), an eleven-point-two percent reduction in U.S. carloadings, and a sickening drop of 94 points on the Dow-Jones index. The economic jolt had ravaged the British balance of payments, and threatened the pound so severely that the Bank of England had been obliged to turn to Latin-American banks for support.

The press army in waiting had grown to eleven hundred and seventy-two journalists, plus the entire corps of *paparazzi* who had hitchhiked from Rome. All of them were fretful and exhausted from the pressure exerted by their home offices. The *Paris-Match* team of sixty-one had been rotated back to Paris for an inspirational talk by the very highest government official, who was worried about the possibility of a recurrence of the loss of face suffered by France when *Match*'s thirty-nine-man team was beaten in its coverage of the Pope's visit to the Holy Land by a lone Texan from the *Ladies' Home Journal*.

Heller crossed through the final entrance compartment to the sound stage and stalked through the assemblage. He was without an ice-cream cone; those relaxed days were gone. His eyes were hard and wary as he mounted a platform and looked out over the hundreds of police, both in and out of costume, at the actors, at McCobb and at the production crew. His voice rang out sternly.

"This is the last day of shooting," he said, "and all of us have every reason to believe that the killer is going to try at least once more. He is on this sound stage among us now. I warn him: Do not persist in this mad plan. The instant the last shot is completed, the film, the cast and the crew will be flown out of Hamburg. Mr. McCobb, Mr. Bryson and Miss Largo will go out on separate planes, whose destinations are known only to Frederic X. Goldberg. If we finish this one day safely, we will have won. But I have this to say to the killer: Not only will we stop you; we will arrest and convict you. Thank you one and all—except for him, of course—and good luck."

"May we begin?" a disheveled and broken McCobb said from his canvas chair.

"Please do."

"I have come to respect you and your men, Inspector," McCobb said shakily, "and therefore I am ashamed that you will have to watch this. Not since *The Kissing Bandit*, not even, I swear to you, since *Jefferson*, has—"

Martin Keys came racing across the great stage yelling, "Mr. McCobb, sir! Mr. Goldberg's voice is about to be amplified through our loudspeaker system here by radio-telephone from New York."

"Oh, *Jesus!*" McCobb shrieked.

At that a massive voice, throaty and opulent, boomed out of the amplifier. The captive audience of hundreds cringed together, much as supplicants did millennia before in the presence of Baal.

Suddenly Caterina was able to identify that voice with a man standing within her view. She stuffed a handkerchief into her mouth so that she would not scream.

"Good morning!" the voice exploded, "and hello out there. This is a recording. This is your president, Frederic X. Goldberg, who wishes to tell you that the picture you are making far surpasses, in its beauty, jollity and sheer wonderment, the greatest musicals in filmdom's Hall of Fame. I tell you, *Bronck's Cheer* will live forever in the hearts of men. I tell you, *Bronck's Cheer* has more soul than *Samson and Delilah*, more wit and excitement than *The Happy Thieves*, more living entertainment than *Noah's Ark*, and more on-target schmaltz for the little people than *The Sound of Music* or *Mary Poppins*. So this is to salute you and to thank from the bottom of my heart Albert McCobb, king of the movie musical. God bless you all."

Mercifully the speakers went dead. Everyone tried not to look at McCobb, who was on the floor kicking his feet in a thrumming tattoo of helpless anger, weeping unashamedly. Martin and Caterina lifted him to his feet and began to move him off to his quarters. As Caterina tottered beside him she tried to decide what to do with the sudden, terrifying knowl-

173

edge that her ear for linguistics had just given her at the sound of Goldberg's voice.

Ty wandered aimlessly through the crowd to the water cooler near the telephone booth. As usual he was very frightened and couldn't keep still. He was terrified of dying and of the fact that Caterina's subconscious knew who the murderer was, but that the self-protectiveness of her conscious mind kept it below the surface. But what terrified him most of all was the prospect of a fourth marriage to her. If there was a hell after death, should a man insist on *four* rehearsals of it before he died? He suddenly found himself staring intently at the beautiful bottom of a scantily clad policewoman from Düsseldorf, and shuddered at the thought of what Caterina would do if he looked at a woman's bottom if they married again. It was all the fault of that bloody murderer. He had been free of Caterina and she of him, and he had been strolling across a lovely lawn of soft mouths, gorgeous bosoms and gasps of appreciation, occasionally pausing to test his long-nurtured ambition to sleep with every female in the world between the ages of eighteen and twenty-four. But that sadistic killer had driven them together again and proved their total dependency on each other, and now all lawn-strolling might be finished forever. Ty's bitterness filled him like lye, and hatred for his relentless pursuer made him shake with anger instead of fear.

In this state he was leaning against the back of the telephone booth beside the water cooler when someone entered it, dialed and began to talk. "Hello, Father Kullers? It's me. Well, another week has gone by. I still can't get out of here to go to confession and with all the women cooped up here I've been having lewd thoughts, so I wondered if you could hear it over the phone, Father. Its pretty bad here; the women have hardly any clothes on. As Yeats wrote, 'The visible world is no longer a reality, and the unseen world is no longer a dream.' "

Ty chilled at the voice. It was the same small voice covered with icy fur which had promised him death and which had now welded him forever, the rotten bastard, to the woman he loved. He ran around to the front of the booth. The man's back was to the door; Ty ripped it open and pulled the man out, spinning him to see his face. He stared at it and almost choked in surprise. It was John O'Gorman, Caterina's make-up man.

At Ty's scream, police swarmed over them. Heller appeared as though from a puff of smoke. Ty, incoherent with rage and shock, babbled at O'Gorman with an accusing finger

174

outstretched. "Make him talk! Hear that voice! It's him. It's the killer—"

"Ty, boy! What are you saying? It's me—Johnny O'Gorman. What's the matter?"

"Speak to them. Say, 'The visible world is no longer a reality—' "

"That's Yeats! I always quote Yeats! I know all of Yeats."

"Say it! Goddammit, say it!"

O'Gorman looked around at all the hostile faces in a world that seemed to have gone mad. " 'The visible world is no longer a reality,' " he recited, " 'and the unseen world is no longer a dream.' "

"Take him downtown," Heller said. "We'll make a few tests." As he watched them lead O'Gorman away, Ty began to plan in his mind the clothes he would wear at the trial and the speech he would make to the jury, but this delicious reverie was interrupted by Martin Keys calling the members of the company back to their places. Albert was about to shoot the final scene of the film.

29

THEY WRAPPED the picture up at nine o'clock that night. The buses and cars were to leave for the airport in two hours.

Caterina walked to her dressing room as if to a guillotine. She was sure she had spotted a false identity, but she could not find the courage to confront the man; her pathological fear of letting go of the slender wisp of security she thought she had, kept her silent. She sat staring into a glass of water, trying to empty her mind by thinking of a blue and cloudless sky. She knew how nearby death was, but she couldn't move to stop anything, could only hope that by her silence she could ward it off.

Someone knocked at her door.

"Yes?" she said apprehensively.

"It's me, luv. Ty."

She unlocked and opened the door. He came in, staring at

her strangely, and closing the door behind him, locked it with the hand behind his back.

"Ty!" She backed away from him. "What are you doing?"

"Locking the door."

"Why?"

"I'm going to make love to you."

Her relief was aphrodisiac. "Oh, yes!" she cried out and ran into his arms.

A thousand asterisks later they chatted languidly while Ty was looking for his socks.

"Ty?"

"Hm?"

"Your plan for Zambia or Nepal is ingenious."

"Northern Sweden should be wonderfully solitary too."

She took a deep breath. "Do you agree that I am good at voices and accents?"

"Of course."

"Then will you believe me when I tell you that Inspector Heller isn't Inspector Heller?"

"All right."

"Do you have any idea who he is?"

"*Two* false Hellers?" he said, incredulous.

"Yes."

"And you know who he really is?"

"I know. I can't believe it, but I know."

"Do you mean . . . is he . . . is he Carl Waldenfon?"

"No Somehow it's even more shocking."

"*More shocking?* Who?"

"Inspector Heller is Frederic X. Goldberg."

"This is not the time for jokes, Caterina."

"No, it's true. It's the same voice. From southern New Jersey. And I'm not guessing. It's a science. Remember *My Fair Lady?*"

He looked at her, pole-axed. His voice meandered as he tried to understand and reply. "If it were anyone else—Barry Goldwater, even Charles de Gaulle—I would believe you, luv. But not Goldberg. Please understand I have every respect, even awe, for your uncanny ability—but for Goldberg to take twelve weeks off? Germany? South America? I mean, power is Goldberg and a little Goldberg corrupts absolutely, but this time, luv, you are dead wrong."

"I'm glad," she said. "Kiss me some more, *bambolo.*"

Ty sat in his trailer taking off his make-up, happier than he had ever been, polishing his plan to fly with Caterina from Hamburg to Zambia or Nepal that night to get married. Then they would double back to northern Sweden for a year to escape from the press, until other catastrophes emerged to dominate the news. They would get word to Goldberg somehow; he could produce Bryson and Largo doubles, stage a monster wedding at someplace like St. Peter's, or even on water skis, and set the press and public loose on them while he and Caterina found peace in a Swedish forest, by the shores of a lake, alone for just once in their lives together. It seemed miraculous, but perhaps they could have a year alone, safe from the savage, simple-minded public.

As he brooded and plotted, tying his tie and whistling softly, a trap door in the floor opened silently behind him. Up the ladder, from a tunnel which was dug twenty-six days before Ty had even known he was going to Hamburg, Moni and Schorschl climbed silently into the room.

Moni hit Ty behind the right ear with a small sap and Schorschl caught him as he fell sideways. They lifted his body and lowered it into the tunnel. Moni closed the trap door behind him, locked it, and by waving a large electromagnet, pulled the metal-lined rug on the floor of Ty's trailer back into position.

Ty regained consciousness in a car. For some reason he felt euphoric. Though his head throbbed, he had a wonderful miles-away feeling, rather as if he had swallowed four stripeys, and his vision seemed capable of extending for hundreds of miles. After a while he looked to the left and right. The car was gliding through a city, and he was seated up front between two large men.

"Hello, Moni. Hello, Schorschl," he said. The deaf-and-dumb Moni answered him, speaking in a Miami-Las Vegas accent.

"Hozzit, Mr. Bryson."

Schorschl, who was driving, said either to Ty or Moni or both, "Shuddup."

"I thought you chaps were deaf-and-dumb," Ty said.

"Wazza joke, Mr. Bryson," Moni said. "You know, like it worked better that way because we can't speak German. Now who needs it, right?"

"Shuddup arreddy," Schorschl said.

"You boys sound like American movie gangsters," Ty said. That pleased Schorschl. He warmed up. "We done eleven months in LA as bodyguards for Dimples Tancredi." Miss Tancredi had been a stripper very much in vogue because she was the beloved of Tommy "Duck Feet" Mongula, a prominent Mafia executive.

"But she was shot to death," Ty said.

"Yeah, we had some bad luck," Moni answered. "But Corrado had his pitcher in *Silvuh Screen*. He was standin' right behind Fillum Czar Jack Valenti at an opening of a new drive-in."

"Who's Corrado?"

"Him," Moni said, indicating the driver. "My brudder. Corrado means Conrad in Eyetalian."

"I got to know Conrad Veidt rather well in his last years," Ty replied serenely. "And your name isn't Moni?"

"Giacobbe. It means like Jake in wop."

The nebulae around the streetlights were very beautiful and the pavement shone exquisitely in the rain. They were driving along the Reeperbahn, and the car passed Der Schmutzige Kniff and its mud wrestlers.

"Where are we going, Corrado?" Ty asked.

"It's a haffa block more."

"*Why* are we going?"

"We'll tell you all about it when we get there, pal. I mean, why say it twice? Right?"

The car stopped at the curb on Schorschl's side, and Ty had to slide out under the steering wheel. They were in front of a grimy two-story building with a sign saying: "INTERNATIONAL TATTOOS." The building was dark; the only light came from the Reeperbahn, half a block away.

One on each side, the twins walked Ty to the door, which Moni opened after several tries with a bunch of keys. They pushed Ty gently in ahead of them and Moni locked the door, leaving the keys in the lock. They walked in single file to a back room filled with placards, stencils and a large, overstuffed barber chair. Schorschl turned on an overhead lamp, Moni closed the door and they put Ty in the barber chair. He sat gazing with interest at the richness and variety of tattooing designs on charts covering every square inch of the walls. Even the drawn window shades were covered with them. They offered fire-breathing gold-and-green dragons, the Dionne quintuplets, Maori moko tattoos, crossed flags and eagles, the head of Balto, who had gotten the serum to Nome, swastikas, butterflies, angels and roses, snakes, several designs saying "Mother" in nine languages, daggers, ships in full sail, a portrait of John F. Kennedy, playing cards, Hokusai paintings, crucifixes, bleeding hearts, anchors, Union Jacks, Hedy Lamarr and Queen Elizabeth.

"We've been on this job a long time," Schorschl said. "Remember that night we chased you and made out like we was shootin' at you after that premeer?"

"We was only supposed to scare you, that night," Moni said. "Not like tonight. You get to yell like bingo tonight."

As he stared at them Ty's emotional euphoria slowly dribbled away, leaving ashes. He could feel his head growing to a sharp point. The room looked morbidly dirty. Moni and Schorschl became callous, sadistic thugs before his eyes. Terror had returned.

"Why are we here?"

"Take it easy, Mr. Bryson," Moni said. "Soon. It'll be all over soon. We got here a little early, is all."

"But why are we here?"

"Because The Man wants you to make a choice of tattoos. He wants you to think about it for a while before he operates on you."

"Does what?"

"He's gonna make you prettier, pal," Schorschl said, grinning widely. He took an envelope out of the pocket of his huge jacket and dropped it in Ty's lap. "Look 'em over, Mr. Bryson," he said. "Take a pick."

Three were glossy color photographs in the envelope. In the first picture a man's head had been tattooed in solid, wide black stripes which ran under his eyes, across his cheeks to his ears and hair, in thick swirls around his mouth, chin and throat. The effect was handsome, but not human.

"That's the Zebra Man, Mr. Bryson," Moni said.

"And it don't come off," Schorschl added. "You can't ever get it off." Ty stared at him in silent terror, then dropped his eyes to the second photograph. Staring up at him through pained eyes was a lewd, contempt-mad face which was determined to make the world look at it. The man's head had been shaved, and bloated cabbage roses decorated the top of his head. The eyes were outlined on the forehead with silly pink polka dots, and with tiny sheaves of green-and-yellow corn on the cheeks. The rest of the face was executed in a demented design of hearts, cherubs, butterflies and cupid arrows. But what was most horrifying was that amid all this grotesquerie it was the mad sadness of the man's eyes that was most conspicuous.

"Hey, Mr. Bryson," Moni said, "keep lookin'."

Looking down at the last picture, Ty had to choke back a scream because he sensed that this tattoo had been chosen for him. It was a color photograph of the great head of a mandrill: a three-colored nose with nostrils like torpedo tubes, above a mouth fully eight inches long—scarlet and blue, curving upward in insane geniality; cheeks covered with gray-and-green fur, tendrils of a mustache, lip whiskers and a

179

chin beard of blond hairs; eyes which seemed smaller than frozen pebbles amid the tattooed fur. His hands trembled violently, and O'Gorman's voice rang inside his head with the force of a steel hammer. Now he knew that O'Gorman was not the man who had conceived these words: *"First I will take your face away—first I will take your face away—first I will take your face away—"*

Ty's mind abandoned reality. He threw himself backward into *Bomb,* his first great action picture, in which he played the aged 8th Dan (karate), 6th Dan (judo), 8th Dan (akido) Hayakawa, who had broken the backs of eleven samurai. He came out of his chair in *jiyukumite,* the wide-open attack. Delivering a crushing roundhouse kick to the side of Moni's neck, he threw him into his brother, then hit Schorschl with a side-thrust kick into his knee, toppling both of them. His heel came up with blurring speed and drove downward into Moni's diaphragm as Schorschl went for his switch knife. Ty hit his arm with a sharp snap kick which sent the knife flying across the room, then stood over them in a powerful straddle position, moved sideways and kicked the two brothers into unconsciousness on the floor of the garish room.

Ty scooped up the knife and dropped it in his side pocket as he careened down the hall leading to the street. He unlocked the door and ran toward the lights of the Reeperbahn. He moved shakily in the shadows, avoiding the streetlights which would make him a target.

Suddenly he saw a sign nailed under a thirty-watt bulb to the door of a building. He was at the back entrance to Der Schmutzige Kniff. He could go through the night club to the entrance on the Reeperbahn side and remain concealed until a doorman found him a taxi.

30

CATERINA waited in her quarters on the sound stage. At first she was impatient; though there had been no mention of a fourth marriage, she knew it had been decided and that Ty would come for her soon. But the longer she waited, the more frightened she became. At last she walked hurriedly through the clumps of police on the sound stage to Ty's dressing room. Two bulky cops were guarding the entrance.

"Is Mr. Bryson in there?"

"Yes, madam."

"Is anyone with him?" It made her nauseated to ask the question.

"No, madam." He knocked at the door and they waited for a response.

"It's all right, officer," Caterina said. "I'll just go right in." She closed the door behind her. Ty wasn't in the living room, dressing room or bedroom, and the lighted bathroom was vacant. In a panic she looked behind the shower curtain, inside closets, and even under the beds and behind the drapes. Finally, sobbing, she ran back to the front door and threw it open. "He's gone. He's not there," she said.

The two policemen pushed past her. One began to search and the other picked up the telephone and called Inspector Winkler. In a daze Caterina walked out of the apartment, across the sound stage, through the semidarkness over the snaking cables until she reached Albert's quarters.

Her mind opened. The terrible need to herself to save Ty had produced the combination that swung it open. Her memory was no longer useless. The power which the fear of Ty's loss had worked upon her dredged up from the depths of her subconscious mind the secret she had been able to conceal from herself all these years since the end of the war. The irony of all this rushing into her mind to save them only an hour before they had almost escaped together overwhelmed her. But ecstasy sustained her; she realized it was only because they had learned they could not live without each other that the secret was released. At last she knew what she had to do.

Albert answered her knock as though he had been waiting for it.

"Albert—" she began, but her voice caught in her throat. He drew her into the apartment and locked the door.

"What's wrong, Caterina?" he asked urgently.

"Ty has vanished."

Albert didn't answer. The ruin of his pendulous face stared back at her hopelessly; his beard was matted, his teeth yellow, and a line of spittle dribbled from the corner of his mouth.

"If Ty is not harmed," Caterina forced herself to say in a choked voice, "I will never tell."

"Tell what, Caterina?"

"That you are Carl Waldenfon."

31

INSPECTOR HELLER faced O'Gorman across his desk at police headquarters while Skutch sat against the wall, his stenographic pad poised. O'Gorman had given vent to his outrage from the beginning, but it still bubbled in him like a thickening porridge. He was reduced to placing his defense on the fact that Caterina Largo was an angel on earth and that no one would believe he would harm a hair on her head.

When he had finished with the questioning, Heller slid a piece of paper across the desk and asked O'Gorman to read from it aloud. The make-up man's hand shook but his voice was steady: *"Bryson! I am going to kill you! It will be a filthy death! First I will take your face away, then I am going to kill you. The visible world is no longer a reality and the unseen world is no longer a dream."*

Heller nooded with approval. O'Gorman said, "Where did you get those lines?"

"One moment, please." Heller pressed a button on one of the two tape recorders on his desk. The voice which had blared from the sound truck crackled out. They listened to the message; then Heller stopped the first machine and started the second. The same voice recited the message, but this time in a quiet, conversational tone.

"Which is your voice?" Heller asked.

"Both of them. But . . . this is terrible."

"Are you ready to make a statement?"

"I am. I have to. I see that."

"Whatever you say will be held against you, et cetera," Heller told him.

"I always quote Yeats. He's my hobby, you could say, and he has been ever since I was a boy in Kilflyn. You know, he was a good man. But anyone who'd want to harm Largo . . . Anyway, I recorded that speech and others something like that for Albert McCobb six years ago, in Kowloon."

32

Ty WALKED across the cellar of Der Schmutzige Kniff as wary as a mountain goat, seeking the staircase that would lead him to the night-club level. Picking his way through straw hampers of muddy bathing suits and an astonishing number of Steinhäger bottles, he finally reached a circular iron staircase. At the top he found himself in an open, barely lit area with stacked flats and ropes; he was obviously backstage. As he groped through the semidarkness he could hear the crowd hooting and whistling from their tables. He moved cautiously toward the noise and in a moment his hand fell upon a doorknob. He opened the door and stepped out into blinding light. A triumphant face shrieked and cackled as he stood there, dazed. Just as his eyes focused on the apparition, he was lifted high into the air and then slammed downward into the viscous mud. He had fallen into the hands of Raddatz.

"Bryson, you son of a bitch! Justice sent you here!" She leaped into the pit after him, her naked skin gleaming in the slime. "This time it's to the death, you miserable bastard!" she shouted.

The crowd loved the zest of the new comedy twist on the old act. Ty couldn't get his footing, Raddatz was barefoot and at home in the mud. She kneed him viciously on the side of the head, then slammed him over with a double arm lock. Clasping her hands together above her head, she struck him across the face as he lay there. He was groggy, but he knew he had to get his shoes off and topple her down into the mud with him. She laughed joyously as he bit her behind the knee, then brought her down. He threw himself across her, and after a struggle, managed to sit on her stomach. He took careful aim and whammed a roundhouse right, a left and another right on her lumpy face. Black mud covered his clothes, and he looked like a minstrel man gone berserk.

With a great heave Raddatz unseated him, grabbed the two ends of his tie and began to strangle him. His eyes were crossing as she said, "I think I have fallen in love with you. And I hate it."

Total revulsion gave him the strength to break her hold, and that was the turning point. Overcome by love, Raddatz threw her arms around his neck and frantically began to kiss his mud-caked face. "Take me, take me, you wonderful, masterful man," she moaned.

It was the first time since reaching puberty that Ty had been sickened by a woman. Suddenly, like the boy who lifted the calf every morning until it grew into a bull, Tynan Bryson tasted the first enthralling fruit of monogamy by re-forming his character, then and there, to spurn the lips of a woman whose hand he did not hold in matrimony. In that same aneling mud Clara Raddatz had become a woman an instant before Bryson forswore adultery forever; and as her heart melted, so did her mighty muscles. Ty measured her for the blow which would put her out of her misery, and he hit her with so much gratitude for what she had given him that he almost tore her head off with the punch. Then she fell face downward, he flipped her over to save her from suffocation; then he climbed panting out of the pit and walked across the tarpaulin and down the main aisle of the night club while the audience, stunned that even trained athletes could maintain such standards of performance for six shows a night, gave him a standing ovation.

Ty was a totally unrecognizable glistening bar of pitch as he walked out the front door and up the Reeperbahn right past Schorschl, who was searching for him frantically. He got into a cab. "What a mess you're making all over my cab," the driver said with enormous pleasure as it pulled away, "and what a big tip that's going to cost you."

"You speak English!"

"You want to hear it in Rumanian maybe?"

"Please—find me a telephone booth." He gave the driver fifty marks for some silver, and in the phone booth a few blocks away he dialed Albert's private number at the studio.

The call was routed swiftly by the efficient electronic device in Albert's quarters to a telephone in the projection booth of the studio's small screening room. There Albert was smiling fondly at Caterina, tied and gagged in a straight-backed chair, as the telephone rang. He picked it up.

"Albert? Thank God you are still there. I was sure the

planes had gone, leaving me behind in this murderous place."

"Ty! Where are you? Everyone has been frantic—"

"I'm all right. I'll get out there within fifteen minutes. Please tell Caterina."

"You may be sure I'll tell Caterina," Albert said, smiling benignly at her. "You were not . . . uh . . . harmed in any way?"

"No, I'm fine, except that I'm unrecognizable. I'll be right there."

"Ty"

"Yes?"

"You'll never get through that cordon of press out at those gates. And at least seven thousand hysterical people have collected since the word got out that you had disappeared."

"Well, then tell Caterina to meet me at the airport. I'll sit in the cab right in front of the baggage entrance. Ask her to bring me a set of dry clothes. I'm a little messy."

"No, we can't do that either. You see, Inspector Heller has caught Waldenfon, and he is about to explain everything to us in the small screening room here. Do you know where that is?"

"He caught Waldenfon! Thank God. Yes, I know it. The small building about a hundred yards from the main stages? Where the cutting room is?"

"Yes, that's it. On the north side of the lot. The building has a delivery entrance. I'll go down to that gate to let you in. Have the cab take you all the way around to that dirt road on the north side, and then walk across the field. No one will see you in the dark. That's much the best way."

"Good. I'll be there in twelve minutes."

Albert hung up and sighed with contentment. "After I had settled you in that fine school with the good sisters in Florence, my dear," he said to Caterina, "I was able to make my way to Lisbon, fortunately, where I soon secured a British passport in the name of Albert McCobb. Then, instead of attempting anything direct, I moved down the coast of Africa as a traveler in surgical instruments. I sailed from Cape Town for Buenos Aires on a Norwegian freighter carrying sheep. I began to learn about sheep and it was well that I did because when I reached Argentina I found it positively packed with escaped Nazis. A little hard thought and a look at a map led me to South Georgia Island, where I became a sheep rancher. To cover all tracks forever, I wrote *Cold!*, my famous but wholly fictional autobiography, and were it not for the happenstance that Goldberg decided to turn it into a film, I might never have returned for you. It is peaceful and pleasant down by the Antarctic."

He sighed, bit off the end of a cigar, then lighted it. "Planning your deaths has been a delicious problem, really. Everyone was so helpful. O'Gorman recorded his voice and I even have a marvelous set of wax impessions of his fingerprints, which I had made into plastic. I'm wearing them now. Had you noticed?" He waved his pudgy fingers at her. "Manderson, one of the special-effects boys, made the two bombs for me, and the explosive side mirror for the car. Guillie Holden, my old-time grip, dug the tunnel and built the trap door in Ty's dressing room. I adored reviving that old gimmick; it's an effect which went out with *The Phantom of the Opera*. I sent Holden and Manderson off to British Honduras before you ever arrived in Hamburg. They won't talk, because they simply don't know what's happening here. On the whole, it's been the best script I've ever directed, and it certainly has given me a magnificent audience for my final effort. And do you know, if it had not been for the accident of O'Gorman telephoning that priest, I could have gone on making pictures long after I'd killed the two of you? As it is, by now O'Gorman is probably telling Heller how that recording was made, but by the time he has it all figured out we'll be dead. So I'll win anyway."

Albert paused to puff on his cigar and stare out the window for the lights of Ty's cab. Then he turned restlessly and continued his monologue. "How could nature have made Ty so beautiful as to impel you to lay your heart at his feet—and he such a silly and unfaithful man? Why was I made so small and ugly, in a shape so repulsive to you? You must be a stupid woman not to be able to see past such things. Well, I blame myself, really. I blame myself for killing your mother and sister before your eyes. I can see that now, but at the time, in the middle of a war, when death was always a matter of improvisation, how could I have foreseen the way I would grow to long for you until eternity?

"But, in passing, it all says something worthwhile about the navy. I tell you, had I shelled your town or bombed it with the planes of my fleet, and killed your mother and sister impersonally from the deck of my flagship, you would never have blamed me. *C'est la guerre,* you would think. That very objectivity of naval officers is what makes them gentlemen. My whole life would have been different if I had been at sea, safe from people, instead of facing what I had to face in the SS."

His eyes welled with tears of regret and self-pity. "It has

186

cost me my beautiful darling daughter, who, like me with you, killed for love and pride. It's all in that line of Yeats which O'Gorman found for me: 'The visible world is no longer a reality, and the unseen world is no longer a dream.' "

The lights of Ty's taxi appeared across the field. Albert clutched at his forehead and stared directly at Caterina for a long moment, his pendulous face ridiculously tragic. Then he slipped out of the projection booth, hurried down the stairs, left the building and unlocked the iron gate to the delivery entrance a few yards away. Within moments, Ty loomed up in the night, and Albert motioned him through the gate and locked it. As they entered the screening-room building, he locked and bolted that door too.

"Heller and his group are on their way, Ty, with Caterina. If you'll take a seat in the little auditorium there, I'll get ready the few things Heller needs." He opened the door, ushered Ty inside and then locked it after him. Quickly he climbed the short flight of steps to the projection booth, walked over to Caterina and kissed her softly on the forehead. Then he untied her from the chair and pulled her to her feet, stood behind her and marched her out of the room and down the stairs to the aisle door on the opposite side of the screening room.

"I am about to consign you to hell," he said. "Good-bye, my darling." He opened the auditorium door, pushed Caterina through and locked it securely from the other side.

Ty turned, the mud now caked all over his face and body. Caterina's hands were still tied behind her back and the gag was almost suffocating her. "Caterina!" he cried in horror and ran crabwise across the row of seats. Using Schorschl's knife, he cut the cords around her wrists and pulled the gag out of her mouth.

"Who did this? What's happening?" he asked in bewilderment.

"Albert. Albert is Waldenfon."

"Albert?"

"He is going to kill us now. Oh, my darling!"

"Don't be silly, luv. I just left Albert. He couldn't have been more friendly."

"He is as insane as the day he killed my mother and sister." Words spilled out of her in a torrent. "But I didn't know —I swear to you right now, when we are about to die, that I had forgotten his face until you told me that you loved me and then disappeared. I knew that he had got you and that
187

you were going to be murdered, and I realized that the only way I might save you was if I remembered."

"Just keep remembering that we're getting out of here and we're getting married in Zambia or Nepal the day after tomorrow," Ty said.

Albert's voice crackled from the loudspeakers behind the screens. "As you may not have had the time to notice," he said, "I have rigged up three screens so that you'll be able to enjoy three great shows simultaneously. First, on the center screen I offer you an uncut version of *Jefferson*."

"No!" Ty shouted.

"Kill us, Albert," Caterina cried, "but not that. You can't!"

"On the right-hand screen you will see various shots we have been able to secure—either by hidden cameras and trick lenses or with the remarkable new remote recording devices —shots of Caterina pursuing her love of money and her hatred for her husband. Lastly, on the left-hand screen you will see, exquisitely photographed, shots of Ty making love to that army of garbage-women he has spent his life courting. In short, all of the total meaning of the lives of both of you."

The three screens came to life simultaneously. On the far left Ty was thrashing about in a large brass hotel bed with a middle-aged chambermaid still wearing her hotel uniform. In the center Ty, in a grotesque powdered wig, was commissioning his secretary to go to Naples to beg, borrow or steal a spaghetti-making machine and somehow smuggle it out of Italy and back to Virginia. On the right screen Caterina was screaming shrewishly over the telephone at what was apparently a real estate dealer, pounding his price down, bullying, yelling, cajoling, making promises, reneging and flirting over an option on a ninety-acre tract of land in Baja California.

They sat and stared at their images, rapt and horrified.

"I wanted you to experience hell before you died," Albert's voice said electronically.

Caterina turned away from the screen and pressed her face into Ty's chest so that she could not see. Ty fought to keep from retching as he watched himself say, from under that large, badly fitted wig, "I don't care how you get it, Billy. Swindle them or beat them up if you have to, but we have to get a *trafila* out of Naples. America must have spaghetti, no matter what the cost!"

In the projection booth Albert dialed Goldberg's secret number in New York, one so private that it rested in a lead-lined safe in Goldberg's library far above Central Park West. It would be about six o'clock there. Albert reasoned, and Goldberg would be shaking, not stirring, his first Dr. Brown's

Celery Tonic of the evening. As the signal went through the Hamburg board it was channeled to a telephone not thirty-eight hundred miles away, as McCobb believed, but only a hundred yards from the projection booth, in the back room of the temporary police post which Goldberg, as Heller, had set up on the sound stage.

The brisk, jolly German voice was gone. Goldberg's face had changed from the merry expression of his role as Heller into an inscrutable mask, and his voice came from far, far back in his throat—rich, round and oozing power.

"Yaaaaaa?"

"Mr. Goldberg?" Albert asked.

"Yaaaaaa. Albert?"

"Don't call me Albert. I am Major Waldenfon, but you may call me Carl."

"It was you? You were trying to kill our actors?" The two policemen in the room with Goldberg were talking to the telephone central, trying to trace the origin of the call on another telephone. One of these men was small, compact and extremely dapper—the true Inspector Heller, who had vanished so early in McCobb's murderous game.

"It was me. And I am going to kill them in a few minutes." Goldberg wrote "He has them" on a large pad and waved the sheet at Inspector Heller who ran over to take it.

"Did you like *Bronck's Cheer*, Mr. Goldberg?"

"It will gross a hundred million dollars the first time around."

"When I burn your actors to death, the only existing negative of *Bronck's Cheer* will burn with them." Goldberg wrote "By fire" on the pad and Inspector Heller handed the slip to Inspector Winkler, who immediately called the Hamburg fire department on his phone. He passed a note back as he dialed and Heller slipped it under Goldberg's eyes as he listened. The note said: "Call traced to small projection room."

Goldberg wrote "GO!" in large letters on his pad. The two police inspectors rushed out of the room.

"And besides burning your actors and your film," Albert was saying, "I wanted you to know that I have canceled all the insurance on them and on the production. Everything goes up together—the goose, the gander and the golden eggs. When I throw the torch in a few minutes, it will mean bankruptcy for you and that mockery, Jetthrow-Goldberg-Pies."

"Now I know you are joking, Albert." Goldberg racked his brain to think of ways to keep Albert talking.

"Carl or Major, please."

"What will happen to you, Albert?"

"I'll burn with them but I will have sent them all to hell—the two people who ruined my life and that film—that execrable film . . . Goddamn you, Goldberg, you should be burning with us. *Ungeschickter Affe! Blöder Sabberer!* May you rot into condemned salami!" As McCobb slammed down the telephone, Goldberg sprinted out of the command post.

Albert had filled the sprinkler system of the theater with kerosene. He turned it on now as the projection machines flashed elderly, nude wardrobe mistresses, raw business deals, early attempts to make spaghetti in Monticello, chases of carhops around seedy motel bedrooms and collusion for tax evasion by Caterina through bribery of an assayer. Then, from a trap door in the ceiling, he dumped yards of explosive celluloid film into the theater, lit a newspaper and thrust it down through the aperture. There was a dull boom as the whole back wall of the theater went up in flames.

Albert laughed manically into the microphone which fed his voice into the theater. "It's only a movie, folks," he cackled. "It's only a movie."

The fire began to lick its way down the rows of seats toward Caterina and Ty, who were forced backward toward the yammering screens. Immediately outside, Goldberg was directing men with crowbars and axes to break through the doors of the projection room to save the negative of *Bronck's Cheer* and, incidentally, apprehend Albert. In addition, the special-effects department was setting up demolitions to blow open the wall of the theater behind the screens.

Ty pulled Caterina behind him down the aisle, barely ahead of the fire, trying frantically to open the switchblade knife as he ran. The sound of sirens on the approaching fire engines could just be heard over the crackle of flames. "Can you hear them?" he yelled as he pulled her after him.

"It's too late," Caterina sobbed hopelessly. "It's no use. It's too late."

On the screen Ty was leering at a supermarket cashier of about fifty-one, Jefferson was begging Washington to urge the passage of a Spaghetti Protection Act, and Caterina was haggling for the rings on the fingers of an emaciated old woman seated on a suitcase on a pier.

Ty slashed a great rent in the screen across the image of his chest where his ever-swelling heart had been, and shoved Caterina through the hole, diving through behind her just as the outside wall of the building collapsed under the detonation.

As they stood gulping the clean night air, Goldberg called out to them. "The negative of *Bronck's Cheer* was saved," he

190

said as five policemen brought Albert through the crowd of firemen. He had been strapped into a strait jacket, and was struggling and shouting wildly as they led him away: "Albert McCobb, Master of Suspense, Prince of Pain and Blood and Violence presents the End of the World in Molten Techni-color!" The door of the police van slammed shut behind him.

Caterina and Ty huddled together in shock, their clothes charred and their eyes glazed. Goldberg came up to them, motioning the others away. "I have to get back to New York," he said, "but I don't want you to feel too badly about Albert, because we have come to the end of his kind of cycle."

They stared at him dumbly until Ty could find his voice. "Inspector Heller," he said icily and stiffly, "Albert McCobb may have had his faults like the rest of us, but—"

Goldberg gestured economically to the compact, sleekly dressed man standing nearby. "There's Inspector Heller," he answered, "the real Heller. Now, wash up and get the ten fifty-five tonight for Los Angeles. My people have your bags already on the way. I want you for a modern-dress version of *Uncle Tom's Cabin.* Mrs. Goldberg feels in her bones that there could be a civil rights cycle coming up, and Larry Oliv-ier has already hinted he would like to play Uncle Tom." He kissed Caterina absent-mindedly on the cheek, shook Ty's hand briefly, then got into a huge Cadillac limousine which had rolled up silently beside him. It zoomed away.

Ty and Caterina faced each other. Tenderly he put his arms around her. They went into a deep clinch, and slowly the whole scene faded away.